Fight Dirty

Dreda Say Mitchell

Big Mo Crime Series Book 2

First published in 2020 by Mitchell and Joseph Ltd

www.dredasaymitchell.com

ISBN: 978-1-9164202-6-7

Book cover Stuart Bache at Books Covered
https://www.bookscovered.co.uk
Formatting Polgarus Studio https://www.polgarusstudio.com
Editorial: Emmy Ellis https://studioenp.com
And Christine Dunlop for casting her expert eye.

Dreda Say Mitchell

International Bestselling Author Of:

SPARE ROOM

'The scariest, creepiest and best
psychological suspense you'll read this year.'

Lee Child

Praise for Award-Winning Author Dreda Say Mitchell

'As good as it gets.' ***Lee Child***

'Great book written by a great girl.' ***Martina Cole***

'A truly original voice.' ***Peter James***

'An exciting new voice in urban fiction.' ***Guardian***

'Zippy, twisty plot… and a bevy of memorable supporting goodies and baddies.' ***The Sunday Times***

'An exciting new voice in urban fiction.' ***Guardian***

'Thrilling.' ***Sunday Express Books of the Year***

'Awesome tale from a talented writer.' ***The Sun***

'Fast paced and full of twists and turns.' ***Crime Scene Magazine***

Amazon Readers Love The Big Mo Crime Series

'Top class.'

'Little Mo captures your heart.'

'Absolutely fantastic read.'

'You must read this book.'

Prologue

Wasting no time, Kristal urgently gripped the bottom of the window frame and shoved it up. Then she scrambled in. One of her six-inch Jimmy Choo's tumbled to the ground outside.

'Heck,' she furiously muttered.

She didn't have the time to go back for it. Instead, Kristal took off her remaining shoe and placed it beneath the window. Now she could creep upstairs on silent feet. The building was dark and cold. It took her a while to get her bearings because it was a rabbit warren of rooms and passageways, including a basement she had only recently realised existed. Finally, she located the foot of the stairs. Gazed up, disgust twisting her lips at the state of the warped banister and dingy carpet.

Kristal took each step quietly, slowly, hoping the aged wood wouldn't creak beneath her weight. She reached the landing. Walked on tiptoes to the door ahead. Sod's law there was no glass in the door, which meant she couldn't sneak a look inside the room to see what was happening.

She waited. Caught her breath. Trembling, her hand touched the round door handle.

One. Two. Three. Kristal burst in, almost swinging off the door. And let out an enormous sigh of relief when she found him inside. He stood in the middle of the room. Alone.

Something was wrong here. Very wrong.

He stalked towards her. 'God! Are you OK?'

She met him halfway, her confusion growing. 'I should be asking you that.'

'I got a text saying you were in trouble.'

'I received the same message about you.'

The hairs on the back of her neck stood to attention when she sensed they were no longer alone. A silhouette appeared in the corridor. Then smoothly stepped inside.

Mo.

Kristal snapped. With an animalistic roar, she flew and leapt onto her stepdaughter. Mo hadn't been expecting that. The force of the attack sent them both crashing to the floor. Frothing at the mouth like a demon risen from Hell, Kristal delivered a resounding smacker to Mo's mouth. The smaller woman's head snapped to the side.

'I hate you,' Kristal screamed in Mo's face.

She was certainly packing some kinda clout because Mo was dazed and dizzy. The room swam, turning upside down. The hideous 70s wallpaper swayed with the motion of a psychedelic acid trip. Her rival pinned her to the floor. Mo tried to clear her head, but Kristal was back at her. This time with an open-handed wallop to the other side of Mo's head.

Kristal continued to spew her hate. 'You had no right taking my son's place.'

Wallop! Smack! Wallop!

'Robbie could've got the whole world in the pudding club as far as I was concerned. But no wrong-side-of-the-blanket spawn of his is taking Damien's seat at the Steele family table.'

Kristal's hand loomed threateningly in the air, intent on inflicting more damage … Despite the buzzing in her ears, Mo reached up and caught her stepmother's arm. Kristal tried her luck with her other hand. Mo caught that too. They struggled, Mo holding on for dear life, Kristal attempting to shake her off.

Frustrated beyond belief, Kristal leant down, wildly doing her best to bite the smaller woman's ear clean off.

So, it's like that, is it? Mo thought. *Fighting dirty.*

Bring. It. On.

Mo blinked rapidly until the room came back to rights. Then she kneed Kristal in her belly. Kristal sucked in a torturous breath against the pain. That was the part where her stepmother should've let go. But this was Kristal Steele. She never let go. A new energy ballooned within her and she dug her talons into Mo's hair. Scrambled off Mo. Still clutching her hair with vicious intent, she dragged her stepdaughter across the room.

'Bitch! Thief! Imposter!' Kristal yelled with feral delight, lips grotesquely and cruelly twisting with every word. 'I'm going to make you rue the day you ever became part of the Steele family!'

Chapter One

2001
One month earlier

The finger pulled back on the trigger. Bang! The target went down. A congratulatory hand cupped the shoulder of the shooter from behind. The hand belonged to fearsome East End gangster, Jimmy Southpaw.

'Nice work, girl,' he complimented his granddaughter, Mo, with pride. 'You need to keep a cool head and a steady hand when you're holding a gun and have a job to do. Always remember that.'

Pleased with herself, Mo, or Big Mo as many were now name-checking her, grinned for all she was worth. She kept her gaze firmly on her next target, a yellow plastic duck in a row at the rifle gallery at the funfair. She squeezed the trigger again.

Bang! Duck down!

Beaming with satisfaction, Mo straightened and shouldered her rifle with a swagger. She gazed up at the man she called Granddad Jimmy with open adoration.

Side by side, granddaughter and grandfather were quite a contrast. Nineteen-year-old Mo had gleaming light-brown skin, courtesy of her Jamaican heritage on her mum's side, with black-brown curls that fell to the tips of her shoulders. She was small, but don't mess with her because she'd come up the hard way, meaning she knew how to use her fists. And her feet. In fact, any part of her body that would give her an advantage over some low-rent nobody who made the mistake of trying it on.

Mo was decked out in denim from her low-slung jeans to her belly top. And, as always, her good luck charm, a spider with knotted legs hung from a piece of black satin ribbon around her neck.

Her grandfather was white, six-foot plus, head shaved, and prowled with the presence of a panther. Jimmy Southpaw was the powerful head of the Steele family and one of the leading figures in the East End's underworld. He'd earned his moniker, 'Southpaw', in his youth as a boxer with a lethal left hand. Jimmy prided himself on being fair, but cross him, owe him …

They had one physical feature in common. Striking silver-grey eyes that seemed to pierce straight through to a person's soul.

The bored voice of the man who operated the funfair rifle range brought Mo back to the present. 'Alright, love, do you want a cuddly toy or a box of chocolates?'

Mo chose a pink teddy bear. She promptly gave it away to a toddler walking by with her mum. The little girl squealed with delight.

When they were gone, Jimmy turned to Mo. He looked like he was having the time of his life. 'I really love bringing the family to Southend every year. You can't beat a day out at the seaside. That's what's wrong with Britain these days, people don't get their buckets and spades together and head off to the beach with the family.'

He stared intently at the overcast skies. 'I even enjoy running around in the rain with a newspaper on my head. It wouldn't be a day at the seaside without a downpour from time to time.'

Spot on! Mo thought. And added, 'At least when it's pissing down the old folks have got something to moan about.'

Today was a Steele family tradition where Jimmy laid on a day trip out for the family. There were a lot of older folk among the many that Jimmy had brought down on his annual charabanc to Southend. His family was spread far and wide and he turned a blind eye to his relations inviting their close friends along even though he was footing the bill. He was good for it. Jimmy ended up booking two coaches to bring them all down. Now his family were wandering the seaside attractions like a school party.

Since her granddad had appointed Mo as heir to his criminal empire, she was expected to make small talk with all the family, even though she only had a vague idea who most of them were. What made it doubly difficult was when they talked and tutted about the dad she'd never known:

'Really sorry that your dad passed on, dear. What a lovely fella.'

'A bit of a rogue was Robbie, mind, but a top geezer.'

'Tragic, really tragic, that fire your dad died in. How did it happen? Don't make sense, does it? Tragic, really tragic.'

Tragic? Mo's mouth tightened. She didn't believe that for a minute. As far as she was concerned that was a pile of dodgy bollocks. Some scumbag had murdered her father, Robbie, in that fire. And she wouldn't rest until she found out who had done the evil deed.

The rambling family left the funfair and headed for the beach. There was Jimmy's surviving son, Harry. He was kitted out in a navy blazer, slacks and canvas shoes with a 'kiss me quick' hat perched at a jaunty angle on his head. As usual, he'd attracted a posse of adoring females of all ages to keep him company. 'Oh, Harry! You're so cheeky! Your ol' man should rap your knuckles!' they cooed.

Not quite so cheerful was Kristal, Robbie Steele's widow. And technically Mo's stepmother, though both women remained zip-lipped at acknowledging that part of their relationship. Mo wasn't heartless and conceded that it must've been a smacker where it hurt Kristal discovering her other half had another kid.

Her stepmother was a busty bottle-blonde who had the type of curvaceous 1950s figure that men openly drooled over. And she knew it. Indoors and out, her slap was always applied to perfection. Robbie had left her nicely provided for, which meant she could still splash the cash on her fave pastime, designer shopping. Today she was dressed in a wine-coloured figure-hugging flash-ya-legs dress and crazy-high Versace heels.

She was unhappily tramping along next to her eighteen-year-old son, Damien, Mo's half-brother. There was only a year between them meaning Robbie Steele had been playing away while he was a married man. As Damien walked, he stuffed his face with his fourth hot dog. He loved a bit of nosh, which showed in the belly spilling through his Hawaiian print shorts. Two things people noticed about him. He leant his neck at a strange angle, giving him an odd look, and he was a bit too lively with his fists. On numerous occasions, Mo had tried to get pally with him, but he'd blanked her. Mo wasn't giving up on him, though. He was her blood whether or not he liked it. Her brother. And family always came first.

Mouth dipping with disdain, Kristal took in the assorted members of the Steele family. 'Half these people should be in a home for the terminally weird,' she sneered beneath her breath to her son.

Her voice lowered even more. If her father-in-law got wind she was having a snide at his family's expense, there was going to be drama with a capital D. 'I dunno why we have to come down here for the day every year. For the same money, Jimmy could fly us to Spain and leave the old crones with a picnic basket and the bus fare to Wanstead Flats.'

Harry and Kristal appeared to be finally getting accustomed to the idea that Mo was second in charge and would become head honcho once Jimmy retired. He wouldn't be completely out of the picture, keeping an eye on Mo and proceedings from a distance, ready with a helping hand if she needed it. She had her own crew, including her chosen minders, her cousin, Delilah, and Mo's former love interest and associate, Josh. Mo was young, no mistake about it, but she was doing a bang-up job of learning the ins and outs about the Steele family crime syndicate. Jimmy was proper chuffed with how she'd stepped up to the mark.

Harry was always unfailingly polite to Mo. Kristal was too, although her good manners always seemed squeezed through gritted teeth.

Jimmy put his arm around Mo's shoulders while they strolled along, trying to avoid the waves crashing onto the beach. 'You're looking a bit mizz, girlie. What's up?'

Forlornly, she glanced out over the beautiful sea. 'I suppose a gathering of another family just reminds me I haven't seen mine since I came to stay with you.'

Jimmy gave her shoulder a sympathetic squeeze. He also tensed up. 'But this is *your* family, you just didn't know it.'

Mo stammered, afraid she'd hurt his feelings, 'Don't get me wrong, Granddad Jimmy, I'm grateful to you from the bottom of my heart for embracing me in my new family.' Mo bit her lip, eyes filling with aching pain. 'My mum. Gramps. I miss them so much.'

When Mo had found out who her father was, she'd had a major-league falling out with her mum, packed her shit and went to stay with Granddad Jimmy. She hadn't seen her mum since. Or her beloved Gramps, known affectionately as Brother Bertie by one and all.

Jimmy gathered his precious granddaughter to his side. 'Break the ice and give your ol' girl a bell? And if she puts the ol' dog down on you, call her again next month. She'll come round, eventually. She's not going to throw her own kid overboard for good. I might have had my problems with Robbie and Harry, but I'd never pull the shutters down. You don't do that, not on your own kids. Family always stands together in the end.'

But why didn't my mum ever tell me about my dad? Mo still hurt so badly that her mum never told her about Robbie. The resentment she harboured towards her mother remained a festering wound. So for now she decided to ignore Granddad Jimmy's advice and best to keep her distance from her mum.

'We're not putting up with this, are we?' Kristal fizzed with fury and not just because she'd broken her overpriced heels on that fecking beach.

Harry's brows flicked up in mock confusion. 'We?'

Flustered, Kristal knew full well why he was giving her the sarky routine. There had never been a 'we' with her brother-in-law. Truth was there was no lovey-dovey love lost between them. With a flick of her Jennifer-Aniston-style bob, she brushed off his manner.

'Putting up with what?' Harry added.

They stood outside a chippy on the seafront. Kristal smoked furiously on a fag.

'That!' She jabbed an irate finger at the function room upstairs where Jimmy was treating his family to a huge spread of cod and chips, bread butties, pickled onions and eggs, followed by ice cream and coffee.

Harry's bafflement grew. 'What? The fish and chips? This is Southend, they don't do Lobster Thermidor here, babe.'

Kristal puffed and hissed, 'I'm not talking about the grub, bruv, I'm talking about *her*.'

The penny dropped. 'Oh! You mean Mo.'

Inwardly, Harry groaned. No wonder his sister-in-law had been ultra-keen for him to join her outside for a smoke. Kristal had more or less had to drag him out here. Now if she'd been talking about a pinch of Snow White up his bugle, he'd have accompanied her outdoors quicker than you can say battered sausage.

She barked on, whipping herself into a proper frothy lather. ''Course, I mean Mo. Miss Slippery Knickers sliming her way in and stealing my Damien's birthright.' She quickly tagged on, 'And yours, of course. I'm thinking about your interests too, don't forget that.'

'Leave it out, Kristal.' As far as Harry was concerned the subject was closed. 'Dad's decision is final. Plus, mixing it with Mo means mixing it with Dad.'

Kristal's lip curled with disgust. 'You're wetter than a day out at the seaside in winter.' Suddenly a cunning gleam lit up her eyes. 'You think if this was Robbie, he would have let this stand? Let that little runt boss the business?'

That made Harry stop and think. Just as Krystal knew it would. If there was one thing that pushed Harry's buttons, caused his heart to pinch in pain, it was others thinking he wasn't as good as Robbie. That he was third-rate when measured against his brother. Harry was still competing against his bro, even though Robbie had been in the ground coming up to a year now.

Pressing her advantage, his sister-in-law cosied up to him. 'Obviously, we can't openly make a move against her—'

'So, what's the point of this one-to-one?'

Kristal sucked hard on her ciggie. Answered, 'What we do is fit up someone else to do the job for us.' Seeing Harry ready to pop another question, she wagged her finger in his face. 'I know what you're thinking: who's going to go up against Mo knowing she's Jimmy Southpaw's newly anointed heir? Easy. We find a clean skin, a young lad who wants to make a name for himself. But he operates far enough away not to know who the Steele family is. And, in turn, Mo and Jimmy won't recognise him either.'

Kristal gave it a few seconds to let her words sink into Harry's loaf. 'We promise this kid the earth and provide him with back-up. He causes mayhem, making Mo look like she's a rank amateur at running Jimmy's empire. The Great Southpaw will have no choice but to put her back in her box and ask us to take over. Geddit?' With a malicious twist of her mouth, she finished, 'Let's face it, she ain't really family anyways.'

Harry mulled over her plan. Then scoffed, 'Where are you going to find a lad who no one's ever heard of to take Mo on? An advert in a newsagent's window?' The taunting incredulity grew in his voice with his rapid-fire probing. 'And where are you going to find someone doolally enough to provide back-up for this lad and his operation? And when the bod providing back-up figures out you've potentially dragged him into a war with Jimmy Southpaw, he'll be doing it in his trousers.'

Flinging her fag into the gutter, Kristal ground out at Harry, 'Bottler. That's what you are. Always were. Always will be.'

With max contempt, she dismissed him, opening the door to the chippy.

Harry surprised her by quietly proposing, 'If you find the right lad and get premier league quality back-up, I'll think about it.'

Yessss! Kristal almost fist-pumped the air. Riding high on jubilation, she entered the shop. Finding a young lad who wasn't known to the family would take time. But make no doubt about it, she wouldn't stop until she found the perfect candidate. The harder part was going to be getting another well-known villain to provide back-up. The problem wasn't that she didn't know who to ask. She did. Her dilemma was if she asked him, it would take her back to memories of where she'd escaped from when she was a teenager.

Acid bile climbed inside her throat and Kristal quickly headed for the ladies'.

Chapter Two

'If the hem of your dress goes any higher your poom-poom will be on show for all to see. You isn't sweet sixteen no more,' Brother Bertie berated his friend, Ruddy, with feeling. His stare travelled disdainfully up her clothes while they sat in the backseat of a very swanky sports convertible.

Nora Baxter, known to most as Ruddy Nora or Ruddy for short, pursed her lips, dissing his pointed comments with a razor-sharp cut of her eyes. Her olive-green minidress was so short it put the mini into dress. A pair of glossy lemon go-go boots reached up to just below her knees. Her ruby-red lippy matched her usual go-to hairstyle, a wobbly beehive wig. The whole get-up was topped off by round sunglasses with daisies embellished around the frame.

Mutton dressed up as lamb, some might sneer, but as far as Ruddy was concerned she was the picture-perfect vision of a cool cat from the Swinging Sixties. And Ruddy didn't think it would be going too far to say she'd probably have given that Bridgitte Bardot, and Jane Fonda in her Barbarella days, a run for their money. She might be getting on in years – Ruddy was always sketchy about how many years that actually was – but that didn't mean she had to be decked out in clobber from a shop with a name like Old Fuddy-Duddies R Us.

'Shut your cakehole, you ol' windbag,' was her vicious response. 'You're just jealous.'

'Jealous? Of you?' Brother Bertie kissed his teeth, stamping his walking stick with feeling against the floor. Then skimmed his fingertips down his natty suit with cocksure pride. 'With sharp threads like these on? No contest, Miss Bandy Legs.'

They shot daggers at each other and, just as quickly, creased up with rib-cracking laughter. The bitching and put-downs were all part of the relationship they'd crafted since meeting in the 60s. How they'd met was still a mystery to many. One story was Bertram Watson, newly arrived from Jamaica, had found himself sitting across from crafty East End girl on the make, Nora Baxter, at a Soho nightclub poker table. Some said she'd fleeced him for everything he was worth, while others insisted it was the other way round. Neither Ruddy nor Brother Bertie would confirm or deny. What people could say with absolute certainty was Bertram Watson and Nora Baxter were devoted to each other.

Today they were off to see their long-time friend, Ted, at an Italian restaurant in South London. He'd been a noted businessman in his day. Much of that business he'd now passed into the hands of his nephew. Ted loved to send a plush motor, plus driver rigged out in classic chauffeur duds to pick up his two friends, so they travelled in style to see him.

The Italian restaurant was packed to the rafters by the time they arrived. No surprise there considering its multi-star rated reputation for both its food and bar facilities. Some diners did a double-take at Ruddy's get-up. She took not a blind bit of notice. As if she gave two stuffs what others thought about her. Besides, Ruddy only had eyes for their friend waiting at a table positioned in a corner with the best lighting.

Most people didn't just call him Ted, he was known as King Ted. Back in the 50s, he'd been king of the Teddy Boys in a section of South London. Nowadays, when it came to his wardrobe, Ted always experienced a twinge of regret when he got his clothes out. During his youth, he'd make sure to thoroughly press all his threads with his mum's iron before stepping out. His frock coat and strides were pressed to perfection. His shirt never dared show a crease. He used a toothbrush to keep his blue suede shoes neatly combed. His bootlace ties, with their genuine American silver buckles, were won in a poker session with a GI in Soho. To get his quiff right, he'd take as long as was needed, which was usually a very long time.

His Teddy Boy days were long behind him. Nevertheless, the tailored suit he wore today had something of the frock about the jacket, something of the drainpipe about the trousers. Ted's tie was narrow. Meeting Brother Bertie and Ruddy was a special occasion, so he'd put on one of his bootlace ties for friends and others to admire. All this was polished off with hair done up in a quiff. He had a full barnet, so why not? Some of his associates might wonder out loud if he'd fallen asleep on the sofa before he came out. But when he gave them the legendary King Ted 'dead-eyed stare' they rapidly changed their tune, made their apologies and swore to his face his hair looked the bizz.

Ted was a big man who loved big gestures, so he got to his feet and opened his arms wide enough to embrace the whole nation. He hugged each of his friends tight.

Once they were seated, they were served mouth-watering dish after mouth-watering dish. Ted didn't scrimp and scrape on the booze either. He liked nothing better than showing off all that he had accumulated over the years. All his wealth helped him to forget the grinding poverty of his childhood. Back then, on days when there was hardly any food around, he always made sure his younger brother Victor ate while he went hungry. Till this day, the memory of the sound of Vic's hiccupping tears of biting hunger made him want to throw up. Ted had learnt to toughen up. Harden his heart. Take what he wanted, satisfying all his urges and screw the consequences.

Ruddy asked, her gaze lighting up in appreciation as the fruity-flavoured brandy went down smooth and nice, 'How's that handsome nephew of yours?'

When his brother, Victor, had unexpectedly passed, Ted had opened his home to his young nephew and teenage niece. After the death of their father, their mother had become consumed by grief, culminating in her dead body found tangled in the muck of the Surrey Canal six months after her husband had been laid to rest.

Ted puffed out his chest in pride. 'That boy is more like

a son to me. He's done me proud. Taken the business to the next level.' He drew in a fortifying breath. 'My only wish is that Victor could've been here to see what his boy's achieved. See what a success he's made of himself.'

Ruddy laid comforting and tender fingertips lightly on the back of his hand. 'Don't you fret. I bet his spirit is watching over his lad every step of the way.'

Ted turned to Brother Bertie. 'Has your granddaughter come to visit yet?'

Brother Bertie's chest shuddered with hurt, knots twisting in his gut. He still couldn't get over his Baby-gal not living at home anymore. That she was living with … He could barely think the man's name. Jimmy Southpaw. If that bastard hurt her …

His gaze sharpened. 'She'll come back when she's ready.'

Ted shook his head. 'Of course, I know exactly how you're feeling.'

And he did. Years back, his niece had done a runner when she was sixteen. He'd never seen her again. Ruddy and Brother Bertie had never met the girl. Ted had been very protective of her when she was growing up. They didn't blame him. The world could be a minefield of cruel and callous traps waiting for girls and young women. Ted had hunted high and low for her with no joy. He'd been heartbroken, worried to death about what was happening to her. The poor, poor man.

Ted's fingers tightened around his steak knife. 'When she left, I didn't worry for myself, but she might as well have taken a blade to her brother's heart.' He shook his head sadly, as if the weight of the world sat atop his shoulders. 'He grieved for her night and day. It took that boy a long, long time to recover from her walking out on him.'

Ruddy's lips thinned with displeasure. If Ted's niece were here, she'd give her what for. He'd spared nothing, *nothing*, so that girl could have the best life possible. And how had she repaid him? Kicked him in the teeth by way of a thank you. What an ungrateful girl!

Now the door to sad memories had been opened they couldn't seem to shut it because Ted softly and wistfully continued, 'It will be over thirty years since Joy was buried.' He made the sign of the cross. 'Rest her soul.'

Ruddy's hand shook, tears welling hot and heavy in her eyes. Now it was Ted's turn to place his palm over hers, offering reassurance.

Joyce had been Ruddy's best friend. Joyce had been called Joy, not just to shorten her name, but she sparkled like the joy of a star on the top of a Christmas tree. Through nights spent in Soho they'd hooked up with King Ted and Brother Bertie. Ted and Joy had fancied each other from the off and were soon an item. He'd been like a father to Joy's little girl, Casey. They were on the cusp of getting married when … God! It still tore Ruddy to shreds thinking about it. Even after thirty years.

Brother Bertie hated seeing his trusted friend in agony like this. 'Don't go there. Nothing good will come of putting your mind back in a place riddled with pain.'

He was so right. Back there was a horror story of epic proportions. Ruddy gulped, her trembling hands wringing frantically in her lap. 'I never understood why she did it. She had a gorgeous daughter. A fantastic bloke in you, Ted.' Ruddy's head fell low, her shoulders bowed in defeat. 'Why did Joy kill herself?'

A crippling silence gripped the table. The crushing blow of hearing how Casey had found her mother dead with her head in the oven was one they'd never recovered from. Especially Ruddy and Ted. What could have tormented Joy so much she'd taken her own life?

Ruddy kept in contact with Casey. Ted didn't. Funny that. Then again, he'd been buried in his own agonised suffering, grieving for his lost love. One of Joy's sisters had taken the girl in and done a bang-up job because Casey was now a teacher in a primary school and had her own happy family. Her mum would be bursting with pure pride. Pure joy.

Out of nowhere, a chip came flying through the air, landing in the middle of their table. Startled, they searched to see where it had come from. But nothing appeared out of the ordinary, the other diners concentrating on their meals and chatting. They considered each other, baffled.

Ruddy picked up the offending vegetable and gave it to a passing waiter, who she told, 'I didn't order chips, darlin', but one seems to have been served, anyway. I hope this ain't the kind of joint where our fellow diners chuck their food around because if they're looking for trouble, they're going to find it. We haven't come here for a chimp's tea party, know what I mean?'

Just as the apologetic waiter turned to leave, another chip

sailed over, but this time it landed in Ruddy's beehive. A rousing cheer rose from a neighbouring table filled with young guys in their twenties.

One of them congratulated the thrower. 'Boom! Bullseye!' They high-fived.

Ted pushed to his feet with righteous indignation. He was going to have it out with those kindergarten toerags.

Ruddy grabbed his arm. 'Leave it out. They're only kids.'

Ted tugged his sleeve back. Plucked the chip from Ruddy's hair. 'I know they're barely out of short pants, that's why they're only going to get a cuff around the head instead of a proper hiding.'

He marched over and immediately zeroed in on the lad who seemed to be the organ grinder. Ted always knew who was in charge in any situation. He chucked the chip in front of the smug kid. Snarled, 'Is that yours?'

'Dunno, Granddad,' came the gobby, taunting reply. 'I've got dementia, see? You'd know all about that, of course.'

Scattered sniggers erupted. Then he made a real drama of examining Ted's quiff. 'What the fuck is that on top of your head? Are you the winner of the OAP's Morrissey lookalike competition?'

The restaurant fell into a deathly silence. Out of the corner of his eye, Ted noticed a few of the waiters coming to his rescue, a few of the diners, men and women alike, shifting their chairs to rise to their feet. They all knew King Ted. He stayed them back with a wave of his hand.

He glowered at the big-mouthed fool before him. 'Big

man, eh? Why don't you get up and we'll see how big your hairless goolies really are?'

The other young guys stiffened in awareness of the shifting tension and atmosphere. The glaring dagger-like gazes levelled their way from staff and diners alike. Suddenly they realised they might be out of their depth.

'Leave it, Jeff, it's not worth it,' one of them advised.

But Jeff wasn't having it. He was loving up his power trip to the hilt.

Insolently, he stood, fronting it off with King Ted. 'Don't you be worrying about the size of my nuts. They're more than big enough to take care of you and that squirrel you've got parked on top of your head.'

'I'll show you what for, you bell-end-faced punk.'

But then Ted did nothing. His face turned ashen, suddenly looking blank. He sharply sucked in a deep breath and then another. His claw-like hands reached out and grabbed a chair to steady himself. He could hear his name being called, but it sounded so far away. Was it Ruddy? Brother Bertie? A film of sweat formed on his forehead. He wrapped both his arms around his chest, letting out a strangled moan of fear. He stumbled forward before collapsing onto the table, sending cutlery, plates and food crashing onto the floor. Ted rolled over, toppled to the floor, desperately gasping for air, his skin marble-white with a bluish tinge.

Ruddy and Brother Bertie were the first to reach him. Waiters and diners who knew Ted rushed over too.

Someone cried, 'Get an ambulance. It must be his ticker.'

By this stage the young lads had scattered back from the table.

A disbelieving Jeff lost his cocksure swagger. His arms spread wide in denial at the accusing gazes. 'What? What? I never touched the ol' codger. You saw! You saw! I never even put a finger on him!'

An inconsolable, wild-eyed Brother Bertie staggered to his feet without the aid of his walking stick. Nearly knocking himself off balance, he lunged towards the youths, intent on doing some serious damage. Hands fought and held him back.

Fighting against being restrained, Brother Bertie bellowed and raged, 'You evil cowards. I'm going to mess you all up. Smash and crush you until your own mother won't recognise you.'

One of Jeff's mates urgently grabbed his arm. 'It's time to bounce, man.'

They ran for it. The lads escaped, but they were going to be sorry. They had no idea who King Ted really was.

Chapter Three

'People are saying that Jimmy Southpaw's losing his marbles. I mean, there's got to be some truth in it, right? Why else would he put that tiny tot in the top spot?'

The pronouncement was made with the loudness of a foghorn, making it hard to hear the music playing, Shaggy's, featuring Rikrok, 'It Wasn't Me'.

Daffy Gates. That was the name of the woman bad talking and giving her two pence worth about East London's premier hardman and his chosen heir, Big Mo Watson. The reason she felt confident enough to blow that trumpet of hers that passed for a mouth was she was inside Mel's, a beauty salon on Roman Road, situated a few minutes' walk away from the legendary market. Of course, she wouldn't have dared in a million years to discuss such matters on the street. Out there, eyes watched, ears listened twentyfourbloodyseven!

It was different inside Mel's. Ladies came to get a proper pampering, a spruce-up, smothered in potions and pastes that made them feel like new again. They also came to let off steam. Natter about anything that was getting on their tits. Straying husbands, wayward kids, money that did vanishing tricks inside their purses. In Daffy's case, the woman was known for moaning and a-groaning about any and anything especially pertaining to having a pop and dig at other folk's business. And misfortunes.

There were only two other customers getting their needs seen to in the salon. While Daffy got her acrylic nails refilled, the other ladies sat in padded black reclining chairs with mechanical massagers having a facial. Their faces were obscured by beauty masks. One's mask was mashed green avocado and Manuka honey, while the other was covered in what was advertised as, 'Ten Years Younger Seaweed-Blue.'

Daffy was never one to take much notice of her surroundings. If she had, she'd have clocked that the colour of Mel, the owner's face, looked worse than one of her beauty masks. Or the way the young girl, who was buffing up Daffy's nails a treat, own hands trembled slightly.

Daffy was in full swing and wasn't about to slow down. 'That's going to be kaput for the Steele family, you mark my words.' She made a big drama of clucking her tongue in fake sadness, mentally relishing the drama of the predicted downfall of one of London's leading families.

Avocado Mask Lady asked, 'I'm new to the area. I'm not familiar with this Steele family. Or this … What did you call him?'

Daffy supplied in a flash, 'Jimmy Southpaw.' There was nothing she loved better than playing to an audience. If her hands weren't already occupied, she'd have rubbed her palms with malicious glee. 'One of the Big Men of the area, know what I mean?'

Avocado Face nodded to show she got exactly where Daffy was coming from.

For a split second, Daffy bit the inside of her cheek, having second thoughts about whether it was her place to be muckraking Southpaw's name from one end of this salon to the other. Then again, she wasn't repeating anything that wasn't already doing the rounds. Even though it had happened last year it remained in the Top Ten Back Fence whisper list.

Shoving her reservations aside, with confident assurance, the loudmouth bulldozed through the Steele family history:

How Jimmy became a boxer.

No one had seen his sister, Sin, in years.

His wife, Mini – the angels above look after her – was a proper lady.

Two sons. Robbie and Harry.

Eldest is Violet. Not the full ticket. No need to waste words on that one.

Robbie married Kristal, a right gobby mare.

Their son, Damien – Yeah! I know! I know! The Omen. *Haha!*

Harry, he's the other son. Flash git.

And Big Mo …

Daffy pulled in a sharp, fortifying breath, properly winded after relaying all that. Her lips rippled with pleasure because she was coming up to the most salacious, scandalous, juicy bit of the tale.

'Poor Robbie dies in a fire in a police station—'

Seaweed-Blue Face cut over, opening her mouth for the

first time. 'Don't you think you've said enough?' The pressure of the harshness of her tone made part of her mask crack.

Said enough? Daffy stared at her in disbelief. She was just getting started! And Avocado Face was in accordance with Daffy because her fingertips gently touched her disgruntled friend's arm as she encouraged, 'Please, carry on with your story.'

Daffy was out of the gates again. 'Thing is, everyone thought Harry or Damien was in the frame to sit at Southpaw's right hand. But Jimmy plays a blinder, don't he? Robbie's got a wrong-side-of-the-blanket kid only Jimmy knows about.' She let out this strange yelping noise of disapproval. 'Robbie's widow must've had kittens. Poor cow. All those years of devotion and Robbie's shagging some black whore.'

Melanie nearly had kittens herself. A strangled noise emitted from her mouth. It appeared she was on the point of having a coronary.

Green Avocado Face asked Daffy, 'What's her being black got to do with it?'

Daffy snapped her neck back defensively, her expression one of horror. 'I ain't pred-jew-diss. Or a race-er-list. Our blood runs the same colour beneath, don't it?' Then her lips smacked together, brow sourly arched. 'All I'm saying is an addition of colour in the Steele bloodlines was the last thing folks were expecting.'

The other woman mulled this over. Then, 'So what's the real problem people have got with Jimmy's grandkid, this Big Mo?'

Daffy cackled. 'The girl's the size of a bottle of milk. Probably without the bottle, you get me? Who in their right nut's gonna be scared of her? Take orders off her?'

Green Face pondered this for a while and then turned to Melanie, who was squirming under her gaze. 'My friend over there' – she pointed to Daffy – 'it would be my honour to pay for her to have a shampoo and set.'

Daffy preened, her chin jutting forward. 'Well, I wouldn't mind if I do. What's your name?'

The other woman never answered. That should've been a warning bell to daft Daffy that something was up here. Five minutes later, while a trembling Melanie washed Daffy's hair, Green Face unceremoniously used a wet wipe to scrub the avocado from her face.

Daffy's eyes were shut, so she never saw Melanie hand over the tap's hose to her other customer. Melanie and her nail technician scarpered to the back room. See no evil. Speak no evil.

Daffy's face scrunched up. The water was getting a bit lively in the ol' temperature department. 'Mel, babe, can you put a bit more cold into that?'

'Oh, it's not Mel. *Babe*. It's that black whore's kid. The tiny tot.'

Daffy sucked in a mortifying breath, her eyes flashing open.

Avocado Green-Face Lady was Big Mo Watson.

Mo was beyond furious. Raging. That this poisonous windbag of shite thought she had the right to chat about her Granddad Jimmy and her newly discovered family sickened her to the core. And her mum? Mo nearly went ballistic when this miserable scum of humanity started having a pop at her mother. Despite their current estrangement, Mo loved her mum to death. And she wasn't standing for anyone, particularly this nonentity, running her mother into the ground.

The trip to the salon was meant to be a treat for her bestie, Twinkle. Last year, Twinkle had had an accident that had changed her life forever. Twinkle looked so down in the mouth lately that Mo had decided to sort her out with a special day of pampering. Now her bestie's day of TLC and forgetting her troubles had been ruined.

Instinctively, Daffy tried to get up. Mo slammed her back down. Daffy screamed with pain as the base of her neck pressed harder into the curve in the sink that had, ironically, been created for the comfort and ease of washing hair.

Mo bared her teeth. Not a pretty sight. 'I wouldn't make any jerking movements, if I was you. Lean too hard back on that sink and your neck could go snap!'

Daffy was terrified, wailing, 'I never meant nuthin' by it. I was only telling ya what everyone's saying—'

Mo didn't have time for excuses. 'Don't think I've got any bottle?'

She didn't give the other woman a chance to explain. Mo stretched a towel over Daffy's mouth and nose. Placed the end of the tap's nozzle over the towel, so it sat right on top of Daffy's gossiping gob. Water gushed over the towel and down the side of Daffy's face. But it was the water that seeped through the material that did the real damage. Daffy felt like she were drowning. The woman's eyeballs nearly left her head as she gasped, brutally coughed and swallowed, trying to shift her head this way and that to get away from the water gushing into her mouth and up her nose.

When Mo pulled the tap and the towel away, Daffy's body arched, horrible wheezing noises coming out of her, gasping for air. Then she coughed and spluttered, water dribbling down her mouth and nose.

Mo leant in close, eyes straight out of Hell, nostrils flaring with raw rage. 'You ever call my mum a whore *ever again* and I'll come gunning for you quicker than you can say wash 'n' go. If you don't like black people, I suggest you go live on Mars with the other aliens.'

Mo slapped the towel back in place and shoved the tap nozzle back. Daffy was gagging again under the onslaught of the water. With satisfaction, Mo gave this nosey parker another dose of her own medicine. By the time she'd finished with Daffy Gates, the woman was a limp, dazed, watery mess slumped sideways in a chair in a beauty salon.

Mo chucked the hose and the towel. A very worried, hand-wringing Melanie appeared. 'Big Mo, all I can do is apologise. I'd have turfed her out as soon as that cack started spewing out of her gutter-gob.'

'What are you saying sorry for?' Mo asked, giving the owner of the shop a polished smile. 'It ain't your fault trouble over there decided to parade her poisonous twenty-four-seven tongue in your place of business.'

Mo pulled out a bundle of twenties and placed them in Melanie's palm. 'Get something nice for you and the kids, eh?'

Money buys loyalty, is what Granddad Jimmy told her. And he was right on that score. In the future, if any other person decided to shout the odds about Jimmy Southpaw and his family here, Mel would be on the blower to Mo giving her the full SP.

Mo gave Daffy Gates one last glance of utter loathing before she collected Twinkle and left the salon.

It didn't matter how much Mo tried to brush it off, that witch of a woman had touched a nerve. What if Jimmy Southpaw had made the wrong decision choosing her to run his empire?

Chapter Four

'Y'know what really pisses me off about boys like you?'

A couple of days later, that was the snarled question Nico Sinclair put to the four young men huddled and squirming in the back of his van. As expected, he didn't get an answer. They were too paralysed with fear to open their mouths.

Nico casually enlightened them. 'It's the time factor. I don't have *time* to waste putting kids like you straight. I'm a busy man and *time* is money. And here's another thing.' He lifted the lapels of his herringbone mohair suit with his thumbs. 'See this? This retails at a couple of grand. Minimum. Do you think I want to get blood, sweat and tears all over gear like this? My dry cleaner's gonna have a mare. And what about these?' Raising his trouser legs, he showed off his handmade Italian leather shoes. 'Do you think I want to get these scrubbed clean after dishing out a kicking?'

When he got no answer, Nico shouted, 'Well, do you?'

The boys shook their heads with rapid-fire desperation.

Nico Sinclair was in his early thirties with square-jaw looks that would take a long time to age, gelled hair that stood jet-black against his olive skin and usually wore a thousand-watt killer smile. Nico was also one of South London's Premier League Faces. A very dangerous man. When word had reached him that his beloved uncle was in the hospital, and how he'd ended up there, Nico had gone on a rampage to find those responsible. These scumbags wanted to thank their lucky stars that the man he loved above all others had collapsed because his blood pressure had gone through the roof rather than anything more serious.

Nico's uncle was King Ted. Nico had taken over his South London criminal empire when his uncle decided it was time to enjoy the finer things in life. Like go to a restaurant for a drink and chinwag with his two dearest friends.

Less than forty-eight hours it had taken Nico to find the filth to blame for putting his uncle in hospital. He'd put the word out on the streets and the word had come back almost at once. Nico's word carried weight. He wasn't a man who liked to do the running, so he'd contacted each one and ordered them to report to his van in a pub car park for a 'light convo'.

Of course, they could've run for it, but they knew Nico would track them down eventually and then it would be much, much worse. Earlier, when Nico had pulled up in his van, he'd found the young men in a little group, shivering in the cold by a recycling bin. He'd opened the back doors. They'd got in.

Nico wasn't an unfair man, so he'd given them an opportunity to tell him what had gone on.

Story number one: they flat-out denied any involvement. Nico arched a sceptical brow at that.

Story number two: another gang did it. Nico clenched his hands with such force it was a wonder his knuckles didn't burst through his skin.

Story number three: they accused each other of starting the trouble.

Frantic, arguing voices filled the van to the brim. Arms folded, Nico observed their antics. It was never a pretty scene when brother betrayed brother. Besides, Nico already had a heads-up about which of the four had played the Big I Am and dared run his uncle down in public. The lad's name was Jeff. And, surprise, surprise, he was the one doing most of the accusing and denying.

Enough with this dicking around! Nico raised his hand. The row stopped in an instant.

He leant forward. 'You know, guys, if I was the law, I wouldn't be interested in who started what. I'd say it was 'joint enterprise' and you'd all be to blame equally. Then I'd put you in front of some magistrates who'd be under orders not to send you to one of these young offender whatnots because there's no room.'

Nico's lip curled with scorn. 'No doubt this would be followed up with sob stories from social workers and probation officers about how you're addressing your challenging behaviour and you need another chance. Then the beaks would let you off with a fine you didn't pay or a community service order you didn't do.'

Nico banged his fist against the side of the van. The

deafening echo put the fear of God inside the younger men, resulting in them nearly jumping out of their skin.

'That's why the streets aren't safe no more.' Nico gritted his teeth. 'They aren't even safe for a well-known local character who can't eat his dinner without getting grief from scrotes like you. You've probably heard of King Ted?'

The look on their faces suggested they hadn't.

'No matter. I'll give you something to stick in your memory box, so you'll remember it in the future.'

He picked up a heavy sports bag. Unzipped it. 'Anyway, that's the straight world's law, not mine. My law keeps the street safe for honourable, upstanding men like my uncle.'

He pulled out a baseball bat and handed it to Jeff. He gave various other hard weapons to the others before finally inviting the baffled gang out into the car park. 'So, here's the deal, boys. I want you to beat the hell out of each other until there's only one man left standing. That man gets to stay on his feet. Call it time off for good behaviour.'

The wary eyes of the young men darted from Nico, to each other, and back again. The grip on their weapons tightened, but none kicked off the action.

Nico lost his rag. 'Are you Mutt 'n' Jeff? Get on with it!'

There were a few half-hearted prods and pushes. Handbags at dawn was tougher than this.

Nico snatched the baseball bat from the ringleader and turned to the others. 'A right bunch of poxy pussycats, you boys are. This is what I'm looking for.' He swung the bat and brought it down with bone-shattering force on Jeff's arm. The sound was like a cricket ball smashing into a bat.

The youngster groped for air and stumbled backwards, his face turning a funny colour. Clutching his arm, he collapsed, legs splayed.

Nico addressed the others. 'See? Like that. Now put some elbow grease into it and don't make me show you again.'

The fight was on. Friendship out the window. A pitched battle began with blows being delivered left, right and centre. Bodies dropped. Cries split the air. On and on it went. Nico checked his texts, glancing up from time to time like a bored referee in a boxing gym to check the progress of proceedings.

Finally, silence.

The gang were sprawled out on the car park ground apart from the winner. Two were out cold. Nico was pleased to see one was that fucker, Jeff. A solitary figure crawled aimlessly towards the pub. The guy still standing was shaken but surprisingly not bruised.

Despite himself, Nico was impressed. 'What's your name, son?'

'My mates call me Charlie.' His dark-brown skin was dotted with bubbles of sweat.

Nico gave the boy's shoes a leisurely perusal. Italian, stylish, single strap and, if Nico wasn't mistaken, made of calfskin. Not the sort of footwear you'd expect one of these Herberts to be sporting. 'Where did you get the brogues?'

The boy was still clearly scared and shocked, his small dreads shaking slightly. 'They were my dad's.'

Nico patted him lightly on the cheek. 'Charlie, you ever in need of work, look me up at the Candy Floss Bar.'

Nico pulled the van door open and sneered over his shoulder, 'Tell your mates they can keep the weapons.'

Nico used his infrared key to open the gates to his villa. Nestled in the countryside, it had handy access to the M25 and M23 so he could slip into town at will or take the family down to the coast as the fancy took him. Handy for the airports too when he saw a weekend break on the last-minute websites or business took him abroad.

Nico adored his wife, daughter and son. Family was everything to him. His uncle, King Ted, had instilled that into him from a young age.

Others might sneer that his home was a dead ringer for the kind of tacky pad a footballer with zero taste would live in, but that was part of the reason Nico had bought it. He was in the Premier League of villains, so needed somewhere to make a statement about who he was.

His substantial house resembled a Spanish villa that had taken a wrong turning and ended up stranded in the English countryside. It was white, long with shuttered windows. It had two classical pillars propping up the porch, so it had something of the Greek temple about it too. Best of all, it was surrounded by mature trees and a stone wall that sheltered it from the prying eyes of the law. You could drive past it on the road and not even notice it was there. Guard dogs that diligently roamed the gardens took care of any parkers who got too nosey.

But, of course, you could never be too careful. Despite taking all the precautions in the world, you could never be sure they would deter unwelcome visitors.

And even as Nico drew up in his drive, he knew he had one. He felt it. No one got as far in his business as he had without sensing danger. He ruled out his wife, Pam, and the kids. They were away at his in-laws for the week.

Nico crept to a window at the rear that opened into his study. He always kept a key to the window on his person as a way of getting into the house unobserved. He crawled through and went to his desk, where he kept a loaded pistol for emergencies. Shooter held in both hands, military style, back against the wall, he went from room to room. Lounge. Den. Morning room. Kitchen. In-house gym.

No one there.

Nico retraced his steps. Moved cautiously up the stairs. He did the same as he had downstairs, checking one room after another. Master bedroom, plus en-suite. Bedroom number two. Three. Guest bedroom. Attic conversion.

No one there.

Flummoxed, Nico couldn't figure this out. Perhaps he was wrong? But it was always better to be safe than sorry. He put the shooter into his waistband.

And that's when he felt it. Something sharp dig into the back of his neck. It didn't break the skin.

A voice behind him mocked, 'You're losing your touch, Nico. Letting a bird get access to your drum and then catching you cold with a blade? Tut! Tut! Tut!'

Chapter Five

Nico reeled in paralysing shock. *This can't be happening. Can't be happening.* His mind chanted his disbelief over and over again. His reaction had nothing to do with the lethal knife resting with threatening intent on the skin of his neck. It was worse than that. It was as if the blade was hacking into his heart.

It was the voice that froze him to the spot. A voice he hadn't heard since he was eight years old. Choking, wrenching emotion whelmed up, lodging in his throat like a stone. Nico was a man who prided himself on keeping his feelings below the radar. Wearing your emotions on your sleeve was dangerous in the business he was in. It could create a chink in your armour that any opponent could exploit to the max, including putting you six feet under. The only people Nico let his guard down for were his cherished wife, children, Uncle Ted.

And *HER*.

The crippling tide of memories of the last time he'd seen her flooded back.

Eight-year-old Nico lay in bed, the blanket tangled about

his waist. He felt so tired, totally wiped out after a day at school and then a game of footie with his mates out on the street. His eyes drooped … he forced them wide open again. He wasn't going to fall asleep before she came in. His sixteen-year-old sister always tucked him up for the night and, if he was lucky, she'd tell him a bedtime story. He loved the stories she told. She had a voice made for spinning a cracking yarn.

Nico was suppressing an enormous yawn when his bedroom door finally opened, and she quietly slipped in. His heart rose. She was everything to him.

His sister smiled that gorgeous smile of hers, sat on the edge of the bed and kissed him on the cheek. The good feelings in his heart dropped to his feet when he caught her eyes. They were red as if she'd been crying. His sister was a natural-born toughie. Even when Mum and Dad had died, she never wept. Well, not in public anyway.

His distressed little voice cried, 'What's wrong?'

Sweeping back his hair off his forehead, that brave smile of hers broadened. 'Wrong?' she scoffed. 'Like anything could be wrong when I'm with the best bruv in the whole universe.'

He frowned hard at her. 'So why have you been crying?'

'Because I'm happy.'

Happy tears? He'd never heard of that before. You laugh when you're happy not start blubbing. Then again, if his sister was saying it was so, it must be the truth. After Mum and Dad went to meet the angels in Heaven, she'd promised never to lie to him. To always look him in the eye and tell him the truth.

She tucked the blanket under his chin. Then Nico forgot all about everything else as she launched into one of her legendary made-up bedtime stories. Her voice was soft and as warm and comforting as the blanket he nestled in. He was fast asleep before the end.

When he woke up in the morning, his sister was gone. Most of her stuff too. Uncle Ted was shattered, Nico devastated. For a whole month, come bedtime, he'd wait up for as long as his eyelids would allow, praying for his beloved sister to materialise like magic and slip into his room. Recite him a bedtime story.

But he'd never seen her again.

Until now.

Nico snapped back to the present. The memories turned his old scars into open wounds. The resentment he'd felt towards her for having dumped him boiled over the surface with the power of a volcano.

In a swift one-two-three move, he reversed their positions. Had her up against the wall, the point of the knife poised beneath her chin. It wasn't lost on him that she'd taught him that defensive move when they were growing up.

He growled in her face. 'Long time no see, Annalisa.'

Not fazed by the knife touching her, she brazenly answered, 'I buried the name Annalisa long ago. People call me Kristal now.'

Kristal couldn't take her eyes off her younger brother as he eased back, giving her the space she needed to move off the wall. Her gaze greedily devoured him. She couldn't get over how big and strapping her little Nico had become. And look at that unforgettable face of his! As gorgeous as a fallen angel.

On the outside, Kristal played it cool to the hilt, but

inside she was a quivering bag of jellied nerves. Convulsively, she swallowed the huge sobs threatening to spill out. She couldn't believe it, just couldn't believe that she was finally standing here with Nico. The baby brother she'd helped bring up. The baby brother she'd had no choice but to leave behind.

'You look different,' Nico fired at her, mostly with contempt, but he couldn't hide his curiosity. Now it was his turn to give her the once-over.

When she'd left her uncle's home all those years ago, her intention had been to board the first train she came across out of London. Her reasoning had been that the country was too big a place for her uncle to search for her. And maybe then she wouldn't need to change her appearance. There she'd been, sitting slumped in a seat on the train going somewhere up north and suddenly it hit – she couldn't leave London. The capital city was her manor, part of her DNA. As the guard had blown the whistle, signalling it was time to depart, Kristal had hightailed it off that train. She'd disappeared into the underbelly of the city's shadows, trying to figure her way forward.

Hide in plain sight, that's what she'd decided to do. She'd dyed her hair from chestnut brown to outrageous blonde. Switched from rake-thin to hourglass-fit. And transformed into a high-gloss, in-your-face, brainy Barbie doll. Even she hadn't recognised herself. Kristal had completed her new life by relocating to the one place they'd never think to search for her – another crime family on the other side of the river. A family that would go all out to protect her if she was ever found out.

First time she'd clocked Robbie, the heir to the Steele family, Kristal had known he was The One. It was no hardship because she'd also fancied the bollocks off him like crazy. Some might say she was taking a chance insinuating herself into another crime dynasty. But only folk who weren't in The Know would think that. The families tended to keep to their own manor and very rarely crossed paths.

'Why did you leave like a thief in the night?' Nico maintained a coldness to hide his anguish.

Kristal had her answer ready. Her lie. 'A boy, of course. Promised to love me for eternity and give me the world. Lasted six months and then I was on my own.'

'Why didn't you come back?'

Nonchalantly, Kristal shrugged. 'By then I got a taste of the independence bug. No way could I have come back and lived under Uncle's rules.' She shook her hair back and plastered on a dreamy smile. 'Then I met Robbie and—'

'Robbie?' a stunned Nico chucked with the explosive power of a grenade. His finger kicked into the air. 'Hold up a minute. You're never the Kristal who was married to Robbie—'

'Steele,' she finished in a cut-glass tone of authority. 'That's me. Kristal Steele. Daughter-in-law of Jimmy Southpaw. Mother of Jimmy's precious grandson.'

She was surprised at the pride brimming in her explanation. Yeah, she was proud of the life she'd made for herself. A runaway could've ended up on the streets, on her back, floating dead just below the surface of the river. The difference between her and those other terrified girls was she knew how to use the head on her shoulders. How to plot and come up with a win, win, win game plan.

Nico abruptly folded his arms, not able to hide the grudging admiration in his voice. 'Sounds like you've landed on your feet like an alley cat with nine lives.'

Kristal kept it schtum, refusing to react to his insult.

'Why are you here? Why now?' he brutally asked.

She caught his eye and wouldn't let go. 'I need your help.'

He threw his head back and roared with laughter. It was one of the ugliest sounds Kristal had heard in a long time. He hacked off his laughter as quickly as he'd switched it on.

'You've got the brass of a disciple of the Devil.'

You best believe it! Kristal thought with feeling, stiffening her spine. For the first time her voice was clipped and tight. 'Where my son's concerned, I'd do anything. Anything.'

Nico's brows slashed together in confusion. Then his eyes widened putting two and two together. He ate up the distance between them, crowding his big sister's space. She stood her ground.

He said, 'The news that's travelling on the waves of the Thames towards my side of the river is that Jimmy Southpaw has discovered a long-lost heir. Not your son. Girl named Maureen, though I hear she likes to be called Big Mo. Your deceased ol' man's bastard-born daughter.'

Kristal's mouth scrunched up, bristling, her rage hot and boiling beneath the surface. She was SO tired of putting a brave face on it all.

Her brother continued in full flow. 'So, tell me if I've hit the nail on the head here? Robbie kicks the bucket in that fire at the cop shop. You're sobbing your heart out, but through your widow's tears there's a silver lining. Your boy will be crowned prince of Jimmy Southpaw's powerful firm—'

Kristal went postal. 'That bitch! No fucking way is she robbing my Damien—'

'The way I hear it, Southpaw's treating this kid as if she's the Second Coming.'

Kristal paced, huffing and puffing with the ferocity of a dragon breathing fire. Finally, she stopped and faced her brother again, her expression knowing and calculating. 'Now if she turns into a disaster, Jimmy will get rid of her as quickly as he found her. That's what needs to happen if my Damien is to assume his rightful place.'

Nico demanded, 'How you planning on doing that?'

Kristal's heels sank into the carpet, moving with the eagerness of the rush of the plan she was about to share with him. 'I need someone to royally fuck up her operations. Turn her into the worst kinda shit in Jimmy's eyes. Let it drill into that numpty skull of his she ain't up for the job.'

Nico asked, 'And who is this *someone*?'

Kristal shook her head. 'Dunno yet. I've put the word out. But he needs to be small fry. Someone trying to get his name lit up in lights.' She held her hand out and then closed it tight as if she were crushing something. 'Someone I can wrap around my little finger.'

Nico glanced at her like she was the embodiment of

crazy. 'And which idiot is going to go up against Jimmy Southpaw's newly crowned heir?'

Kristal smiled darkly. 'You leave that to me.' She wet her lips. Casually dropped, 'He'll need back-up. Some muscle. Shooters. Hardware—'

Finally understanding what his long-lost sister was doing here, Nico couldn't hide his stunned expression. *Was she having a laugh?* His restraining palm in the air stopped her. 'You want *me* to provide this back-up? To get involved in an all-out war with *Jimmy Southpaw*?'

Kristal took a breath. Plunged on, manner soft and persuasive. 'You wouldn't be physically involved.' She placed her fingers gently on his arm. 'You'd be behind the scenes. All you'll be doing is backing up my Chosen One from a distance. Jimmy won't be able to trace it back to you. Plus, the heat's going to be falling on Mo not Jimmy.'

Nico's gaze flashed at the person he'd once treasured more than anyone else in the universe. The person his younger, innocent self had looked up to. Uncle Ted said that bitterness was one of the most terrible things to hold in your heart. As corrosive as acid, eating you alive from the inside. Nico couldn't help it. The bitterness he felt towards this woman who now called herself Kristal Steele was heavy. And it hurt.

Kristal recognised that her brother was wrestling with his demons She caught his wrists in her hands. 'I wronged you. I should never have left the way I did. I was out of order.' She choked up. 'I didn't want to go—'

'Then why did you?' Nico slammed back, the pain of a

young boy in his words. 'Uncle Ted searched high and low for you, from one place to the next. It wasn't just me you kicked to the kerb. He never said a word against you, only had the brightest and best words to lay at your absent feet.' Steel entered his tone. 'But he couldn't hide the hurt from me. He promised our dad, his brother on his deathbed, that he would take care of us. Shelter us. Protect us.'

Kristal dropped her hands, trying to move back, but Nico's fingers captured her resisting wrists. He leant down close, his hot breath beating in her ear. 'He's in the ozzie. Had a funny turn with his—'

With all the will she possessed, Kristal wrenched out of his grasp. The buzz of her heart beating in her ears, she let rip. 'I've got another boy in my care now. My. Son.' She stabbed a finger with pride into her chest. 'No way am I going to let him down. Not like I did you. I'm going to do every last thing in my power to see that he gets what he's due. But I can't do that without you.'

Her arms fell limply to her sides. 'I'm begging you to help. Not for me. But for my boy. Your own blood.'

It was the pleading in her voice that got him in the end. It pierced Nico with the intensity and crippling pain of a shard of jagged glass right in his already bleeding heart. She might have left him all those years ago, but she was still his sister. His blood.

Family.

And you stood behind family one hundred and ten percent.

Nevertheless, there still needed to be ground rules. So, he

told her, 'Whoever you find can't be a rank idiot. At the same time, he can't be too clever in the upper storey.' He tapped his temple. 'But he's still got to be able to use his loaf.'

Nico moved to stand in front of his sister. 'I'm going to need to check out the guy you choose before I commit. The last thing I need is World War Three breaking out with Jimmy Southpaw.'

Chapter Six

Mo stopped dead in her tracks when she caught sight of her adored Gramps on his allotment. She choked up. God, she'd missed him something chronic. Missed the way his battered pork-pie hat sat at a jaunty, youthful slant. Missed the walking stick with the silver top engraved with a Lion of Judah that was his constant companion. Missed his 'don't mess with me' tongue. A lump of pure heaven lodged in her throat as she observed him leaning heavily on his shovel, taking a breather and wiping his forehead, standing next to one of his ginormous pumpkins.

Brother Bertie, her mum's father, was the one she'd always turned to when life got a touch too tough. His arms always open wide, his shoulder available to cry on. That didn't mean he wasn't willing to put her straight with a few choice home truths if need be. Kindness and love mixed with in-your-eye honesty was his straight-up policy.

After Mo discovered that Robbie Steele was her father she'd gone at it hammer and tongs with her mum, the result of which was Mo had given her mum the finger, packed her gear and left the home she'd shared with Gramps and her mother on the Isle of Dogs and gone to live with her newfound grandfather, Jimmy Southpaw.

Two granddads. Who'd have thought it, eh? The kid with no dad ends up with two grandfathers. Mo still shook her head in wonder and disbelief at the extraordinary turn of events.

She resumed walking, bolstering her courage at the same time because she would need it. What she'd come to speak to Gramps about was no easy matter.

Mo was overwhelmed with a desperate need to fly into his arms … A hard glint in his rheumy gaze screamed at her to back off. Brother Bertie smacked his lips with disapproval, narrowing his hard stare.

Clinging more casually to the shovel's handle, he pronounced, 'Well! Well! Well! Lookee at what the donkey dragged in.'

Inwardly Mo winced. Gramps' expression told its own story – he wasn't pleased one bit. He looked stern and guarded. She wouldn't be surprised if he picked up the shovel and chased after her with it.

Mo nervously wet her lips. Slapped on a tentative smile. 'Wotcha, Gramps. How's tricks?'

Brother Bertie tilted his chin. 'When you left, I kept this' – a bony finger patted his lips – 'sealed tight. I tells myself, I sez, *Bertie! Bertie! Baby-gal's all grown up. She's a big woman now. If she wants to leave her mother's yard and make her way in the world, wish her the best of luck. Let her make her own decisions.*' Brother Bertie deliberately paused. Then, '*Let her make her own mistakes.*'

His words soured the air between them.

He continued, 'I also sez to meself: *Bertie! Bertie! If Baby-gal's a big woman now, why did she disrespect her mother by leaving the way she did?*' He turned, giving Mo the full force of his thunderous expression. '*Bertie, Baby-gal never even stopped to say goodbye to her own granddaddy. Never even stopped to kiss his wrinkled cheek goodbye.*'

He held up his hands, the skin thick and criss-crossed with the scars of manual labour. They shook. 'I sez, *Bertie! Bertie! You see these? When they placed Baby-gal in these arms after she was born, man, the tears fell from my eye. God had never sent a more beautiful baby to walk this earth. I loved her. Cherished her. Hugged her with all the love I had to give—*'

And that's what Mo did, covered the distance between them and threw herself into his arms with all the love she had to give. Brother Bertie hadn't even realised that tears rolled down his weathered cheeks. The very thought that she'd caused her precious Gramps so much excruciating pain left Mo feeling lower than the dirt beneath their feet.

His body sagged against her with the weight of his worry at her leaving. 'I can hardly catch any sleep at night because I've been so worried about you.'

She whispered with all the fibre of her being, 'I'm sorry, Gramps.' Mo pulled in a hard breath because what she had to say next was the reason she was here. 'After … After I found out who my dad was, I couldn't understand why Mum never told me about Robbie. And then she wouldn't tell me the whole story. Plus, she seemed to hate Granddad Jimmy's guts.'

Brother Bertie harshly sucked in a sharp breath. Hearing his granddaughter call another man 'granddad' wasn't easy. He'd been her only grandfather. Now he was going to have to share her.

Mo eased away from him, hands still clinging to his waist. 'That ain't right, Gramps. Ain't right at all. Mum's got no right to keep what she knows from me—'

'She's suffering—'

'So. Am. I,' Mo practically yelled back. With her next breath, calm but shaky, she added, 'I want you to tell me about Robbie Steele. I need to find out who murdered him.'

Lord Creator's reggae classic, 'Kingston Town', played on Brother Bertie's old-style small radio as he sat next to his granddaughter. He sat in his Jamaican flag patterned deck chair while Mo sat in the Union Jack one that was usually reserved for Ruddy. They relaxed back, each with a glass of his legendary 'Lord Have Mercy Rum Punch', a lethal mash-up of Wray and Nephew white rum seasoned and mellowed with potent ganja steeped into it for a month. Brother Bertie grew his own weed on the allotment, in a secluded patch away from prying eyes.

The sun was bright, but all Brother Bertie saw was the muddy water waiting for him to wade through if he answered his Baby-gal about what he knew about Robbie Steele. What sickened him was he couldn't tell her the truth about her parents' relationship. If she knew the real story of why her mum and dad had split up, he would lose her respect.

Mo's face screwed up after she took another tentative sip of his classic rum punch. 'I don't know how you drink this stuff and still manage to walk on your own two. It's enough to pickle your insides.'

Brother Bertie silently cursed when Mo put her hardly touched glass on the grass. He'd deliberately given her the drink, topped up to the rim, hoping the combo of booze and weed would make her woozy, letting her need to find out more about her dad drift away in the laziness of the sun. He should've known better. Wasn't he the one who'd trained Mo to be focused?

'One hand can't clap,' that's what he'd taught her over and over.

Mo didn't disappoint his teaching. 'What was Robbie Steele like?'

Brother Bertie stared straight ahead with a lengthy sigh. 'Only saw him once, from a distance. Came to pick Precious up in some flash set of wheels. She raved about him until one day she didn't.' *Nicely done! Short 'n' sweet!*

Mo shifted, searching his profile. 'Why did she stop talking about him?'

He still wouldn't gaze at his Baby-gal. Instead, he drank deeply of his special Caribbean brew. 'I figured they must've had some kinda bust up and stopped walking out with each other—'

'Did you disapprove of them seeing each other?'

That got him looking at her, the corners of his aged eyes crinkling in confusion. 'Whatcha mean, disapprove?'

Mo wore the expression of a dog that wasn't giving up

until they got the bone. She tucked her legs under herself, leaning her weight into the side of the deck chair. 'You know. Coz he was white and Mum was black?'

Brother Bertie's jaw worked, but no words came out, so gut-shocked was he at her meaning. 'Girl, did you have dumb-dumb flakes for brekkie this morning? Are you implying I'm prejudiced? Don't cotton to a person because of the colour of their skin?' The blood surfaced beneath his dark-brown cheeks. 'Wicked, wicked girl. As if I could ever be like them blasted racists. You've seen my friends, they come from all shades of the rainbow.'

Alertness left Mo. She slumped back in her seat. 'I know that, especially since Ruddy's your bestie.' Frustration crept into her tone. 'I just don't get it. Granddad Jimmy's shown me pictures of Robbie, and the guy was a stunner. Mum's a stunner. What would make two beautiful people break up so badly?'

Brother Bertie's back teeth scraped together when the word 'Jimmy' put in another appearance. Jimmy Scumbag Southpaw. What would Mo say if she knew he couldn't stomach the man? Hated his guts to the core? If he opened up to her he'd have to confess about his own misspent youth. His own criminal past. And the awful rest.

Weariness descended over Brother Bertie. A tiredness that had sod all to do with the rum and weed. Brother Bertie felt every year he'd lived in the East End come back to haunt him. As if that wasn't enough, also eating away at him was he hadn't been able to visit Ted in the hospital yet. The hospital was insisting only family was allowed at the moment. Didn't the hospital get it? He was Ted's family. They were brothers. Blood wasn't the only thing that made people family. He was so worried about his friend. His shoulders drooped, the skin sagged on his face, and his bones held the heaviness of lead inside his skin. God, to shut his eyes and not wake up for an eternity would be a blessing.

'Gramps? Gramps?'

His granddaughter's distant, worried voice pulled him back to the allotment.

He downed some more rum before he gave her a weak, world-weary smile. 'I travelled over here from Jamaica with a group of good friends. All men. Most of them, all they could think about was what type of jobs they would find.' He laughed quietly. 'I wanted a job too, but I also wanted to party from sun up to sun down. Find me some fine ladies to whine on the dance floor.' Whining was some heavy-duty sexy Caribbean dancing.

A bleakness clouded his face, making him look so very sad. 'I found me a very, very special lady and I don't mean your grandmother – rest her beloved soul. What a lucky man I am to have loved two wonderful women.'

'What happened?' Mo's voice was so quiet.

Even though he tried his best, Brother Bertie couldn't stop the sorrow seeping into his every word. 'It was the wrong time for our love. The tide against us was too strong. Sometimes love just isn't enough.' He caught her gaze and held it. 'Maybe that's the truth of your mum and dad – whatever they had wasn't enough.'

Mo adamantly shook her head. 'Nah! I know it was more

than that. There's a whole history here and I'm gonna dig it up. With my bare hands if I have to.'

Abruptly, it dawned on him what else she said she was trying to find out. It left him very troubled indeed. 'What makes you think Robbie Steele was murdered?'

Mo's expression was one of determined defiance. 'Everyone else managed to get out of the fire. *Everyone*. Accept Robbie Steele? Nah! His death's as fishy as a Friday at the chippy.'

Mo spoke her final words as if Brother Bertie was no longer there. 'If it's the last thing I do, I'm going to find out who cut short the life of my father.'

Chapter Seven

'I thought you was a goner for sure,' Ruddy wailed before she threw her arms around Ted, almost smothering him in the hospital bed.

Brother Bertie would usually tell her to stop ladling on the drama so thick. Not today though. There was none of his sarky-sharp tongue now. It was nearly a week on from the incident at the restaurant. This was their first visit to see their old friend.

Brother Bertie's eyes glistened with unshed tears. Lord Jeezuus! He couldn't get the image of Ted lying prone on the floor fighting for breath out of his mind. He'd thought his friend was done for. Gone forever. Gone! At the restaurant, paying no mind to his dodgy hip, he'd dropped to his knees beside Ted in a mad panic, inconsolably calling his friend's name over and over. Ruddy and Brother Bertie had wrapped their arms about each other, drawing strength as they helplessly watched the paramedics work on their friend and eventually stretcher him away.

Thank God it turned out that Ted had had a funny turn because of his blood pressure. The doctors didn't think it was anything serious, but best be on the safe side, so they were running some tests and keeping him in for observation. Whatever the outcome, he was going to be in the hospital for at least a month.

When Ruddy let Ted come up for air, the two men watched each other, their chests heaving with emotion. It was as if they were the only people in the room. Brother Bertie couldn't speak because his throat was clogged with apprehension.

Ted could see that his friend was fighting his feelings and losing the battle. Ted tried to reassure him with a killer smile that ended with a tiny wince of pain. 'Come here, you old fool.'

He beckoned with his work-roughened hand. Brother Bertie limped over and took it. Their foreheads touched. These two men had aged side by side, experiencing the ups and downs of life. Simply put, they were as tight as brothers.

They'd met during that never to be forgotten winter of 63, one of the most savage winters on record. It still brought the shivers out in Brother Bertie just thinking about it. Back then he would wake up in the tiny room he rented with the sensation of ice in his bones, icicles on the single window and the water in the communal toilet bowl frozen over.

When he had initially arrived in England, Bertram Watson had every intention of looking for a respectable job like the other members of the Windrush Generation. Making a new home in England was his chance to turn over a new leaf, leaving his bad boy ways behind. Brother Bertie had got tangled up in some dangerous shit back in Jamaica.

Very dangerous indeed. If his older sister, who was already settled in England, hadn't sent him the money to purchase a ticket to the Motherland, Brother Bertie doubted he'd be alive now.

Landing in England had been a shock to the system. He'd been led to believe that the new immigrants, the Queen's subjects, would be welcomed with open arms ... Well, that wasn't exactly how it had played out. He didn't mind the stares of curiosity, but the name-calling – 'You black so-and-so' – made his fist stiffen at his side with the need to break a face or two. His sister had cautioned him to pay 'those ignorant jackasses' no mind, keep his head and eyes straight and walk tall.

And stay well clear of the nightclubs or any blues parties.

That was Brother Bertie's weakness – the nightlife. He was a party boy, a blues man who loved nothing better than dancing the night away with a rum 'n' Coke in one hand and a lady in the other. Women found him drop-dead gorgeous because he had oodles of style and charm that they found irresistible. Out of respect for his big sis, for a time, Brother Bertie had turned his back on the nightlife. Plus, the last thing he needed was to bring trouble to his family's door. But the winter of 63 had tested his resolve. He'd trudged through bitter snow, skidding on ice, looking for work. In-your-face racism and abuse meant that Brother Bertie had got so many knockbacks on the work front he was losing faith.

He was at an all-time low when he decided to lift his spirits by going down to this basement club in Notting Hill.

He wasn't going to stay long, just enough time to drop foot to a couple of tunes, wet his tongue with a single glass of stout and then be on his way. Problem was, the old life sucked him back in. It didn't take him long to become the life and soul of the party, not just Bertie but everyone's brother with his arm slung over their shoulder in friendship. He hadn't left until coming up to two in the morning, singing Prince Buster's Ska classic, 'Enjoy Yourself It's Later Than You Think,' letting loose some serious dance moves as he and his pork pie hat merrily weaved their way through the streets of West London. He was back to being the original Rude Boy.

And that's when it happened. A blow to the side of the head had him reeling into a wall, crying out in pain. He couldn't see. His vision dizzy in the dark. He shook his head until the world came back into focus, and what he saw made the blood in his veins run as cold as the snow at his feet. Four men dressed to impress with the rebellious quiffs of Teddy Boys. Grinning and jeering, they crowded him, their intent clear – do him some serious damage. Maybe even kill him.

It wasn't the first time that Brother Bertie had found himself in this situation, so he knew the first thing to do was identify the leader. Brother Bertie didn't have long to wait. One of them stepped forward, distinguishing himself from his pack of attack dogs. Barrel-chested, with glossy black hair, moving like his balls were the biggest in London town.

He spoke, threatening and low. 'What you doing in my end of town without my permission?'

Brother Bertie already decided to give as good as he got.

If he was going to get a kicking, then best go down with his pride still intact. He punched off the wall, so he stood on his own two feet. Leaning back could be seen as a sign of weakness, and no way on this earth was he going to come over as someone who'd lost his bottle.

Brother Bertie fronted his attacker out. And laughed with scorn. The man and his thugs looked shocked. 'If you let me go home, maybe I can get my mother to write me a permission slip and bring it back for you.'

The man chuckled, checking the faces of his gang as he slyly slung back, 'We've got a real joker on our hands here, boys.' The night went deathly still when he produced a cutthroat razor. He held it up, its wicked sharpness glinting in the moonlight. 'Why don't I slice you a new grin, from ear to ear? Eh?'

Others might be shitting a brick at this stage. Not Brother Bertie. This two-bit prick didn't scare him. What he'd run from in Jamaica, now *that* terrified the piss out of him.

The other youth couldn't stop the surprise slamming onto his face when Brother Bertie stepped closer instead of cringing away. 'One-on-one,' he dared.

One of the other guys growled in disgust. 'Are we gonna batter the …' a foul racist word spewed out of his mouth, 'or what?'

The youth with the razor swung round violently to face his gang. Between his teeth he warned the one who'd used such vile language, 'Cut it out. You know I don't deal with that type of lingo. We've all got red blood running under our skin.' He twisted back to his cornered quarry. 'And let's see how claret this one's is.'

Brother Bertie got in there quick. 'Like I said. Me and you. Man to man.'

'Now why would I do that with this beauty' – the guy shook the razor – 'in my hand?'

'Because I've got one of them too.' Before his opponent could catch up with his words, Brother Bertie had his own razor in his hand, gleaming in the night. It was one of the first things he'd bought in England. He'd been warned that England was a place where you sometimes had no alternative but to protect your back.

The other guy's gang stepped forward. He waved them back. Grinned. Bent slightly, his blade thrust out, so did Brother Bertie. They circled each other, the air heavy, thickening with tension. Then they suddenly both chucked their weapons aside and jumped on each other. They fought hard and long. Brother Bertie knocked him down. He knocked Brother Bertie down. Punch after punch. They slogged it out in the snow until they were both bloodied, out of breath, lying on the icy ground. They each tried to get up but collapsed back down again.

Finally, the other man rolled to his side. He gazed at the damage he'd done to Brother Bertie. 'My name's Edward, but everyone calls me King Ted.'

Brother Bertie took a couple of breaths, his ribs hurting like crazy. 'Bertram. But everyone calls me Brother Bertie.'

'You looking for a job, Brother Bertie?'

'You've still got the power in your hand.' Brother Bertie

realised that it was Ted's voice he was hearing, but it was Ted decades later in a hospital bed. His friend's tired eyes twinkled as he cheekily added, 'I never told you, but I let you win that night.'

'You wish.' Brother Bertie playfully kissed his teeth. 'If I hadn't downed so many stouts at that blues club I'd have licked your raas all across London.'

Seriousness and emotion overcame Ted. 'I'd take every one of those blows again and again if it meant I'd end up with you as my friend, you ol' bastard.'

The men held on to each other. Nothing would ever break their bond of brothership. Nothing.

Ruddy told Ted, 'We've got a little relish for you.'

Ted rubbed his hands together in delightful anticipation. 'I hope it's that potato and leek soup of yours. Between me and you, Oliver Twist would turn his nose up at the slop they serve in here.'

Ruddy winked. 'I'll bring some soup the next time. A proper treat is what I've got.' She whipped out a quart bottle of Brother Bertie's 'Lord Have Mercy Rum Punch'. Ruddy knew full well that booze was strictly a no-no for Ted, but, come on, a little tipple wouldn't hurt him. That weed would probably speed up his recovery.

Ted let out a heavenly sigh of pleasure. 'Bless you, both. They've been pouring chicken soup down my neck. Thought I was going to grow feathers soon.'

Brother Bertie slowly eased the door open a slither to check that none of the staff were coming to the room. Triumphantly, he reported, 'Coast clear. Although I wouldn't want to tangle with that sister over there, she looks handy with her fists.'

Ruddy raised the rum punch bottle with much ceremony. 'Here's to Ted. The best mate a lady could ever have. I'll always stand by his side through thick and thin—'

'Ted will have died of thirst by the time you finish,' Brother Bertie cut in, eyes rolling.

Taking the hint, Ruddy passed Ted the bottle. He took a deep swig, his eyes watering with gratification. Then they passed the bottle around. It was only meant to be the one round, but they got carried away …

The door burst open.

'Shit,' Brother Bertie cursed, trying to shove the bottle under the blankets. What he actually succeeded in doing was tipping himself onto the bed.

'What the hell's going on here then?' a voice roared.

When the three very guilty senior citizens looked up, it wasn't a nurse, or the dreaded ward sister. It was Ted's nephew.

Nico Sinclair.

Huge grin splitting his handsome face, Nico closed the door and watched as Brother Bertie righted himself. It gladdened his heart to see his uncle's closest friends by his side. He'd only got to know them when Annalisa – Kristal, he must remember she was called Kristal now – did a flit. They offered comfort to Uncle Ted when she'd disappeared. Nico pushed the pain down. It's bitter agony still churned deep in him thinking of her leaving him behind.

King Ted's face lit up at the sight of his nephew. 'How

you been, son? The business running smoothly?'

Go on! Tell him. Tell him you've found Annalisa. Nico didn't. How could he when the old man was lying sick in a hospital bed? Probably give him another seizure.

Instead, he reported, 'Everything's a-grooving and a-moving.' His gaze took in each one of them in turn. 'In fact, you'll all be pleased to hear I had *words* with the tosspots who fucked up in the restaurant. And, believe you me, they'll be minding their table manners from now on.'

Chapter Eight

Sister Aggi wasn't in the mood to take any backchat cheek from the three eleven-year-olds lined up in front of her in the back office at the food bank. Now and again, parents dragged their kids, sometimes by the ear, to the nun for a good ol' talking to if they'd stepped out of line. It was part of her duty to see the next generation straight.

This lot had been caught doing the five-finger discount in a shop on Whitechapel High Street. Nothing big – sticky fingers and dirty fingernails in the pick 'n' mix – but parents around these parts recognised if you didn't nip it in the bud it could escalate into their child walking the path of more ruinous things later on. Although Sister Aggi was only too willing to roll up her sleeves to help her community out, regardless of whether they showed their faces in church come Sunday, she sometimes felt they expected her to have a magic wand hidden up her habit. Wave it in the air and, abracadabra, their naughty kids have transformed into goody-two-shoes, goofy grins an' all.

Sadly, the East End was no Disney movie.

Two of the children before her, the boys, wore expressions

of repentance and scuffed their feet in embarrassment. But the girl was a hard nutcase. She stared at Sister Aggi blatantly right back in the eye. Her brow was insolently arched, mouth mulishly set and posed in a way that shouted she was planning to be queen of the world one day. The bad world.

The unrepentant kid reminded Sister Aggi of another girl. Small and fierce. A girl who had taken on the playground bullies and despite being knocked on her arse time after time she'd defiantly climbed to her feet, fists locked tight in front, ready to slog it out.

'Sister Argy Bargy giving you a tongue-lashing,' a voice intruded from the open doorway.

Talk of the devil. Fancy that, her memories must've conjured up the girl. Slightly stumped, Sister Aggi found the small, bullish figure of Maureen Watson cockily leaning, arms folded, against the doorframe. Mo, or Big Mo as the nun had been hearing people calling her lately, was the only person who called her Sister Argy Bargy in recognition that the nun wasn't afraid to get stuck in, including putting herself in harm's way if it protected one of her flock.

Mo sauntered past the nun she'd known since school days who had also been her needlework teacher. She stopped in front of the line of children and gave them *the look*.

Mo told them, voice dead serious, 'Dunno whatcha gone and done, but you wanna listen to this here lady.' She stabbed her thumb in the older woman's direction.

The boys had the decency to cast their shame-filled gazes to the floor, but the girl … now she was a different breed entirely. Her regard was steady and unnerved, boldly sticking to Mo's face. 'How come you never listened to her advice?'

'You what?' Mo was not only baffled but put out by the kid's bald-faced cheek.

The girl's eyes suddenly lit up with admiration. 'You're Big Mo, ain'tcha? Mister Southpaw's new grandkid.'

The force of the child's adoration almost toppled Mo backwards. No one had stared at her that way before, as if she were the maker of glittering dreams. Mind you, after Jimmy's public announcement that she was his heir, it hadn't taken long for some folks to start bowing and scraping to her.

Mo should've felt on top of the world. Hadn't this been what she'd been gunning for all the time? Praise. Admiration. Maximum respect. But the last thing she felt was elation. This was pure scary shit. People were going to be looking up to her, their expectations running high.

Daffy, the woman from the beauty salon's hateful words came back to her: *'The girl's the size of a bottle of milk. Probably without the bottle, you get me? Who in their right nut's going to be scared of her? Take orders off her?'*

Mo squared her shoulders, shoving off her doubts. She ruffled a hand through the girl's pixie cut. 'What's your name, sweetheart?'

The girl's grin was slow and long, leaving her mouth wriggling like a worm. 'I'm the girl who's gonna take away your crown when I grow up.'

What a sauce! Before Mo could muster a retort, the three naughties scampered out of the room, laughing and joshing each other.

'You've got a proper live wire there, that's for sure,' Mo

told Sister Aggi, referring to the mouthy girl.

The nun sighed, knowingly raising her eyebrows. 'Puts me in mind of another child I knew years back who vowed to take the East End by storm.' Her brows fell. 'And word is she's ended up in a nest made of Steele.'

Seeing Mo about to go on the defensive, the nun put her hand up as a sign of peace. 'Let's get some air.'

Once in the alley out back, Sister Aggi pulled out the one vice she couldn't ditch from her old life, a pack of ciggies. Mo took the one on offer, and soon both were puffing away, leaning against the scarred brick wall.

Sister Aggi asked, as gentle as can be, 'Has it sunk in yet that your Jimmy Southpaw's granddaughter?'

Mo's spine curved heavily into the hard wall. 'Truth? I still feel like I've been hit by a truck and then it's come back and run over me again. I've been left on the ground while the world happily goes on around me.'

Neither of them spoke. The traffic on the Commercial Road was noisy at the other end of the alley. The Commercial Road was one of the main roads into the city and as such it rarely seemed to sleep.

Finally, Sister Aggi cautioned, 'You can still be his granddaughter and have nothing to do with his business enterprises.' With an urgency, she positioned herself in front of Mo. 'There's plenty of families around here where half are grafting and doing an honest day's toil and the other half wouldn't know how to spell honest much less live it. Bottom line is though, both halves love each other. You could do that with—'

'I haven't come here to talk about Granddad Jimmy. I want to ask you about my dad,' Mo butted in.

Confusion appeared like a rash all over Sister Aggi's face. She dropped the ciggie butt and ground it with her soft, black flats. 'Robbie? Robbie Steele?'

The air thundered in Mo's chest as she insisted, 'Someone killed him in that police station. Burnt him to a crisp in a cell.' She drew in a tremendous breath. 'And I'm going to find out who did it.'

Suddenly the nun became silent and still, but her gaze was busy checking over Mo like she'd never seen her before. Then she spoke ever so slowly and faintly as if in a daze. 'I should've noticed. How did it escape me? You've got Jimmy Southpaw's eyes.' She shook herself slightly like she was clearing her head and pulled up tall. 'I'm so sorry for your loss, Mo. But why would I know anything about Robbie Steele's passing?'

'Coz you know everything that goes on around here. You hear the lot.' She beseeched the woman who had taken a tiny, battered girl under her wing years ago. 'If you know anything, please tell me.'

'I do not.' Sister Aggi wasn't finished. 'But if I did, I wouldn't tell you. Murder. Thou shall not kill. The unlawful taking of another's life. Mo, this is dangerous. Stay away from this. I beg you.'

Pissed, Mo stalked through the food bank towards the exit, so full of fiery frustration she wanted to punch something. Hard. Anything to get rid of this wagonload of defeat that she'd never discover what happened to Robbie Steele. It still rocked her universe to think what his last moments must've been like. Poisonous fumes choking and burning his eyes. Kicking and screaming for air. Wicked and lethal flames sweeping under the door. The idea that was how the father she'd never got a chance to kiss on the cheek, hug tight, had had his life cut short, almost had Mo crashing, broken, to her knees.

Maybe Granddad Jimmy was right, and it was all an accident. The police station's dodgy electrics. Still, Mo couldn't let it go. What were the odds of everyone in the building getting out and the only person who didn't was the son of the local crime lord? The son who was next in line to take over? And, from all accounts, Robbie was a man with a smart head on his shoulders and a nifty nose for recognising the stench of trouble. And shouldn't a police station be one of the safest places a person could be?

Nah! What had gone on just wasn't adding up.

Mo let out a long overdue sigh. She passed the young woman on the reception and neared the entrance door … and collided with someone coming into the building. Mo recoiled in disgust, her nose wrinkling at the stink. What the fecking hell had she bumped into?

'Sorry, lovely lady,' leered a man who was as grizzled as an old bear and …

Mo made a face at the ripe whiff coming off him and reared back. By way of reply he chuckled, flashing a mouth that was more gum than teeth. Mo dismissed him, ready to be on her way. Then stopped dead when she heard the conversation between stinky grizzly bear and the receptionist.

'Surprised to see you, Pockets,' the receptionist brightly greeted. 'Heard you were stopping with your sister in Gravesend after you got caught in that fire last year.'

Willie 'Pockets' Robinson's chest rumbled with a chuckle. 'My sister can't cook to please a fart, not like the food around here. Anyroad, she was doing my nut in, her and those feral kids of hers.'

The receptionist clucked her tongue. 'A bad business that fire. In a police station of all places.'

His voice lowered, his cloudy eyes furtively darting about before he confided, 'I was in the cell next door to the poor sod who never made it out. They opened up my cell and let me go. I don't get it. Why didn't they unlock his cell door too?'

Mo gasped. A horrible sensation slid down her spine. Then a ray of hope hit. She rushed outside to her motor, a shiny light-blue Mini Convertible where her muscle, Dell and Josh, waited up front.

Mo slipped urgently into the back. 'I've got a job I need you both to do.'

Chapter Nine

Eyes closed, Eileen Dripsey gripped the middle-aged man's hand so tight she nearly dragged him across the table in her sitting room in the prefab she lived in. She let out a long drawn-out moan, swaying slightly.

'Your ol' mam says to forget the dim-witted bimbos you usually hang out with. Her spirit says you need a relationship with a slightly older woman. Someone more mature.' The pressure of her grip increased. 'Perhaps someone on a higher spiritual plane. And who's desperate to see the musical, Mamma Mia!'

Eileen was doing her Madam Amon-Ra routine, giving Monty here a special one-to-one séance to commune with his dear mum who had met her maker last summer at the grand old age of ninety-one. In her role as a psychic healer to the East End, Eileen had been offering him spiritual counselling, fortune telling, in fact any service that would see Monty come waltzing through her front door. Eileen had fancied the pants off him ever since he'd set up his fish stall in Chrisp Street Market fifteen years back. She'd worshipped him from afar with a heavy sigh; no way would a good-looking bloke like him be interested in a dumpy Doris like her. Well, that's what Eileen told herself. Monty had been heartbroken with grief when his mum passed over to the world of the angels. When he came seeking spiritual enlightenment, Eileen had seen her chance and taken it.

And used her bogus channelling of his mum's 'spirit' to push him in the right direction with his love life. Earlier, she'd spent eons at her dressing table, putting the finishing touches to her slap. None of the eccentric outfits she usually wore for sessions for yummy Monty. He got Uncensored Eileen in her LBD. Some might scoff that she was a little on the old side to be wearing gear like that, but Eileen was confident she still had the legs for it, especially after she'd shed a few pounds after watching her fave daytime telly host, Floyd Plunker's, chat show weight loss special: *The Greyhound Diet. Eat what a greyhound eats because you never see a fat greyhound.*

Eileen Dripsey was very lonely. Even a spiritual adviser needed some hot loving from time to time.

A bemused Monty asked, 'My mum's saying that? That I need a more mature lady?'

Eileen snapped with a bat of her eyelashes, 'Are you suggesting your mother's spirit isn't whispering that in my ear?'

'No! No, of course not. It just doesn't sound like something my mum would say.'

Her Right Said Fred's 'I'm Too Sexy' front doorbell chimed. Who the heck could that be? Eileen stubbornly compressed her lips. Whoever it was could buzz right off.

She was going to make her move tonight on Monty. Go in for the kill. And nothing was getting in her way.

Chrissakes! Whoever was at her door wouldn't let up.

Monty lifted his brows. 'Don't you think you should get that?'

'Nah! Probably my neighbour, Ruddy, wanting a bowl of sugar—'

She never finished because an insistent and impatient tapping at the window caught both their attention. When she saw who was staring at her through the window, Eileen inwardly groaned. Kristal fecking Steele. Madam Drama Queen. Monty was on his feet, visibly shaken at the apparition of Jimmy Southpaw's daughter-in-law at the window. The last thing he wanted was trouble.

Swallowing convulsively, he let out, 'Madam Amon-Ra, I'll come over another time.'

No! No! Eileen stretched out her arm beseechingly to him, but Monty was gone with the speed of his mum's spirit chasing him. Eileen's heart pinched, her arm falling limply and dejectedly to her side. She was crestfallen. She might never get another chance to tell Monty how she felt.

'Madam Amon-Ra?' came Kristal's sing-song enquiring voice from the open front doorway. 'May I come in? You did an exorcism for me the last time, casting out a very pesky pushy demon from my boy Damien?'

Eileen remembered alright. Truth was, seeing Monty depart like that had taken the wind out of her sails. Wearily she got up and moved to the front door where Kristal hovered. 'I'm sorry, Kristal, but I'm afraid you've called at rather a bad time. If you need to see me for anything, you will need to book an appointment online.'

Running her gaze over Eileen, Kristal slowly studied her legs and figure-hugging, super-short little black number. 'Gone on the game, have you? I don't blame you, babe, I hear it's good money.'

This was too much for Eileen. She was curt. 'Book online, Mrs Steele.'

She tried to close the door, but Kristal shoved one of her Dior sparkling sapphire sling-back shoes in the way. 'Come on, love, you can give a good customer like me an emergency service, surely? I'll pay double.' Kristal took out a bulging brown envelope from her metallic-silver Ted Baker handbag and waved it under Eileen's nose. 'You know I'm good for it. I'll pony up whatever it takes.'

Eileen's gaze was glued to the envelope. There was no doubt Kristal was good for it. And Eileen could always use the dough.

'Mrs Steele, this is most irregular, but if it's urgent, I suppose I could make an exception in this case.'

'Oh, it's urgent, babe, you don't want to worry about that.'

Eileen escorted Kristal to the main room where the lights were already dimmed from the earlier séance. She left Kristal and returned a few minutes later kitted out in one of her purple gowns with its yellow and white sun and moon symbols and matching pointed hat, which was in reality a magician's outfit.

'What can I do for you? Another problem with your son?'

Kristal leant forward and whispered, 'Not this time. I was wondering where you are on curses?'

'Curses?' Madam Amon-Ra batted her eyelashes.

'Putting the hex on people and that. I think you've done one for me before.' Her voice grew grim. 'There's one enemy in particular I need messed up.'

Kristal ferreted around in her designer bag and produced a doll. A Cabbage Patch Doll. Its expression was very glum indeed with its tight-lipped mouth. 'Mo' was scrawled in black felt tip on its forehead.

'There are other people I want worked over, but Mo's my priority. I mean, obviously I don't want you to off her or nuthin'. If I want someone whacked, I'll sort that out myself. But if you could just,' Kristal waved casually in the air, 'mess her up with a couple of quick curses, I'd be very grateful.'

Eileen knew she was getting into very dangerous territory. She knew exactly which 'Mo' Kristal Steele was referring to. Jimmy Southpaw's heir. She was going to have to play this very, very delicately.

She played dumb. 'Mess her up?'

'Make some terrible badness bomb into her life. Y'know, Chronic back pain, hair falling out, a plague of locusts buzzing after her every time she steps out. That sort of thing. If you could make a carbuncle grow on Mo's cheek there'd definitely be a drink in it for you.'

Eileen took the doll from Kristal and stared at it. 'Well, as I'm sure you understand, this is highly specialised work. And very expensive. It's also the case that curses require regular topping up, so I'll probably need a financial retainer on a monthly basis. You also need to know that curses take some time to bed in, so don't expect any immediate results.'

Kristal took her brown envelope and firmly placed it on a coffee table. 'There's a grand for starters, and I'll pay whatever it takes. And if the next time I see Mo she's going a bit thin on top, you can bet there'll be a bonus in it for you.'

After excusing herself, Eileen went off to the airing cupboard where she kept her sewing machine. She found some needles and pins in her sewing basket. On her return, she scattered her pins and needles on the table and then picked up an especially vicious-looking one along with the Mo doll.

'Kristal, I'm going to need you to focus for me. I want you to close your eyes and imagine Mo. She's standing against a black background and there are wispy shafts of red light casting shadows over her face. I need you to keep that vision in your head at all times because if you fail for one moment, my spell will fail too and you will have wasted your time and money. Are you focused?'

'You better believe I'm focused.'

'You may hear me make some distressing noises, but there's no need to be alarmed. It's all part of the ritual. Do you understand?'

Eyes shut tight, Kristal nodded.

What a numpty! Eileen thought, gazing heavenward, shaking her head with a wry smile. After a few moments of silence, Eileen let out a high-pitched scream.

Kristal gasped. Eyes flashing open. 'Are you alright there?'

Eileen was furious. 'Are you deaf? I said shut your noise and focus!'

'Yes, sorry.'

Eileen stared at her fingernails while making ominous squeals, howls and groans that suggested she was in agony. Then she realised it sounded like she was having an orgasm, so she switched to moans of, 'Help! Help me! What's wrong with my back? My feet. I can't feel my feet. Oh, my hair, my beautiful locks are falling to the floor!'

Her voice tailed off into a whisper, a ghostly whisper of, 'Noooooooo!'

After a minute's silence, Eileen's voice rose again, cold and metallic. 'Kristal, focus on Mo. Focus hard. She's tumbling into a long black pit, over and over into the abyss.'

Eileen decided to skip the noises this time. She silently padded her way to her kitchen and stared out of the window. When she was back in her chair, she adopted a pose and stretched out her palms. 'You may now open your eyes, Kristal.'

An anxious Kristal opened one eye. 'Are we done?'

'Yes. Chaos and mayhem are winging their way through the ether to your sworn enemy, Mo.'

'Only I didn't hear the Mo doll make any noises. Or screams.'

Eileen let her hands drop. 'Some pain is too deep to be expressed. The Other and Unseen World is now in motion and can't be called back.'

'Fair enough.'

When Eileen opened her front door to mercifully shoo

Kristal on her way, a darkened figure appeared at the gate. For a moment it seemed Kristal thought it was a visitor from the Other and Unseen World.

Stepping outside, she called out in horror, 'Oi! Whatcha playing at? Who's that out there waiting for me?'

A sheepish Monty emerged from the shadows. He shuffled uncomfortably, peering at Eileen. 'I was a bit worried about you. Thought you seemed a bit off when I left.'

Eileen didn't give him a chance to think. She grabbed Monty by the arm, licked her lips and dragged him into her prefab and slammed the door shut.

Chapter Ten

The usual sound of flesh on flesh and moans of pleasure couldn't mask the sharp shriek that shattered the air, followed by an agonising, choked sob inside the Mighty Minge brass house in Canning Town. Lucky Lucy, the madam of the brothel, fisted her hands tightly in her lap as she sat in her office near the reception. She knew what those sounds meant – one of her girls was getting the stuffing beaten out of her. Lucky didn't countenance violence inside her house. Once you let that through the door, word got around, and before you know it, all the other weirdos and creeps were lined up outside wanting to ply their filthy trade within your four walls.

In normal circumstances, Madam Lucky wouldn't have bothered with knocking, she'd have been in that room in two seconds flat, grabbed the fella by his short and curlies and thrown him in the gutter as naked as the day he was born with a lasting kick to the ribs as a reminder never to darken her door again. The problem was, these weren't everyday circumstances. The customer with her girl wasn't your run-of-the-mill Joe Bloggs.

Carlos Donahoe was his name. She'd heard on the crime vine that he was making a name for himself in South London. A name as an enforcer who was willing to not only do other folks' dirty work but clean up so that not a speck of evidence was left behind. The bastard mainly tidied up after Nico Sinclair, a name to be reckoned with.

Tiptoe very delicately around the issue, that's what Lucky was going to have to do. But know this, she wasn't putting up with some twisted tosser trashing her girls. She would never forget the feel of her dad's fists on her child's body after he came home from the boozer most nights. Physically the scars were long gone, but they remained in her brain, coming alive and festering at times like these.

A deep voice at the door pulled her back to the present. 'You want me to sort that out?'

Lucky looked up at Benny in the doorway. He was her muscle who ensured that punters understood the rules of the house and, more importantly, what hellfire would be unleashed upon them if they stepped over the line. A huge guy, built like a house, downright scary to those who didn't know him. Lucky had known him long enough to realise that beneath all that muscle was a total sweetheart. A gentle giant who hated to see the girls being harmed in any way.

Lucky paused, mulling over his question. She'd love nothing better than to see Benny bash the brains out of Carlos Donahoe, but she recognised she couldn't do that. What was needed here was a combo of girly-girly flirtation and firmness.

She smiled gratefully at him. 'Never you mind, Benny

babe. I'll have a little word in his ear and have it all as smooth as a baby's bot in no time.'

Suddenly his bushy brows hitched up. 'When what's-his-name gets here, he ain't gonna be best pleased.'

Lucky's face fell. Bouncing balls! She'd totally forgotten about *him*. Benny was bang to rights about that. The issue was the girl had a regular customer who it was very important for Lucy to keep on side. He'd go bloody maracas-crackers if he got wind Charmaine had been used as another punter's punchbag.

Ten minutes later, Lucy heard Charmaine's door open and the heavy footsteps of Carlos Donahoe making his way towards the reception. She managed to get there before him. She squinted knowingly at the woman who managed the front desk, who took the hint and disappeared.

Lucy strategically positioned herself in front of the main door with a fake face-splitting smile stretched from ear to ear. She'd been bestowing that smile on guys since she was fifteen. 'I take it Charmaine nicely fulfilled all your requirements?' she preened.

And rippled with disgust inside. In this game Lucy had seen all types of faces – lopsided, minus an eye, wicked burns. In fact, her place had a reputation for offering tea, sympathy and oodles of humpalicious sex to men who were feeling out of sorts because of their physical appearance. This guy was in a league of his own. He was the poster child of ugly. It looked like someone had put his face through a sausage grinder and then plonked it willy-nilly back together. He'd make a mint in Hollywood as the monster in a horror movie. It wasn't his features that bothered her so much. What made him particularly ugly was his twisted nature.

Carlos Donahoe didn't smile back. Instead, he gave her a quelling glance that was meant to put her in her place. 'There's more life in a stiff down the morgue than that Charmaine. Think I'll sample something that at least sounds like it's breathing next time.'

Next time? Touch one of her girls again? Not on your effing life, matey!

Lucy allowed her smile to congeal slightly. She considered her words very, very carefully. 'Thing is, my business is built on my reputation. A reputation of having princesses who give a new meaning to the word 'regal'. Picture perfect they are, ready for David Bailey to snap.' She placed a gentle finger on his arm. 'I think we understand what I'm talking about.'

He grabbed her finger and bent it back. She gulped in pain. He hauled her mercilessly close. His spit hit her face. 'Princesses! Slags and sluts, every last one of 'em. They should be thankful a bloke like me allows his knob anywhere near their filthy gashes.' Viciously, he twisted her finger, and she howled. 'I'm going to spread it around that the clap's breeding in here. Let everyone know that, come here and there's a chance your cock's going to fall off—'

Benny grabbed him in a chokehold and swung him around like a toy.

Lucy forgot all about the hot, shooting pain in her finger, shouting, 'Stop it, Benny. Put him fucking down.'

A gasping Carlos was instantly dropped to the floor.

Benny stood over him, breathing heavily.

Lucy pointed her throbbing finger at Carlos. 'I want you. Out!' Now it was her turn to be menacing. 'You say a false word against this house, and I'll have Jimmy Southpaw on you like a catcher on a rat.'

The blood drained from his face at the mention of the legendary Southpaw. Slowly, he struggled to his feet, never taking his mean, beady eyes off her.

He jeered, 'I wouldn't touch one of your scrubbers with a barge pole. I wouldn't come back here if the lotto jackpot waited for me to collect up one of your slapper's snatches.'

And with that, he was gone.

Lucy's legs wobbled, making her collapse against the wall. She could barely catch her breath.

Benny asked, 'You alright, boss lady?'

She couldn't even speak, so nodded instead. This life was going to be the death of her. At least the cretin wouldn't dare show his mug here again. Then she remembered Charmaine's regular. He was very possessive of her. And, if that wasn't bad enough, he had a temper on him. The last thing she needed now was more aggro.

Lucy clamped her teeth firmly together. She was going to have to warn Charmaine to keep her trap well and truly airtight shut.

Shooting his load, Damien groaned with toe-curling pleasure and slumped heavily on top of Charmaine. His exertions made his breath hot and harsh in the curve of her neck. She certainly knew how to put him through his paces.

Wring the toothpaste completely out of his tube.

When he flopped on his back, Charmaine leapt out of the bed as if the hounds of Hell were on her tail. She whipped on her baby doll dressing gown in a flash. Damien scowled. What the heck was going on? Since he'd arrived, he'd got the distinct impression something was up with her. Usually, their session kicked off with Charmaine offering him a perfect cuppa, and they'd relax back for a half-hour chat. Today, she'd wanted to get right down to business. His mum would probably have a fit and box his ears bloody if she knew one of his closest friends was a Covent Garden nun.

'Tarts are only for afters,' was what his mum tried to drum into his head.

He wasn't stupid enough to fall for Charmaine. It wasn't like that between them. What made them close was she was the only one who knew about his secret. Clever lady had figured it out during their second session together. Even his mum, with all her bluster and knowhow hadn't twigged he was hiding something from her. And Charmaine, bless her, hadn't breathed a word to a soul.

He sat up, his brows slashing together, carefully observing her. After they had sex, usually, she'd take her time getting out of bed and make a big show of parading in front of him, playfully and teasingly showing off her assets before seductively putting on her dressing gown.

He said, 'Sharm, what's up, baby?'

She averted her blue gaze from him. 'Nuthin'.' Then glanced back. The smile she fixed to her lips was as false as her long lashes. 'How can anything be wrong after making love with you, lover?'

Damien stiffened. Now he definitely knew something was up. They never referred to what they did as making love. They were too straight up with each other for that. It was always sex. They didn't delude each other about that. Besides, most of the pleasure he derived from his visits was from sitting and talking to her. She listened to him in a way his mum never did. Never interrupted him either.

Since his dad had died, Charmaine had been like a rock. Damien had worshipped the ground his dad walked on. Had looked up to him in all ways. His dad hadn't minded how he sometimes oddly held his head. Robbie Steele had made him feel loved. Now he was gone, and only Charmaine provided him with a shoulder to grieve on.

Damien got out of the bed and walked over to her. She tried to look away, but he gently tucked a finger under her chin, turning her to face him. That's when he noticed what he should've as soon as he'd first seen her. He would've if he hadn't been thinking with his dick. Charmaine's face was plastered with powder, especially around her gorgeous, big eyes.

Damien raised his hand.

Charmaine flinched back. 'Please don't,' she begged.

His nostrils flared and he grimly pressed his lips together. He didn't drop his hand but placed it against her cringing face and used the pad of his thumb to wipe away the cosmetics near her eye. Damien gasped at the ugly bruise hidden beneath.

He saw red. Blind fury consumed him. 'Who did this to you? Was it Benny?'

Charmaine rolled her eyes at that. 'Benny? He don't touch the girls even when they're shooting him come-hither looks for a quickie between customers.'

Damien took her by the hand and perched her next to him on the bed. 'Who put their stinking hands on you?'

Charmaine initially clamped up. She was under strict instructions from Madam Lucky to keep the story under lock and key. Especially from Damien. Jimmy Southpaw's grandkid. Still, he was so kind to her. After punters washed themselves – house rules – they were on her like men who hadn't eaten for a year. Huffing and puffing for England, dripping sweat, not giving a stuff that the only way she could deal with being prodded and poked was to be lubricated beforehand to the hilt. All that mattered to them was their needs were met.

Not this sweet lad, though.

He took time to listen to her woes. Tipped her a bit on the side to help with her son's schooling. Charmaine knew full well she was playing silly beggers getting emotionally entangled with a client, especially one with the surname 'Steele'. The trouble was, this boy had somehow wrapped himself around her jaded heart. He didn't make her feel dirty and used up like so many of the other johns.

So, she told him, gripping his hand. The horrible story poured out. Being duffed over was a hazard of the flesh trade. Nevertheless, that didn't make her telling of the violence that had been inflicted on her body in this very room any easier. It was as if that bastard was thumping her up all over again.

Charmaine was in tears by the end. Damien took her into his arms and rocked her.

And whispered, 'What's the name of this fuckwit?'

'Carlos Donahoe.' Her mouth suddenly snapped shut. Maybe she shouldn't have told him that. 'You can't do nuthin' about it.'

Damien patted her back as his anger turned to silent vengeance. 'Don't you worry your head about a thing.'

Silently he vowed: *I'll sort out that fucker Carlos Donahoe.*

Chapter Eleven

Willie 'Pockets' Robinson, of no fixed abode, greedily gulped down the contents of the bottle of hand sanitiser, weaving his way through a dark street in the back of Mile End near the old cemetery. He smacked his lips, a dreamy, satisfied gleam in his eyes, lapping up every last drop of the liquid. He didn't have a clue what the time was. He never did when the booze got into him and, let's face it, that's how it was most days.

The cravings came upon him more and more these days. When that happened, he found himself down the offy in record time buying a bottle of voddy. The stuff was like manna from Heaven. It warmed his belly up and made the memories of a life badly lived disappear. The only problem was when he'd drained every drop, the heartache all came back. But he didn't have any money left, so he'd gone down to Mile End Hospital and nicked more of the hand sanitiser, which contained enough alcohol to help him drown his sorrows again.

Once upon a time, back in the day when he'd had a wife and three kids and a gorgeous home in Stepney Green, he'd cared about his drinking, done his best to control it. Then

Pockets had been laid off, and instead of feeding the family, the dough he'd got off the social went down his throat. He was so rat-faced the day his wife packed up his kids and left, he still couldn't fully recall what went on. After that it didn't take long for him to be turfed out in the street, the life of the homeless welcoming him with dodgy open arms.

High as a kite, Pockets suddenly spread his arms wide and started singing 'Nessun Dorma' in a comical parody of The Three Tenors. He'd learnt the song off by heart, in Italian, in a drying-out clinic many years ago to try to keep his mind off the demon drink. His operatic voice sounded more like 'Who Let the Dogs Out'. Pockets didn't give a toss.

That's why he never heard the swift footsteps gaining ground behind him. A baton viciously struck him in the back of his knee. His legs went from beneath him and he crashed to the hard street. He cried out with fright when two figures loomed over him. Clothed in black from head to toe, the both of them. Had the Grim Reaper sent spirits from the cemetery to come get him?

Trembling with fright, Willie's bladder let loose a warm stream of urine. He held his arms up defensively, pleading, 'I ain't done nuthin'. Please! Leave me al—'

The remainder of his words strangled in his throat as the demons took an arm each and dragged him down the street to a waiting car. He was unceremoniously dumped inside the boot.

Delilah gagged, her tummy recoiling in disgust. She slapped her palm firmly over her nose and mouth, fighting to keep the sick down. The stench coming off Pockets was beyond nauseating, and it wasn't all down to him pissing his pants. How people could live like he did, she'd never know.

Pockets had been lifted off the streets by Mo's two minders, Dell and Josh. Dell wasn't a girly-girl, preferring trousers and a simple top. She didn't subscribe to straightening her hair, so it was always natural and done up in twists which some mistook for dreads. Josh, on the other hand, got many of his clothes tailor-made. He was a charmer with one of the most gorgeous faces around. Truth be told, he swanned about like he was some sex icon. Well, that's how Dell viewed it.

Dell and Josh hated each other on sight. Hated even more that they had to work together.

They turned their attention to Pockets. The old soak cringed on the floor of the hotel. It was one of those hotels where you placed a thick enough bundle of smackaroos at the reception, no questions were asked. Instructions were simple. Clean and sober him up. Well, as much as possible in the hour they'd been given to do it.

Dell clucked her tongue with supreme annoyance, flashing a heated gaze at Josh. 'How the frigging hell are we going to de-booze his tank? The guy smells rank, like he's been squatting in a barrel of Jack D for the last year.'

'What?' Josh messed his gorgeous face up with a sneer. They both knew his expression of disdain was directed at her and had nothing to do with the terrified man on the floor. 'You frightened of getting those soft hands of yours dirty?'

Dell took that the way it was intended, as a jibe. She

kissed her teeth as if he were lower than dirt, cocking her head and a hip to the side, turning into the trademark South London-Jamaican gal she was.

'Scared? As if! Then again, knowing your background you've probably been dealing with booze heads your whole miserable life.'

'You what?' Dell smugly smiled at his fired-up response. It was so easy to take the rise out of Josh. He continued, dander well and truly up. 'You saying something about my family? About my mum?'

Touchy! Obviously, his mum was a sore spot. Dell backed up a bit. She might get a real tickle out of messing with his mind, but no way was she out to diss anyone's mother. Mums were important. They were often the backbone of a family, keeping it together through lean and tough times. Where would she be if her mum hadn't sent her to England on a one-way ticket to Croydon?

Dell couldn't hide her curiosity. Josh clenched his jaw at her comment about his mother. 'Something happen to your mum?' She couldn't resist adding under her breath, 'Other than the misfortune of giving birth to you.'

Josh inhaled harshly through his nose. 'Nothing you need to be worrying your interfering nut over.'

Dell's sympathy fled. 'At least my face ain't as pretty as a Miss Universe contestant.'

And they were off! Their mouths out of the gates, forgetting the business at hand, instead lobbing insults at each other. Despite Dell and Josh having been given equal power by Jimmy Southpaw to guard his newly found granddaughter, the twosome were often tearing at each other's throats. Neither would admit it, but they were jealous of each other, rivals in wanting to be Mo's main confidant. Her number one muscle.

Pockets momentarily forgot the dangerous situation he found himself in, his eyes bouncing from one to the other like a tennis match at Wimbledon, the insults flying thick and fast.

Abruptly the atmosphere changed. In a nifty move, Dell crossed her arms over her head and down her back, unzipped the rucksack she carried with her everywhere and pulled out one of her constant travelling companions – a wicked machete.

Willie's heart crashed and cried out. She loomed large and fearsome like a pirate with a cutlass ready to carve him up worse than a Sunday roast. Probably dump his butchered remains in the river. And he still had no sodding clue what he'd done.

The air whooshed out of him in merciful relief when she merely used her deadly weapon to slice through the tape that bound his hands together. Pockets didn't have time to enjoy the feel of the blood pulsating properly in his arms again because he was yanked to his feet by Josh and dragged into the bathroom. He was dumped onto the floor of the shower which Dell turned on. Full force. He shivered and shook with the shock of the ice-cold water.

Dell and Josh watched him dispassionately from the corner of the cubicle.

Josh casually commented, 'That should sober the fucker up.'

Del added, 'What does Big Mo want with him, anyway?'

A voice from the bathroom doorway caught them both off guard. 'That's for me to know and you two to be told on a need-to-know basis.'

Big Mo stood there taking in the scene. She pointed a finger at the quaking mess Pockets was in the shower. 'Get him kitted out in some clobber and pour some coffee down his neck.'

'I want you to tell me what happened in the fire inside that cop shop.'

Mo wasn't hanging about. She got down to business once Pockets faced her in the chair opposite in the hotel room. She was jittery, could barely sit still with the thought of what she might discover. She wasn't ready to bring her cousin and Josh into her confidence about what she was doing, so they were both stationed outside in the corridor.

Pockets' wizened face checked her out. 'Who the bloody hell are you then?'

Mo almost jerked threateningly forward, allowing her nerves to get the better of her. Almost. She stopped the motion in time. She was Jimmy Southpaw's heir now, which meant she had to conduct herself in a particular way. Cool and ultra-calm on the outside, while her brain did all the work on the inside. So that's how Mo played it, relaxing back into the lumpy stuffing in the armchair.

'I'm the one asking questions here, not you, matey.'

Pockets tucked his neck into his chest, his eyes suddenly wide. 'I don't know nuthin' about nuthin'. How the heck would I know what happened at that fire?'

Now she leant forward, so he got a close-up of her deadly expression. Let him understand she wasn't fucking around. 'Now, we both know that's a load of ol' cockle.' Mo shifted back, crossing her legs with ease. 'In fact, a little birdie swears you was in the cell next door to the cell where the man died in the fire.'

An expression of such stark horror spread across his face. Mo thought he was about to keel over. The words flew out of Pockets' mouth so quickly it was hard to keep up with them. 'I never … I swear … How was I meant to know that next door is Robbie Steele …?' His lips snapped shut so tight it looked like his jaw was glued together.

'Jimmy Southpaw's son?' she softly finished for him.

Mo surprised Pockets by not demanding an answer but easing to her feet instead. She slow-walked to the camper-sized fridge and took out a bottle of really expensive fizz. Inwardly Mo smugly smiled, knowing full well what had grabbed Pockets' attention. The bottle of booze. Mo made a big production of taking her time opening it. Pockets looked on with horrified greedy dismay when the champagne bubbled over and slid down the side. Probably wished his mouth was under it to catch every last drop. *Good!* That's exactly the reaction Mo was after. The temptation of liquor to a seasoned alkie she hoped would make him tell her what he knew about the fire.

Mo sauntered back to the uncomfy chair and waved the Dom Perignon at him. 'This is all yours.' With a thud, she placed it on the side table. 'All you've got to do is tell me what happened inside the police station that night.'

His tongue flicked out, wetting his cracked lips. He grabbed the bottle with such ferocity it almost tipped over. Pockets angled it to his lips, tipping his head back. His Adam's apple bobbed as he ravenously drank his fill. He sucked at the bottle like a baby at its mother's breast.

Mo let him feast for a while, then, 'Tell me what happened.'

With the back of his hand, Pockets wiped his mouth and belched loudly. 'I got picked up by the plod for a non-payment of a fine—'

'Let's skip the *This is Your Life* section. Tell me why your cell was unlocked, and Robbie Steele's wasn't.'

Pockets squinted at her with suspicion. 'I never said that—'

'Know what your problem is, Pockets?' Mo confronted him with. 'You've got a big trap. And word has reached me that you're telling anyone with an ear you was let out of your cell while Robbie was kept locked in his.'

He reared half out of his seat in indignation. 'Whoever said that is blowing porkies straight outta their lying arse—'

Mo got in his face, so he tumbled back down. 'I heard you at the food bank, with my own ears speaking to the girl on reception. Now, one of us is lying big-time here … and it isn't me. Got it?'

His eyelids lowered, checking her out below the cover of his lashes. His jaundiced-coloured fingers clenched and unclenched in his lap. His head abruptly shot up and he stared starkly at her. 'I nearly choked to death myself in there, I did. Black smoke coming in like a phantom raised up from the dead. I start banging on the door and no one comes. No one. Banging and banging, I'm like a madman.'

Mo's heart rate kicked up at the dreadful picture he created. It must've been awful. Stuck in a tomb with no way out. That's how it must've been for Robbie. Her dad.

He continued, 'Thought I was done for, didn't I. Then I hear the key and the door opened—'

'Who opened it?' Mo jumped in. Because whoever this person was they hadn't done the same with her dad's cell. She tensed up, eagerly waiting for Pockets to drop the name.

But he said, 'Couldn't see who it was. Smoke was so thick. You didn't need to tell me twice to get out of there.'

Mo wouldn't let it go. 'Are you sure you never saw who had the keys?'

Pockets crossed his heart. 'As the Lord is my witness! Like I said, young lady, the smoke was as thick as a peasouper.'

If Mo had known Pockets better, she would've witnessed how his features shifted from wide-eyed innocence to calculating craftiness. Would've sussed he was holding out on her. And mentally rubbing his hands with glee because he figured he could do a spot of blackmailing. Squeeze money out of a certain someone who wouldn't want him to tell Mo what he knew about the death of her father.

But Mo missed all of that. With a tormented growl, she picked up the bottle of champagne and hurled it with all her might against the wall.

Chapter Twelve

'You look like a total slapper.'

Kristal purposely ignored Damien's condemning and contemptuous comment as she put the finishing touches to the raspberry-crush coloured lip gloss on her pouting lips. He stood stiffly just inside her bedroom. He was very annoyed, the strange leaning angle of his neck more prominent.

'Are you listening to me, Mum? I've seen less leg on a turkey at the butcher's. You can't go out looking like that.'

Kristal tried her best to tune her kid out. Who was he to keep giving it all that? Who did he think he flaming well was? Her lord and master? Anyroad, she was dressing downmarket on purpose to help him. Kristal had kept him in the dark about her latest plans to bag him his rightful place in the Steele family empire. She gazed down at her leather mini. It was indeed ultra-short, more like a big belt, really. But that was OK. She still had the pins for it.

Beneath hooded eyes, she caught the reflection of her son's face in the chunky Italian marble dressing table mirror. If he got any redder, he was going to go pop!

'Your tits are hanging out. Like two puppies posing for a

photo.' His fists gripped together. 'Are you listening to me? You can't go out like that. Dad would never allow it.'

His dad! His fecking dad! Kristal nearly threw a hairbrush at Damien. They were only in this mess because Robbie had snuffed it, allowing *that frigging girl* to take their son's place next to his Granddaddy Southpaw. If Damien knew what was good for him, he wouldn't let the word 'dad' pass by his lips while he remained in her boudoir.

Kristal picked up a bottle of knock-off perfume. She had plenty of the good stuff but wasn't wasting them on the kind of guys she was planning to meet tonight. Rental boys like that wouldn't know the difference, anyway.

'A complete and utter scrubber.' Damien was like a stuck record.

Kristal dabbed her neck, biting back, 'Give it a rest, son.'

'Where the hell are you going, anyway?'

Kristal added lashings of hairspray to her barnet. 'It's none of your beeswax.'

Damien was like a bull about ready to charge. All he was missing was the stamping of his hooves. 'It is my business if my ol' dear goes out looking like some low-rent Slaggie Maggie who needs to top up her benefits money with a little freelance tarting. Supposing someone I know sees you? I'll be a laughingstock.'

Kristal put the spray can down and turned her nose up at her boy's continued stream of insults. Plus, his outrage showed she'd got the look she wanted down to a T. Kristal topped it off with a pair of cheap, thigh-high, patent black boots.

'You don't need to worry, hun. I'm going somewhere very select tonight, so the kind of boys you hang out with wouldn't get in anyway.'

Damien gave up.

Kristal grabbed a fake Chanel handbag, the stitching already coming apart. Then stood up. 'I'll probably be back late, so don't wait up.'

'Have a good time, Mum,' Damien taunted.

Slightly unsteady in her boots, Kristal gave him an arched smile. 'Don't you worry, I will.'

Kristal's car navigation system was having trouble finding the Scarlet Lady pub, almost as if it were as miffed as Damien's doubts about his mum's night out. It turned out that the boozer was tucked away on a B road outside Grays. Kristal knew when she finally found it without seeing the sign, which featured a woman in a flowing red dress on a horse. In the car park middle-aged people milled around. The ladies were done up a treat although they weren't dressed as upfront as Kristal. The men, on the other hand, were a sorry spectacle. Plenty of dyed hair and the occasional comb-over. No amount of designer clobber and flashy gold chains could hide their paunches or sagging rear ends.

Prominently displayed in a window was a notice:

Every Thursday.

Over 40s Disco.

Ladies free before 10.00 p.m.

Dress to Impress!

Kristal ignored the information as she swung out of her

motor. She wasn't here for an aging disco. Clutching her bag, she briskly walked through the car park crowd and the leering glances of the blokes. Kristal strolled into the Scarlet Lady. Sylvester's 'You Make Me Feel' boomed down a staircase from an upstairs room, rocking the building. Kristal scowled upwards and then went into the saloon bar. Much quieter in here, only with a scattering of drinkers. She did a quick sweep around even though she had no idea what her quarry looked like.

The barman gave her the eye. 'The Grab-a-Granny night, it's upstairs in the function room.'

Kristal feigned confusion. 'Grab-a-Granny?'

'The over-40s disco. Mature singles night. Grab-a-Granny is what it's called locally. No offence intended.'

'None taken.' She bestowed on him her second-best smile. Her best she was reserving for another man tonight. 'You're right, I am here for the Grab-a-Granny night, but I thought I'd get a drink down here first. Y'know, to steady my nerves. A Campari and soda.' While he poured, she casually added, 'Any chance that Dean's in the house tonight?'

'Who wants to know?' The barman was now suspicious.

Her tone sharpened. 'I'm a friend of his mum's. I know he drinks in here, so I thought I'd check him out while I'm in the neighbourhood.'

He abandoned her drink and took the measure of her. 'His mum's dead. What are you? The law or something?'

Kristal rested her upper half on the counter, giving the barman a bird's-eye view of her cleavage. 'Do I look like the law?'

He shrugged, though his gaze didn't waver from her boobs. 'You could be undercover.'

Kristal leant into his face. In a tone that had floored better men than him, she hissed, 'Is he here? Or ain't he?'

The barman thought about it before nodding to a table tucked away in a corner. A group of lads sat around it. One of them she knew was Dean Forest.

Her target. The patsy she was going to set up to run Mo out of town.

Kristal instantly identified Dean. A real looker with bleached-blond hair and a gold looped earring. His tight white T-shirt showed off his pecs and six-pack. Black jeans were tight too, and a pair of upmarket slip-on shoes with no socks. Kristal knew that kinda guy well. Small-timer with big ideas, but no clout to get into the underworld proper. A cocky little sod who fancied himself as a demon with the ladies. The kind of young man who liked his women classy but didn't know the meaning of the word. The kind of guy who might come good later, but now wasn't his time.

It was almost a nailed description of the young lad Kristal had put the discreet word out she was searching for. It hadn't taken long for Dean Forest's name to be chucked into the mix. Of course, she'd checked him out before coming here. Petty drug dealer that hung out at the Scarlet Lady in Essex with his crew of no-marks.

The Grab-a-Granny over-40s disco provided a perfect cover for her being here. Now it was only a matter of attracting his attention. And Kristal knew exactly how to do that. She was in no doubt that if she dished it up on a plate for a boy like Dean, he'd get his knife and fork out.

As confident as a cat hunting a mouse, Kristal took her Campari and soda and positioned herself at an empty table directly in Dean's eyeline. Deliberately she crossed her legs, so the hem of her skirt rode higher, almost showing off her very skimpy thong. Kristal waited. And waited. It soon became apparent that Dean was too deep in convo with his boys, holding his hand over his mouth so any undercover cops wouldn't be able to lipread his words. Probably picked that idea up from a true crime documentary. Kristal sadly shook her head. Poor deluded Dean. Like the Bill would be interested in small fry like him.

Being subtle wasn't working. Time to put dinner right under his nose.

Kristal took her empty glass back to the bar and then used a roundabout route to get to the mature singles night upstairs. She walked directly past Dean's table, but he didn't look up because he was too busy muttering with fury behind his hand, 'The geezer's way out of line. We'll have to get a shooter and show him what it's like.'

When Kristal got to the door, she used her side-eye to check behind. Shit! The kid hadn't even noticed her at all. Kristal wasn't giving up yet. Ferreting around in her purse, she took out a pound coin, returned to the bar and popped it in a charity box. Then she moved using her best catwalk strut to a window near Dean's table and peered out at nothing for a count of ten. Back she turned, but this time as she sashayed by, Kristal gently cuffed Dean's blond head with her elbow.

Lashes fluttering like windscreen wipers, Kristal stopped short with a smiley apology. 'Sorry, handsome, didn't notice you there.' Now she applied her number one best smile. 'Although I should have noticed a suave, sharp man like you.'

Kristal tilted her head and shoulders backwards, pushing her kitty-kats front and centre. She thrust one knee forward, so he copped an eyeful of legs too.

Dean finally noticed her and with a cheeky smile remarked, 'Don't worry about it, babe.'

She gently touched her top lip with the tip of her tongue. Meaningfully, she stared upwards to the sound of music coming from above. Back at Dean. Then, very slowly, pivoted around and drifted towards the door while she felt Dean's eyes burning into her backside. As she reached the door, she turned and gave her target a long lingering glance before disappearing.

He'd follow. She knew he would.

Irritated, Kristal checked her watch. Again. She was starting to wonder if this Dean Forest was going to be a no-show. If he was planning to put in an appearance, he was certainly taking his time about it. The cocky little bastard. If it weren't for the fact that Dean was central to her plans, she'd be long gone.

This Grab-a-Granny night was hell on earth. All the grannies had quickly decided none of the men were worth the time of day, so they were bobbing around their bags to the Village People and ABBA. The men were holding pints and watching them do it. Kristal knew how the girls felt. She was stuck with one of these cretins at the bar. She'd tried giving him the brush-off, but he wasn't getting the message. Kristal didn't want to make a scene, so she heard him out.

'Yeah, the missus left me two years ago. The utter bitch.'

'Did she? I wonder why.' Kristal's sarky response flew over his head.

The bloke grunted and slurped on his pint, then barked, 'Coz she's an utter bitch, that's why.'

Gimme strength! Where the hell was Dean? Short of walking past Dean Forest stark bollock naked, Kristal couldn't have made it any plainer that she was interested in him. As if on cue, a figure appeared out of the crowd and wedged between her and the guy whose 'utter bitch' of a wife had left him.

The older man sputtered, 'Do you mind, sonny? Me and the lady are together.'

Dean put his hand on the other man's chest, shoving him backwards. 'Look, bruv, why don't you go for a walk before you get hurt?'

The other guy pushed his chest out. 'Who the hell do you think you are?'

Dean was giving it the big 'un. 'If you want to know who I am, just make some enquiries with regulars. They'll tell you. I pretty much boss this pub. Now do one.'

The bloke hesitated for a few moments, then followed Dean's advice to buzz off.

Kristal slithered back into her femme fatale persona. 'So, you're Dean, are you? You don't look old enough to be at an over-40s disco.'

She was expecting him to say 'Neither do you, darlin',' and was put out when he instead declared, 'Age is just a number, babe. So, tell me, what's your name? I bet it's a beautiful one for such a beautiful lady.'

He was young, naff and almost like a comedian's piss-take of a Jack the Lad character. In other words, perfect for what Kristal had in mind.

'Can I top you up, babe?'

'You can top me up anytime.' Kristal smiled with flirty-flirty coyness. 'Campari and soda.'

Kristal spent the next hour spinning Dean around the dance floor. Her fingers dug deep into his buttocks, her legs massaging his. When The Commodores' 'Three Times a Lady' signalled the last dance, Kristal wrapped her arms octopus-style around Dean to make sure he couldn't get away.

The problem was, he hadn't invited her back to his place. Blimey! She was going to have to take the initiative. *Again.*

'I bet you've got somewhere where we can continue the party? I'm having too much fun for it to stop now.' Her tongue did a sexy circuit of her lips. 'I really want you.'

Chapter Thirteen

'Wakey, wakey, slugabed,' a woman's voice purred. 'Rise and shine.'

Dean groaned deeply, having trouble getting his eyes open. When he focused, there was a woman next to him. Wearing one of his silk shirts with the front open so all her strawberry creams spilled out. Who the heck was she?

Then he remembered. It all came flooding back.

'Not at the moment, Kristal. I'm a bit knackered to tell the honest truth. Why don't you let yourself out? I'll see you around sometime.'

He closed his eyes, but even Dean had enough sense to feel the sudden chill in the air. He opened them again. 'Or do you want me to take you for some brekkie down a caff? I'm easy.'

Kristal held her temper. She didn't much care for being treated like a dockside doxy by a chancer like Dean. Nor did she much care for Dean worrying she was the kind of girl who thought getting your leg over with a stranger meant they were suddenly in a long-term relationship. She was here on business, not pleasure. Although, if she was being honest, sex with this young, fit and eager man had been a very, very delicious slice of hottie-heaven.

Kristal shook her hair back. 'Breakfast would be lovely. It'll give me a chance to get to know the real Dean. Although I can already see you're a young man with a big and bright future ahead of him.'

Dean's brows shifted together, his expression perplexed. 'Can you?' Then he recovered himself, remembering he was playing the Big I Am. 'A boy's gotta do what a boy's gotta do. Y'know, ducking and diving and that.'

Kristal shook her head slowly to allow what she was about to say to sink in. 'I don't think a bright spark like you should be ducking and diving. You should be getting others to duck and dive on your behalf.'

'I'm running my own crew if that's what you mean?'

Kristal was stern. 'No! That's not what I mean.'

No warning given, Kristal swept the duvet clean off him. 'Come on. Get your kit on. Let's get some breakfast where I'll give you chapter and verse about exactly what I mean.'

Dean's place was a flat in a new build on the road into Tilbury. He claimed he owned it, but Kristal already knew that was a bald-faced porkie. She'd already been up for an hour before waking Dean, snooping around his flat to see what she could find out about him. She found his rental agreement in a drawer in the kitchen along with other interesting things that enabled her to compile a mental dossier about him:

Twenty-three-years old.

Had attended various college courses but had dropped out or been kicked off.

He kept a number of 'business' phones around the flat.

Small quantities of coke and weed about the place too.

He was broke.

Living heavily off credit cards.

His motor was a second-hand Golf GTI that he was struggling to keep up the payments for.

In other words, Dean really was bang-on perfect for what she had in mind.

Kristal drove him into Grays and bought him breakfast. For herself she only ordered a latte.

She fired off the questions as soon as they sat down. 'What do you do for a living?'

Dean, who was wolfing down his Monster Big Breakfast as if he was in a hurry to get this over with so he could go back to bed, puffed himself up. 'Can't talk about that, babe. Let's just say I've got various irons in various fires, know what I mean?'

Kristal looked him dead in the eye. 'You mean you're a criminal?'

Dean stared straight back as innocent as a newborn babe. 'No way! I'm not a crim. I'm a businessman. All my trading is totally legit.' A mischievous glint sparkled in his eye. 'Although, I dare say the local magistrates would say different.'

'Magistrates?' she questioned with contempt. 'You mean you've never been up in front of a judge? Not much of a player then, are you?'

Dean stopped wolfing down his food, needled by Kristal's jibe. His fork clattered into his plate.

He leant towards her. 'What is this? Have a Go at Dean

day? Let me tell you something, babe, if I haven't been up at the Bailey, that's because I'm always one step ahead of the law. And don't think they haven't tried to take me down coz they have. There's an entire team of the Essex Constabulary keeping an eye on me, but I'm too clever for them.'

Kristal suspected that this team was probably comprised of traffic wardens. But she played along. 'Really?'

Dean picked up his fork, tucking in again. Then it occurred to him. 'What do you know about judges and magistrates?'

'I know a lot about how to avoid getting sentenced by them.' She pointedly sipped her latte. 'You see, I'm a very well-connected lady, with the biggest firms in town.'

He was doubtful. 'Yeah? Like who?'

Her brows delicately and meaningfully rose. 'They wouldn't thank me for dropping their names around. It's not the done thing. But let's just say they're very big operators indeed.'

Dean rolled his eyes, shrugging. 'I don't believe you.'

Kristal had expected this. She eased open her fake Chanel bag. Dean nearly jumped out of his skin when she carefully placed an automatic on the table by the salt and pepper shakers.

'That believable enough for you?'

'What the fuck? What the actual fuck?' Nervously, his gaze darted about. 'You can't put that there. If the waitress clocks it and calls the coppers, we're going away for five years. Minimum.'

Kristal left it sitting where it was. Dean had lost his

appetite. In fact, he felt like throwing up. He was out of his seat in a hurry. 'I've got to go. Got people to see. Things to do. Ta for the brekkie.'

Kristal pointed a red-nailed finger at his chair. 'Sit down, hun.' It was more of a command than a request, and, like he was under her spell, Dean did as he was told.

He rearranged the salt and pepper pots, the mayonnaise and the red sauce to hide Kristal's shooter from prying eyes.

'Let me ask you a question, cowboy,' Kristal started. 'Don't you ever get tired of struggling? Of living in a shit-hole one-bed flat? Of making a living fencing nicked tellies and selling your mates tiny portions of gear? Don't you want to make something of yourself?'

Kristal resisted a congratulatory smile because Dean was lapping up every last word she told him. She pressed her advantage.

'When I saw you last night down the pub, I said to myself, *Now there goes a young man who's going places. All he needs is someone to help him find his way, a gangster's moll, if you like.* I can be that gangster's moll if you've got what it takes. I can introduce you to the right people, join some dots, vouch for you and show you the ropes.'

Kristal paused to down the dregs of her coffee. 'Here's my dilemma, though. I'm asking myself, was I mistaken? Is Dean a big guy in the making?'

'Is this a wind-up or do you really mean it?'

In that simple statement, Kristal heard all his pent-up yearning to be someone other than Dean Forest from Tilbury.

'Just imagine it, Dean. Living in a country house with a snooker room indoors and a swimming pool out back. Proper hard nuts under your command. Everyone pissing their panties, terrified of getting on Dean Forest's wrong side. Your word is the law. Can you imagine that?'

Dean looked pensive. 'Yeah! I can see it.' He gazed longingly into the distance and nodded. 'I can imagine it.'

Then he took Kristal by utter surprise by getting to his feet. 'But I ain't interested, thank you very much. I'm doing alright on my own.'

Kristal exploded in fury, her words chasing him across the café as he strode away. 'You ponce. You small-time ASBO kid. I thought I was dealing with a real man, not a fecking frightened little boy. And yeah, you're crap in bed with your titchy-witchy todger.'

The door slammed. Fit to burst, Kristal watched through the window as Dean hurried down the street, ruining her plan to get rid of Mo.

'Don't start! I'm not in the mood!'

Kristal followed through by hurling her fake handbag across the hallway. Kicked the table against the wall. Ripped the mirror down. Her son stood watching hurricane Kristal blow.

Damien was ready to demand answers from his mum about where she'd been all night, but she cut him short. 'Just shut up, alright?'

Damien knew better than to row with her when she was on one like this. 'I was only going to ask where you'd been, that's all. I was worried.'

Kristal stomped up the stairs to her bedroom. She stripped off her Grab-a-Granny gear as if it were infected with a disease. That fecking Dean needed a severe kicking. Tosser! Loser! He'd taken advantage of her, although a tiny voice inside Kristal reminded her it was *she* who'd been trying to manipulate *him*.

'Shut. Up,' she responded to the voice, quickly shutting it down.

She was of a mind to bombard that fuckwit with texts to tell him about his business … Kristal's mind stopped swirling and started thinking calmly again. Dean was too perfect for the role she needed him to play for her to give up on him. She convinced herself all he'd done was fluff his lines and suffer from stage fright while eating his breakfast. Dean just needed more carrot and less stick.

Kristal tracked Damien down in the kitchen. 'Are you still driving the SUV?'

'Yeah,' he mumbled around a triple-deck ploughman's sarnie.

'Take it down the carwash and get it cleaned and polished to the max. Then bring it straight back.'

'Eh?'

Even though she had a plan, Kristal was still doing some serious 'tude. 'Don't ask questions, you little scrote, just do it!'

Damien did as told.

By the time he returned, his mum was kitted out in a charcoal-grey Burberry skirt suit heavily laden with her most expensive jewellery, topped off with Blahnik fuchsia-pink heels. Kristal led Damien outside to where his newly buffed truck was parked. She climbed onto it and draped herself over its bonnet in all her finery.

'Take some photos of me on it.'

Damien wasn't asking questions anymore. He raised his high-tech digi camera. Snap! Snap! Snap!

Kristal jumped off the car. 'I want you to help me attach these photos to an email.'

Damien sent his mum a quizzical look. 'Who you emailing?'

'Just do it.'

After he loaded them to Kristal's computer, she shooed him from the downstairs office. She added Dean's email address with the message:

Wouldn't you rather be driving one of these than that MOT failure you clank around in? I can make it happen. Think about it.

Kristal waited for half an hour … No answer.

With grim determination, she yelled for her son. She wasn't done with Dean by a long shot.

Next, she photographed Damien in his flashiest suit and blinged out in gold chains and rings. She emailed the images across with: *You're a good-looking boy. But even a good-looking boy looks even better with some tom like this around his neck and on his fingers. I can make it happen. Think about it.*

No answer.

Kristal didn't give up, she never did.

'Damien, ring that brass house you go to.'

Her son pinked over with embarrassment.

'Come on, I know you visit the Mighty Minge in Canning Town. Tell Lucky Lucy to send over her most expensive girls on her books.' She levelled a warning finger. 'I don't want the kind of crackhead who hangs around underneath the arches in fishnet tights and fake leather miniskirts.'

The two ladies who came around later that afternoon Kristal wasn't entirely happy with, but they were going to have to do. Damien was barred from the room.

'Alright, ladies, this'll be the easiest dosh you'll ever earn. All I want you to do is sit on my sofa. I want one of you to stick your hand up the other's skirt while the other one fondles her mate's Yorkshire puds. Then I want some serious snogging while I take a few pixxies. That's all.'

Photos done, ladies gone, Kristal tried to cover her son's eyes while he loaded the photos to the computer. He was thoroughly fed up by now.

Finally, he demanded, 'Mum, I want to know what's going on.'

Kristal bit her lip. Then, 'I'm doing this for you, sweets. All for you.' More quietly she added, 'Do you trust me?'

'I miss Dad.'

His unexpected response nearly broke Kristal in two. She knew how much her boy worshipped his father. Kristal embraced her son tightly, whispering, 'I'm going to put you in a position where your dad will be proud of you. You hear me?'

Damien pulled back from his mother and kissed her on the cheek.

Once he was gone, Kristal's tender moment with her son fired her up even more about her plans for Dean. Her email message read: *Shouldn't you be in between these two lovely ladies? With the money you'll make with me, that could be you every night. Think about it.*

No answer.

Kristal cursed a blue streak. She took out a bottle of pink gin, tilted it to her mouth and slogged it back. She'd played all her cards. She slumped, defeated and dejected, in the chair.

Suddenly the computer screen lit up.

You've got mail.

Dean: *Dunno. Let's have a meet and a chat. D.*

Hook, line and sinker!

Gotcha!

Chapter Fourteen

'Let me give you a bit of advice, Dammy boy. When you're in a ruck, always make sure you've got something about your person to surprise the oppo,' Robbie Steele advised his seven-year-old son.

Young Damien lay in bed staring at his father with open adoration. While other kids got bedtime stories about the land of make believe in fairy tales, princesses getting rescued by princes, witches and orphaned kids, Damien Steele got real-life tales about how to survive in the East End.

'They'll be expecting you to carry a blade. They might even think you're packing heat. But will they be expecting you to have a knuckleduster to give your fist that little bit of extra heft? What are they gonna do when you pull a bicycle chain out of a deep pocket and wrap that round their loaf? Know what I'm saying?'

Damien nodded, lapping up every wise word his dad gave him.

'They might be expecting you in their regular haunts, but will they be ready for you when you're waiting outside their granny's after they've paid a visit of an afternoon? Remember Napoleon Bonaparte. He always turned up with his boys where they were least expected.'

The words of his father all those years ago accompanied Damien as he made his way to the door of the snooker hall. He'd bought a knuckleduster from an army surplus store, nicked a motorbike chain from a garage and borrowed an extendable baton from a mate of his. Then he'd gone gunning for Carlos Donahoe. He'd teach the wanker a very, very painful lesson he wouldn't forget about putting his hands on Charmaine. So what if she was a working girl? That didn't give anyone the right to turn her into a punchbag.

Damien was honest enough with himself to admit this wasn't only about avenging Charmaine. He was going to have to prove himself with his fists if he was ever going to get a sniff of a position in Granddad Southpaw's various operations. He suspected his mum was planning something, but she wasn't letting on. Besides, he didn't need to hang on to his mum's apron strings. He was going to do something on his own to get his granddad to notice him.

Damien wanted to smash something when he thought about Granddad Southpaw giving that fecking girl the job of running his firm. Jimmy Southpaw must have gone soft in the head. Surely it was only a matter of time before his granddad realised his mistake? When legendary hardman Jimmy Southpaw got his marbles back, his grandson would be in pole position for the gig at the top.

'Don't go around bragging when you've taken someone down, it shows a lack of class. Word will get around on the grapevine, and no one does grapevines like the underworld.' His dad's pearls of wisdom again.

Damien had made a list of the places where the woman-beater hung out. Apparently the geezer thought he was somebody and liked to hold court in his local snooker hall, where the management knew better than to tell him to put a cork in his antics. Carlos took precautions with his security everywhere, but he was a bit slack when he was playing a table. So Damien decided that was the ideal place to have a go. Damien might be a touch muddled in the brain department every now and again, but even he knew Carlos would probably be mob-handed. Would have his mates close by. Damien's dad had given him a steer on that type of situation as well:

'One against the many? What counts when you're in a battle is who's the one and who's the many. Put the boss guy down first and the many will soon run for it.'

Damien pushed the double door to the snooker hall open. There was a drop lock on it and a kiosk to monitor the CCTV outside, but it was early so the door was unlocked and the kiosk empty. He'd chosen his time well. Damien climbed the stairs, wheezing by the time he reached midway. Fact of the matter was he was carrying one too many pounds, especially around the midriff section. When he was a kid his mum was always threatening to drag him out of bed in the morning to join Mr Motivator on brekkie TV. Then again, it was his mum who was always shovelling all manner of relishes down his throat because he was, as she put it, 'a growing lad.'

When he reached the top, Damien had to take a few seconds out for a breather. Ahead was a long hall with a bar at one end that was open but unattended. A dozen snooker tables were dark and only two were lit. Two young guys played at one while five others watched.

Damien had never met this Carlos twat before, but he fingered who the prick was straight off. The ponce clutching a snooker cue like it was his second dick. He was one of the ugliest fellas Damien had clapped eyes on in his life. Damien's lips tightened. He was going to have that ug-mug bastard.

Damien swaggered between the tables until he stood a couple of paces in front of Carlos. The guy was clearly puzzled for a few moments. 'Do you mind, mate? You're blocking my view of the game.'

Damien stood his ground. 'I wanna word with you.'

Carlos shouldered his snooker cue. 'Do you now? And who are you exactly?'

Damien's lip curled. 'I'm your worst nightmare, is who I am.'

Without looking up, the other player hit a ball and explained to Carlos, 'His name is Damien. He's Jimmy Southpaw's grandson.'

Carlos sniggered. 'Jimmy Southpaw? If I were you, Damien, I'd pop off home and wipe the old man's bum for him. I hear he's a bit gaga these days. Didn't he give up his business and hand it over to some slip of a girl? Mind you, if the alternative was handing it over to a muppet like you, I can see why he might have done that.'

The others were openly laughing. Carlos pulled up close to Damien. 'So what's the problem here, mate? You don't wanna start something with a guy like me, do you? It's a bit above your pay grade.'

Damien's temper rose like a ball of fire. He despised being laughed at. It took him straight back to his schooldays when the other kids mocked him, calling him dumb. It wasn't his fault he was no good at lessons.

Hissing through his teeth, he growled, 'You shouldn't have put your hands on Charmaine.'

Carlos' neck pulled back and he scowled with confusion. He obviously didn't have a cuckoo who Charmaine was. Then the light bulb went on.

Wearing a large, mean grin, he told his men, 'The poor chump's got a crush. On some slag. He's come down here to defend her *honour*, which is anyone's for a nicker a time.' Carlos screwed his face up at Damien. 'Look, mate, I ain't got time to waste on a pillock like you. Now why don't you piss off back across the river before you get hurt?'

Enough with the talking! Damien whipped his bike chain out of a long pocket in his tracksuit and swung it like a silver flash that lashed his enemy's face. Carlos reeled backwards, feet tangled, and he went down. Gingerly, he touched the side of his face with his fingers. Teeth bared, he struggled to his feet. Damien basked in his triumph, which meant that he forgot one of his dad's critical pieces of advice: *'Always hit the enemy when he's down. Use your advantage to grind him into the dirt.'*

Carlos snatched a snooker cue while Damien took another swing with his chain. It whistled through the air, missing its target. A blow from the cue crushed Damien's arm. The shock of it meant he felt no pain. His arm went numb, hanging limply by his side, no power left in it. On a backswing, Carlos took out his other arm. Carlos chucked his cue away. Seized a dazed Damien by his jacket and slammed him on the table. Lips curved in a satisfied, cocky grin he rained blow after blow into Damien's face. Climbing onto the green baize, Carlos finished the job with kicks to Damien's ribs. Grabbing him by the collar like a kitten, Carlos jerked Damien off the table and flung him into a heap on the floor.

Carlos paused to catch his breath. 'Here, boys, chuck the rubbish out, will ya? It's bin day tomorrow. I don't think he's a member, anyway.'

Blood thick in his mouth, bruised and battered, Damien was half in, half out of consciousness as they dragged him down the club's stairs by his ankles. Then he was slung into the gutter outside.

Instead of proving himself to his Granddad Southpaw, Damien lay beaten and ashamed. Damien realised, despite his dad's teachings, he still had a lot to learn.

Chapter Fifteen

Kristal was pulling her hair out. 'No! No! No! When I said walk like you're not in a hurry, I meant walk like you're not in a hurry, not like an old codger with a dodgy hip replacement.'

Turning Dean into a top-flight villain was proving to be harder than Kristal expected. True, he looked the part now she'd taken him Up West to Jermyn Street to buy some expensive whistles and a flash new hairdo. Despite all of that, getting him to actually perform the part was proving a monumental headache.

Dean's training was taking place in a duplex apartment in Wapping with commanding views out over the river in both directions. The lounge was connected to an upper level by one of those spiral staircases she thought would be well dodgy after a skinful down you. Kristal told Dean that she lived there. In truth, the developer had been on the in with Robbie, so he was letting her rent it for a month. No way could Dean ever discover where she truly lived.

Damien had accompanied her, lounging on the thing that passed for a sofa but was as uncomfortable as a bed of nails. He read the paper, barely able to stifle a chuckle at

Dean's antics prancing around the place playing the hard nut. Damien had been fighting again, and he wouldn't tell her who with. She was worried about her boy. Had been worried about him since Robbie died.

Damien picked himself up on the way to the kitchen for a bevvy from the fridge. Walking past his frustrated mother, he shot, 'I don't know what you're playing at here, Mum, but if you're hoping to pass this plonker off as a gangland Face, I think you're throwing darts at the wrong board.'

'Shut up, you little weasel before I drag your goolies over your face. Why don't you help instead of making narky remarks?'

'He's beyond help, Mum. I mean, look at him. He couldn't scare a nursery class. The tiny tots would have him over and chase him out in five seconds flat.'

Displeasure flashed in her eyes. She fired back, 'I'm not listening. But keep talking. I enjoy the way your voice makes my ears bleed.' She ended on a growled, 'Now bleeding well bugger off.'

Dean demanded her attention again. 'I don't see why I have to walk slowly, anyways?'

Kristal glared daggers. 'I didn't say you had to walk *slowly*. I said walk as if you're never in a rush. Never in a hurry. You play it cool like ...'

She nearly said 'Jimmy Southpaw' but caught herself in time. She still couldn't be sure that Dean hadn't heard of the patriarch of the Steele family. But she'd taken a risk giving him her and Damien's real names, calculating he wouldn't make the connection to a high-profile London crime family.

Besides, her son could barely remember his own name sometimes. Giving Damien a fake name without him slipping up was tempting fate, a chance Kristal couldn't take.

She let out a mammoth punch of air. She was properly done in. 'Alright, Dean, let's take five. Have a fag and we'll go again.'

Dean shook his head. 'I don't smoke, babe. It's bad for you.'

A raucous peal of laughter burst from the kitchen.

Dean got the nark, not best pleased by some kid who was plainly younger than him taking the rise. 'Who's the chunky boy? He's starting to get on my wick.'

Kristal gamely tried to carry on. 'Never you mind about him, he's just one of my runners.' She raised her voice meaningfully. 'A bit of an idiot, if we're being honest, who will be leaving shortly.'

Which Damien did, along with a can of brew and the parting shot, 'Chunky boy has left the building.'

'So, who's this Mo lady?' Dean asked her. 'Why do you want me to put her out of business?'

It wasn't the first time Dean had put Kristal on the spot with this question. It was to be expected after all. Kristal had her answer prepared as usual, coupled with a sparkling smile. 'She's small fry and just the start of getting you hooked up with the big boys. After you've dealt with her, sky's the limit, baby.'

The security intercom went a few minutes later. Kristal checked out the video screen before pressing the buzzer to let her visitor in.

She explained to Dean, 'I've asked someone to drop by for a meet 'n' greet. He's a top guy in the London world.' She tapped the side of her nose. 'Know what I mean? He's going to be a crucial contact for you. Which means you're going to need to impress him. So, don't forget what I told you. Play it cool, play it calm, play it confident. Treat him with respect, but like an equal.'

Kristal finished with a jaunty, 'What's our motto?'

'Fake it till I make it.'

Trilling, she clapped her hands in gleeful triumph. 'Bullseye!'

Then she cupped his face and tongued him for all she was worth. His palms eagerly grabbed and kneaded her bum. Keeping up the sexy-loving was an important part of keeping Dean on a leash. And they'd developed a mutually very, very interesting sex life. The knock at the door pulled Kristal out of his arms.

A bored-looking Harry waited in the immaculately kept carpeted corridor. His clothes were straight out of the current gangland movie, *Snatched*, with his beige trench coat and slim-line trousers. He also sported a new gold signet ring which Kristal couldn't make out but would swear was engraved with an initial. Did Harry have a sweetheart he was hiding away?

He peered over her shoulder at the expensive fixtures and fittings. 'This is where you're training up your Essex wide boy as the new Mister London Gangland? Must have cost a few bob.'

Kristal kept schtum about Robbie's developer mate. Her

dead husband's business contacts were for her to know and others to never find out. She joked, 'Don't worry about the money, bruv, I'll claim it back on expenses when we take over from Mo.'

Harry stepped inside. 'Where is he then?'

Talking, she guided him to the lounge. 'Don't forget to cut him a bit of slack. He's still learning.'

Harry peered through a gap in the door to where Dean practiced various sitting positions, pinpointing which made him appear suitably tough.

Concerned, Harry turned to Kristal. 'This lad's very young.'

'So is Mo,' she lobbed back stubbornly.

'And he's a bit of a pretty boy.'

'And Mo's a pretty girl. What's your point?'

Harry strolled in. Dean forgot all about not rushing as he leapt out of his seat. Kristal could've throttled him.

He extended a hand to Harry. 'Alright, mate? Nice to meet you.'

Harry gave Dean a slow perusal that seemed to take an age. Then Harry ignored the offered hand and took a seat.

Mortified, Dean gazed stupefied at his empty hand. He sat down, then shot to his feet again as if he wasn't sure he should take a pew before Harry had invited him to do so. Finally, Harry pointed to the chair, so Dean parked himself back down. Harry kept quiet while he again gave the lad the once-over, more leisurely this time, which was freaking Dean out. The youngster fidgeted while glancing meaningfully at Kristal for support.

At last Harry broke the silence. 'I hear you're a rising star, my young friend. So, tell me, what kind of business are you in?'

The question seemed to throw Dean, who wasn't quite sure what kind of business he was in. He shot another urgent glance at Kristal that screamed, 'help!'

'Dean's in import-export,' she quickly supplied.

Grateful, Dean gave a knowing smile. 'That's right. I'm in import-export.'

Harry nodded, doing his part to appear impressed. 'That's a good business to be in.' Then after a long pause he added, 'So what exactly is it you import and export?'

Dean was back seeking help from Kristal. This time he received a killer glare for his troubles. He got the message loud and clear: *answer your own effing questions.*

'Well, you know,' he stuttered, 'anything that turns a dollar. Obviously, I can't say too much. You know, you might be wearing a wire or something.'

Harry was incredulous. 'You think I might be tapping you? Perhaps you should have searched me when I came in?'

Dean realised his mistake, but it was too late. 'Nah! Of course not.' Then he compounded his error by tagging on, 'You can't be too careful, now can you? I mean, walls have ears and that.'

Harry painstakingly turned to his sister-in-law. 'Can I have a word? In private?'

The two plotters went off to the kitchen and closed the door. Harry wore the gobsmacked expression of a fitness expert who'd just been asked to turn an overweight, wheezy twenty-a-day guy into an Olympic marathon runner.

'Are you serious?' He blasted low so Dean didn't hear. 'You really think anyone's going to believe that oik is some kind of underworld big shot who's got the clout to take down Mo? You're having a buzz.'

She delivered him a quelling set down with her eyes. 'Have you got a better idea? We can't take her on openly without the brown stuff hitting the fan. We have to do it behind the cover of someone else. Like him.' She gesticulated in the direction of the lounge.

Harry ran his fingers impatiently through his hair. He should've known better than Kristal of all people having the solution to a problem called Mo.

He put her on the spot. 'Tell me, my dear sister-in-law, has Dean got an army of cutthroats and desperadoes ready to do battle with Mo and her crew? To take her off her perch? Because at first sight, that doesn't appear to be the case.' His voice hardened. 'You promised me you'd get him back-up.'

Kristal averted her sheepish gaze. Harry had hit on what was currently the flaw in her plan. 'I'm speaking to a certain someone at the moment. He can provide the muscle and weapons. I just need to persuade him that it's in his interests, that's all.'

Harry wasn't convinced. 'And does this *certain someone* know you're going to use his people to go up against Mo? And, by way of her, Jimmy Southpaw?'

'He knows.'

Harry considered her words. Then heavily shrugged.

'Brave man. Either that or he's as thick as my dad's police record.'

Kristal took ultra-delight in relaying to him, 'Believe you me, he's one of the smartest geezers around.' Her Nico was as sharp as the lash of a whip and as deadly as a bullet between the eyes.

Harry said, 'Keep me posted on developments.'

Kristal grabbed his trench coat and jerked him towards her. 'Oh no you don't, buster! I ain't keeping you posted on sweet FA. Either you're in or you're out. I ain't having you dobbing me in it to Mo and blabbing that this was all down to me if things go belly up. That ain't happening.'

Harry feigned hurt. 'What a suspicious mind you have.' He yanked free of her considerable hold. 'I've said I'm on your side, which means I'm on your side. Now, you'd better get back to rehearsals with Laurence Olivier out there. Looks like it could be a long day.'

But as he turned to leave, he added, 'Although I'm very interested to hear who's going to be providing Dean with back-up. I hope he knows what he's getting into.'

Kristal never gave him an answer.

An hour later, finally alone, Kristal crashed on the sofa with a ciggie and Campari topped up with gin. Fuck me! What a rough day!

After a few reviving puffs on her smoke, she called, 'Are you coming down then or what?'

'Are you sure they've gone?' came the answer from the floor above.

'It's just me and you, hun.'

A figure made his way down the spiral stairs, slowly and coolly, the exact style Kristal had been trying to drum into Dean. His green-and-grey tonic suit changed colour when the light fell on it. His shoes were Cuban heels while his shirt was tight enough to show his taut torso without hugging it. His black hair was gelled back, a few wisps flopping on his forehead. His unshaven face seemed as if a barber had spent hours making it look that way. On anyone else, the image would've appeared naff.

But Nico Sinclair, South London Bad Boy Boss Number One, was the spit of a rock star.

He crossed the room, fetched a whisky from a decanter and joined his big sister on the sofa. It was strange after all this time how they'd slipped so comfortably back into an easy relationship despite Kristal remaining tight-lipped about why she'd done a runner all those years ago.

He gave her a rueful and sympathetic smile. 'It isn't going to work, sis. Face it. I'm sure if Dean had a spell as an intern with a gangland boss, he might pick it up eventually, but you haven't got time for that. Cut your losses and send him back to sell wraps of leaf on street corners.'

Kristal got the hump, mostly because she knew he was right. She felt like a proper wally. She'd invited Nico over to earwig on her session with Dean in an effort to persuade him to provide the back-up Dean needed to bring Mo down. And what a dog's dinner that had turned into.

'He'll be fine.' Even she didn't believe her assurances. 'Are you going to help me out here or not?'

Her younger brother plucked the cigarette from her fingers and took a few puffs. Her heart twisted at his gestures. That's what she'd missed out on when she'd run away and left him behind. Sharing things with him.

Nico pulled a face. 'I want to give you a dig out, I really do. But this isn't going to work. You can see that. He's hopeless. And even if he wasn't, sooner or later, Big Mo's going to work out I'm up to my hairline in this. You know what the underworld's like. Secrets have a way of rising to the surface pretty quickly. If Southpaw finds out I'm involved, he'll make it personal. I've got a good little number going with my various rackets, I can't afford to blow it coz I put myself where I should never have been - in some madcap family melodrama.'

When he didn't get an answer, he added, 'Come on, play fair, Annalisa—'

'Kristal,' she bit out. 'Annalisa is dead and gone.' Her face turned to marble. 'And she's never coming back.'

Nico was shocked. He touched his sister's bare arm. Her flesh felt frozen.

Kristal got up, moved to the large floor-to-ceiling window and watched the river's lazy waving motion. 'Annalisa might be dead, that doesn't mean your sister is.'

She walked back to him and hunkered down by his side. Took his hand and rubbed the back of it against her cheek. 'I'm your flesh and blood. Whatever happens, whatever has come and gone in the past, I'm still your big sis. I'm in trouble and I need your help. That's what brothers are for. *Family* is for.'

She knew from the way he looked shamefully down at his Cuban heels that she'd won. Kristal kissed his cheek.

Nico nodded. 'I'll provide Dean with back-up.' Beneath his breath he added, 'God help us all if Jimmy Southpaw finds out.'

Chapter Sixteen

'I hate taking orders from that ginger nut, limping retard.'

The spiteful, poisonous words dripped with malicious intent off the tongue of Lindy who bitched and witched to her friend, Josie, for all she was worth inside the staff ladies' loo in Club Class. As well as being a trendy and very groovy West End nightspot, Club Class was Big Mo's HQ. Jimmy Southpaw had given over the place to her as a welcome-to-the-family gift. Lindy and her mate worked behind the bar on the glitzy dance floor. Both ladies – though calling them 'ladies' was cutting it a touch fine – were pampering and preening, admiring their reflections as they touched up their slap. Mind you, their make-up was shovelled on so thick it would take a chisel to unearth the skin beneath.

Josie pouted and settled her features into a picture of displeasure. 'It's wicked to use those words. My baby sister was bullied by a group of kids who would corner her, spitting those horrible words at her. Anyways, we don't use bad words like that no more. We're all civilised now, ain't we.'

Lindy applied a circle of burgundy-coloured lippy,

tutted, the words flying out of her always on-the-go gob. 'I meant every word of it. What's the world coming to when we've got to follow the say-so of some half-wit who walks like she's dying to take a shit. She'd fall flat on that ugly moosh of hers without that gross walking stick.'

Josie stared at Lindy, her false lashes blinking and blinking, thinking hard. 'Well, I don't think she's too bad.' Her voice pitched lower. 'Way I heard it she caught an unlucky break. Fell in this very club and smashed her hip up good 'n' proper. Remember, last year, some clowns turned up and tried to do the place over?'

Lindy pursed her lips, checking her reflection this way and that. ''Course I recall it. I ain't been dead, y'know. Whatever the circumstances, it ain't natural for us to be taking orders from someone who walks like Quasi-ho-dough.'

Josie delicately sponged translucent powder to the tip of her nose. 'Quasi-ho-dough? Who's that then? Someone from North London?'

'Nah! That hunchback geezer. Y'know, from Paris. Hunchback of Nostradamus.'

Josie rolled her eyes, clucking her tongue. Her friend really was ignorant. No culture. She corrected Lindy. 'You mean the Hunchback of Notre Dame. Quasimodo.'

'That's what I said. Quasi-ho-dough.'

Josie let out a giggle that was a dead ringer of a puppy yapping. She soon stopped, though, when she spotted that laugh lines were cracking up her concealer. 'Modo. Not ho-dough, ya idiot. Ho-dough is a hunchback who's a whore.'

Lindy's brow arched. 'Maybe I'm bang to rights then coz,

let's face it, the only way her with the walking stick is ever gonna get her good leg over is to whore herself out.'

The pair cracked up so much they could barely get the door open to the corridor to start their shift getting the bar ready for later on.

Their merriment dying away into the distance, the door of a loo stall creaked open. The partial gap revealed Twinkle, Mo's best friend. Carefully she checked that the room was empty. Realising the coast was clear, instead of coming out, she clutched tight to her walking stick and slumped, dejected, against the wall. The tears swam hot and unwanted, bulging in the bottoms of her eyes. Wave after wave of humiliation stained her face a ghastly red. To have to hide cringing in this cubicle while she heard the vile and repulsive names that Lindy had called her was simply horrible.

Since the accident last year when she'd literally crash-landed to earth in the club, life had never been the same for Twinkle. Even though she'd stayed in the hospital a good while to allow the medical team to sort her hip out as best as they could, it hadn't been enough. When she was told she'd always walk with a limp, Twinkle had put a courageous face on. Limp? That was a kind word for it as far as she was concerned. Her hip was so damaged that every time she lifted her leg it shifted to the side as if it had a mind of its own and then came back in line again. Like a strange, monstrous slow dance.

And if that wasn't enough, nursing herself back to health in the flat she shared with her mum was a total nightmare.

In front of an audience, Sheena Brodie played the dedicated and devoted mum to the hilt. As soon as their front door was shut, it was nasty game-on as usual. Snapping at her daughter in blatant disgust, calling her 'gimp' and vowing, 'First sign I'm expected to wipe your arse, I'll have the council cart you off to one of their homes for wrong uns.' The absolute pits was her mum sickeningly suggesting, 'Shame you didn't lose your leg. I've got a client who gets a real tickle out of fucking girls with one leg. Likes her artificial limb lying in the bed right next to them while they're doing their business.'

On discovering the torment Twinkle's mum was inflicting on her, Mo had gone ballistic. By way of rescuing her from the clutches of her sick, evil parent, Mo had asked her to manage the bar staff at the club. Twinkle had zilch experience of managing staff, but it was either take up Mo's offer or be subjected to the increasing vindictive bile her mum spewed at her on a daily basis.

Twinkle might not be the brightest match in the box, but she knew full well that Mo had also offered her the job for another reason. Her best friend felt guilty. Mo thought she was to blame for Twinkle having the accident in the first place. No matter how many times Twinkle tried to put her straight, Mo still carried that burden of guilt.

Heavily supported by her walking stick, Twinkle moved to the sink. Splashed water on her colourless cheeks. Stared at her reflection. Lindy was right. No man would ever want her. She was as dull as drain water with bright-ginger hair and freckles to boot. What a combo. Though Mo said often enough her red hair was a glittering crown of orange-gold. Aww, bless her! However, Twinkle knew the truth. She wasn't the kind of girl fellas went head over heels for. Now, her leg had made that worse.

And the bar staff despised her. A right proper coven of witches spelt with a 'b' she was expected to manage. Grinning Colgate-bright in her face while sharpening their knives ready to shaft her behind her back.

Twinkle straightened her backbone. Mo had put her in charge of the bar and those who didn't like it, well, tough shit. Let them take it up with Big Mo. 'Course they never did. *Sling your work-shy hook*, that's what Big Mo would tell them. On top of that, they all knew their boss would never go against her bestie.

Twinkle pulled out her heavy-duty painkillers and dry-swallowed a couple. She had to watch her intake because the doc had warned her they were addictive. It wasn't that easy, though, sometimes the pain was that excruciating she had to go slightly over her limit. Not too many, mind, she always reminded herself.

Twinkle settled her shoulders back and popped on an easy-going smile as she entered the main room. Cor! She still found it hard to get her head around the fact that Mo owned all of this. At night, what a picture it was with multicoloured lights flashing and rolling on the dance floor, plush seating, one wall dominated by a huge screen playing the latest music videos and, of course, the bar, Twinkle's domain.

Come evening, the bar lit up like something futuristic out of a sci-fi movie, the whole length of it glowing with electric-blue lighting. The ceiling was done up with neon-pink individual LED lights shaped into a huge fan that reflected on the glossy floor behind the bar. And when things started really rocking on the dance floor, the lighting changed and moved, turning the place Twinkle worked in into a wonderland.

Thinking of her one true mate made Twinkle's heartstrings twist. If it wasn't for this job, Twinkle didn't know what she'd make of her life.

Who the hell would give a job to someone with a wonky leg like hers?

When she reached the bar, Twinkle was startled by the unexpected appearance of a group of men. She sensed trouble coming. She'd been around long enough to know they were toughs, decked out all in black, baseball caps and shades to hide their features. Strutting instead of walking. How the hell had they got in here? The security at the club was tighter than Twinkle and Mo's friendship. A state-of-the-art security cam system covered the whole building, the outside too. A couple of bouncers were always stationed at the door … No! That wasn't strictly true. The bouncers would turn up in about an hour. Mo wasn't in residence, which meant her constant protectors, Josh and Dell, weren't present either.

Something terrible was going to happen. Twinkle could feel it in her bones.

Everyone froze, silent and tense. One of the intruders swaggered like he was the mutt's nuts. Clearly the leader.

Linford, the club's manager, warily stepped forward.

'The club is currently closed, gentlemen.' He underscored the last word with acid emphasis. He knew, as well as they did, they were no gents. 'If you want to see the owner, best make an appointment.'

The leader said nothing, taking his sweet time observing Linford, his head insolently cocked to the side. Talk about brass neck! In a low voice he finally mocked, 'I like a man with plenty of bottle. But I like this more.'

He whipped out a retractable baton. With a vicious flick of his wrist, it extended to full length and laid into Linford with two solid licks about his head. Twinkle and everyone else gasped in open horror. Club Class' manager crumbled to the floor, unconscious, head seeping blood.

The place erupted, the club's workers bolting every which way to get out. They were in for a nasty shock. Each exit was strategically blocked by a member of the gang. Twinkle was the only one to hold her ground. It had nothing to do with the fact her leg would probably have hampered her swift escape. This was her bestie's club. It was Twinkle's job to defend the place when Mo wasn't here.

Her heart was almost in her mouth, but she didn't let that deter her. Gripping her walking stick with renewed determination, she carefully moved so she was in the vicious thug's radar. 'What do you want?'

His lips curled, his gaze running the length of her in disbelief. 'Big Mo sending cripples to defend her patch, is she?' He hooted with nasty laughter. Twinkle's face heated at the insult that felt like spit gobbed in her face. 'Then again, I ain't surprised. All mouth and frilly knickers is so-called Big Mo. That's what you get for putting a bird in charge.' A wicked glint shone from his eyes. 'But that's all about to change.'

Before Twinkle could ask him more, the man and his crew set about smashing up the club. Twinkle and the others dived for cover. Some people whimpered and sobbed in distress. Twinkle did neither, instead keeping an eagle eye on the men's destructive path across the room. Chairs and tables broken against the wall. Glasses and bottles smashed until the floor glittered with splintered glass, running thick with alcohol. Blades and razors slashed to ribbons the classy seats in The VIP lounge. The gang rampaged with the frenzy of animals let out of the zoo. When they were finished, the main room of Mo's gorgeous club lay in ruins.

The leader got well cocky and downed Cognac neat from a bottle at the bar, surveying the violent chaos he'd wrought to Mo's HQ. He let the bottle slip from his fingers, accompanied by a mocking, 'Oops,' when it shattered against the floor.

Twinkle clung to her walking stick and unsteadily got to her feet. Hot pain sliced through her leg. Despite this, she confronted him. 'I'll ask you again, what do you want?'

He turned his gaze to her, his eyes hidden by the shades. He pointed his baton with menace at her. 'You tell Mo Watson that I'm taking over. I'm gonna be the king of her manor. She's got till the end of this month to pack up her shit and to fuck the hell off.'

Gasps of consternation and outrage filled the air. Was this guy off his trolley? Run Big Mo out of town?

Twinkle held her nerve putting into words what the

others were thinking. 'You do know who Big Mo is backed up by? Whose blood she is?'

He sauntered over to Twinkle and then placed the end of the baton at the tip of her nose. 'And I'm backed up by Satan—'

Cutting over his bragging bullshit, Twinkle whacked him with all her might in his kneecap with her walking stick. They both went down. Twinkle's co-workers' jaws dropped, eyes bulged, disbelieving what they'd just witnessed. Shy, soft-spoken Twinkle had just laid that ponce low. They held their breaths because no way was the thug going to take that lying down. Although he was lying down, thanks to Twinkle. He was going to batter Twinkle this side of Sunday. A few of her colleagues considered coming to her aid … Then again, that would put them in the firing line.

No one came to her rescue.

Twinkle knew she was done for. She didn't regret it. That's what you did to bullies, brought them back down to size. Now she was going to have to pay the piper. Twinkle knew there was no escape, the excruciating pain in her leg so bad she thought she was about to pass out.

'You bitch! You fucking bitch,' the brute cursed over and over. Then he was over Twinkle, his fist raised high like a battering ram.

She screwed up her eyes tight. Waited.

The blow never came. Cautiously, she opened her eyes to find another member of the gang behind the guy, staying his fist in a tight grip. The guy whispered rapidly in her attacker's ear. He dropped his fist.

And shook his shoulders. Addressed the room. 'Remember what I said. Give Big Mo the message. Every part of her empire is going to be mine.'

He let his crew exit first. Then, when he reached the door, he pulled out something. Threw it into the room.

A hand grenade.

Chapter Seventeen

'When I get my hands on the scumbag scrote-sack who did this, I'm going to shove his arms so far down his throat he'll be pissing fingers for a whole week.'

Mo's raging, blistering threat of retribution hung ominously in the air as she surveyed the destruction in her club. It bore a chilling resemblance to twister hurricanes having torn through it. The glass on the entrance door and windows were totally blown out. Some fucker had chucked a hand grenade in, not caring who he might hurt. Thank God no one had been.

Alongside her fury, Mo was filled with shattered shock. It was her manager who'd phoned with the bad news. The poor sod had been in a right ol' state thinking that Mo was going to blame him. And, by rights, she should. It was his job to have eyes in the front and back of his head to ensure that everything remained all tickety-boo. The security level of the club meant that he should never be caught on the hop.

So that was Mo's first question: How had the gang got past the security system?

Feeling Dell's presence close by, Mo half-turned her furious stare to her cousin. Dell wasn't one to wear her emotions on her sleeve, but even she couldn't hold back her open dismay at the scene before her.

Her cousin demanded, 'You can't let this stand. You're going to have to—'

Josh smartly butted in, 'Big Mo doesn't need an instruction manual from you about what she's got to do. What you need to be asking is how can you help her track down the arsewipe and his fuckwit crew?'

The two glared daggers at each other, as per usual. Mo wasn't in the mood for their antics. She directed a sour stare their way. 'Knock it on the head, will ya.'

Dismissing them, Mo marched over to Linford for a further accounting of what had gone on. Mo couldn't wrap her head around who the heck would do such a thing to her headquarters. Proclaim they were going to take over her operations? The fool must be batshit bananas! Didn't they know that Jimmy Southpaw was her grandfather?

Add to that, she'd only taken up the reins of being his heir recently, hardly time enough to make enemies. Unless, of course, this was an enemy from the days before she'd found out who her dad and grandfather were. Sure, she'd been a teen tearaway with her own crew of juvie delinquents, putting their sticky fingers where they shouldn't. But they'd been low-level, not exactly Al Capone.

While Mo cast her perplexed gaze around, watching her staff trying to tidy up, doing their best to turn bad to right, it dawned her that one person was missing. Her heart jumped into her throat. If something had happened to her best friend …?

'Where's Twinkle?' she asked her manager.

'In the ladies with—'

Mo was gone before he finished, motoring with purpose towards the lav, her tummy flip-flopping with dread. A cloud of doom descended above her. If something terrible had befallen Twinkle, she'd never forgive herself. What the fuck had she been thinking? Mo berated herself. *Giving my BFF a job in the same place where she'd smashed her hip and changed her life forever*? Mo felt like banging her forehead against the wall. Then again, she reminded herself, she'd given Twinkle the job to get away from that vindictive, malicious mother of hers.

Mo pushed the loo door back. Gasped loudly at the sight that greeted her. Two of the women who worked the bar hovered and fussed over Twinkle. Lindy and Josie, she recalled their names. One pressed a cooling flannel to the side of Twinkle's face.

Mo flew across the room to be by her best friend's side. 'Did that bastard put his hands on you?'

Lindy gazed at Twinkle with awe. 'Twinkle's our hero. She whacked him one with her stick. Dropped like a sack of spuds, he did.'

Josie quickly added, 'The rest of us were looking after number one while Twinkle was taking care of everyone else.' Her palm gently ran the length of Twinkle's arm. 'We're so proud to have her as our bar manager. Ain't we, Lindy?'

Lindy nodded. 'You betcha cotton socks.'

The way Twinkle had taken on that gorilla had left Lindy gawking in amazement. And shame. Not long ago she'd been mouthing off about Twinkle being flat-out useless. And Twinkle's walking stick had saved the day. Just went to show that those sometimes you pegged as the weakest were actually the strongest amongst us.

When the other two women left, Mo and Twinkle fell into in each other's arms.

'I ain't happy you put yourself in harm's way,' Mo half told her bestie off.

Twinkle eased back, gazing into Mo's unhappy face. 'I'm not a fragile piece of glass.'

Mo didn't hear the cloaked resentment in her closest friend's reply. Truth was, Twinkle was fed up to the back teeth of Mo's smothering overprotection. Mo's guilt was on a par with the pity Twinkle often saw in strangers' faces when they copped a load of her awkward walk. She knew that Mo was only doing it out of the goodness of her heart. Still, it rankled. She wasn't a bloody charity case.

Twinkle continued, her resentment now overridden by righteous indignation. 'I wasn't prepared to stand idly by and let some wanker off the street play Rambo on your manor and diss you to the max. No way.'

Staring into Twinkle's eyes, Mo whispered, 'East End Girls Forever.'

'East End Girls Forever,' her bestie said back.

This was their special phrase that they used to bolster each other when things were at the grimmer end of life.

Neither of them heard the door open. But they heard the voice, commanding, growling with anger. A very displeased Jimmy Southpaw loomed in the doorway, his fists balled by his sides. And his words knocked Mo for six.

'Maybe I chose the wrong grandkid to run my empire?'

Mo went into damage limitation control mode immediately, despite feeling like the bottom of her world was crumbling beneath her feet. She was with Granddad Jimmy in her basement office in the club. No way on this earth could she let him think she wasn't up to the task of running his ship when he hung up his captain's cap. The problem was, the attack on her HQ had left her appearing weak. Vulnerable. She'd been so consumed with finding out how her dad died in that fire that she'd taken her eye off the business. Mo mentally beat herself up on that score. How could she have been so stupid?

She made a decision. Robbie Steele's death was going to have to go on the back burner. For now.

The door opened, revealing Kristal and Harry. Kristal was done up to the nines in a sparkling-gold feathered top and white jeans that made her bum cheeks look like a work of art. Harry wore black jeans and a red leather shirt. His dad gazed at the leather shirt with disdain. Jimmy thought his son was doing a dead accurate impression of a peacock. What was wrong with the boy?

With enough drama to win a BAFTA and an Oscar rolled into one, Kristal rushed on tippy-toes across the room to Mo and took her dead husband's wrong-side-of-the-blanket daughter into her arms. Then she buzzed a kiss on both her cheeks.

Kristal drew back, her expression one of extreme

concern. 'When I heard what happened I dropped what I was doing and rushed over here as quick as my little legs could carry me.' Her fingers fluttered against her bottom lip in consternation. 'Upstairs is a bomb site.'

'That's because it was a grenade,' Mo supplied. Kristal gasped as Mo continued. 'And I'm not talking the stun grenade variety either. It's a blessing no one was hurt.'

Her stepmummy's face was a picture of pure holy horror. 'Who would do such a thing?'

Kristal had to restrain herself from crowing with insane laughter. Dean plus the back-up provided by Nico had done a bang-up job of wrecking Mo's joint.

Harry joined in, his face an absolute storm. 'When I get my hands on the bastard—'

Mo held her hand up. 'Hang on a minute. This is *my* show. I'm the one who's going to hunt him down.'

To her embarrassment, her Uncle Harry came over and ruffled his fingers through her curls as if she was some kid. 'Don't you worry, young un, you leave it to your Uncle Harry. You concentrate on fixing this place up.'

Kristal jumped in. 'Harry, she manages her own affairs. You butt out of it. It's not as if this shows she's weak. Or that the security at her HQ is crap. Or she hasn't got a clue what's going on. Give the girl space to breathe.'

Mo wasn't experienced enough in the bizz yet to realise that Kristal and her uncle might appear to be backing her up, whereas, in reality, they were playing a crafty game of undermining her in front of Jimmy. Harry, rustling his fingers through her hair, was as good as patting her on the head as if she were a child. In a classic backhanded fashion, Kristal had called her 'weak', 'crap', 'didn't know what was going on', planting the seeds of doubt about Mo's capabilities in Jimmy's mind.

Mo lowered her head slightly so she could flick her gaze beneath her lashes at Kristal and Harry. They seemed to be offering her support ... Nevertheless, there was something strange about their words. Right! She needed to show Granddad Jimmy two hundred percent she had the situation under control.

With determination, Mo proclaimed her power by sitting in the large exec chair behind the desk. She'd observed her granddad do this many times in his HQ at the betting shop on Commercial Road. Using a finger, she gestured for Jimmy to take a seat. She left the other two standing. Kristal and Uncle Harry needed to understand once and for all that on her manor she was the one calling the shots. The one wearing the crown.

She looked over at Uncle Harry. 'Pour Granddad Jimmy a malt.'

Harry hesitated, balking and bristling slightly at her order. Mo had acted deliberately. It was her turn to treat him like a runny-nosed kid. She had to show Jimmy that she was in the driver's seat.

While Harry poured the drink, Mo slowly turned her cool gaze to Kristal. 'I appreciate you coming over and offering your support ... stepmama. The best support you can give me now is to help put the place to rights. I'm sure someone upstairs can find you a dustpan and brush to help clean up.'

The corners of Kristal's mouth paled at the word, 'stepmama'. She laughed nervously at Mo's instruction. 'You want me to do what?'

Mo leant forward. 'No worries if you can't help tidy up. I mean, if you've just had your nails done and are frightened of rolling up your sleeves and getting your hands dirty. Not a problem.'

Kristal's mouth flapped like a floundered fish in astonishment. Mo had deliberately called her out. If Kristal refused to go upstairs, it might come across that she was indeed more into her beauty regime that the business. Not a good look in front of Jimmy Southpaw.

A fake smile fixed to her face, she perked a finely plucked brow up at Mo. 'Of course, honey-honey. Anything to get you back on an even keel.'

Once his drink was delivered, Jimmy ordered his son, 'Go with Kristal. Have a word in the ear of the staff. Dig up as much as you can and then pass the info on to Mo.'

Harry's dour expression showed he was less than happy, but he left with Kristal.

Jimmy told his granddaughter, 'That was smartly done. Getting rid of Kristal like that. That's why I put you in your father's seat, my right hand at the top table.' He drank deeply from his glass. 'But I've got to tell you, what I've seen here today makes me think I made a big-time mistake.'

Mo calmed her breathing before responding. 'Something's at play here. I can feel it in the air—'

'In the air?' Jimmy scoffed with a dismissive shake of his head. 'Next you'll be telling me we need to consult a crystal ball and have a sit-down with Mystic frigging Meg.'

Mo didn't let his sarky response throw her off. She kept her cool and held his silver-eyed gaze that matched her own with steadfast conviction. 'The only way someone had the brass to come here, fuck the place over and leave a message that they're planning to take over is if someone else is pulling their strings. Someone with more clout than they have. More powerful.'

'I hadn't thought of that.' Her grandfather slowly and carefully placed his glass on the desk. 'Who would have the hardware and nuts to do that?'

Mo shook her head, slumping back. 'Dunno. But I'll tell you this much: I won't sleep until I hunt and put them down.'

Jimmy Southpaw gulped the last of the malt. Slammed down the glass and got to his feet.

He turned his laser-like glare onto his granddaughter. 'You better find who it is because I'll tell you this for nothing. If this happens again, I'm going to have to reconsider who I want to be sitting next to me at the top table.'

Chapter Eighteen

Dean's eyes bugged out of his skull as he copped an eyeful of Kristal on his doorstep. She was practically grinding herself against the doorframe. One fishnet leg was hitched seductively so high it was a wonder he didn't get a flash of her Jackie Danny. Her hips worked the doorframe like a pole dancer; up, down, side to side. Most of her body was covered by a vintage, swing chestnut fur coat with a fox fur collar and stiletto-heeled black patent boots. The top of the boots disappeared where he'd give his right stone to stick his head right now – under the coat's hemline.

Dean yanked her unceremoniously inside, his jittery and panicked gaze searching along the communal balcony, worried that one or more of his neighbours might be doing the ol' twitchy net curtain routine, taking note of everything happening. There were plenty of prying eyes around here. He winced from the pain still throbbing in his knee, courtesy of a walking stick of all things.

Since sleeping with him on the first night they'd met, Kristal had made sure to do the dirty with Dean any chance she could get. Her tongue peeped out and with slo-mo seduction licked a leisurely route around those luscious cosmetically plumped-up lips of hers. The lad looked like he was about ready to offload in his pants. She leant into him, her expensive perfume wafting in his face. Her motion pushed him into the wall.

She laid her hands flat on his chest, her exaggerated Marilyn-Monroe-style breathing making her boobs rise and fall. Dean swallowed hard, hypnotised by her heaving flesh. He could gaze at those yummy mummies for eternity.

'I think you deserve a very special present after the damage you did to Mo's club.'

'It was easy-peasy. Nuthin' to it,' he answered breathlessly.

'You done good,' Kristal purred. 'The ultimate gangster.'

When the pads of her thumbs caressed and circled his nipples beneath his polo shirt, an aching moan burst from Dean's lips. He tried to speak, but desire smothered the words deep in his throat. Kristal's palm flashed down and landed on his aching knob. Dean's eyes rolled back. Her hand did wicked, wicked things to him. Sweat pooled on his face, breathing turning ragged. His body shook from his hairline to the tips of his toes.

Kristal chuckled. This young man was like putty in her hands. It hadn't taken her long to discover that Dean got his rocks off when she ordered him to do kinky shit during sex. The rougher she was, the more he lapped it up. Kristal's clit had gone into meltdown. There was nothing she loved better than playing the part of Miss Bossy Boots in the bedroom.

Her honeymoon had been one disappointment after another. Robbie had climbed on top of her, put it in … and almost put her to sleep. Where was the exciting and experimental lover he'd been before they'd exchanged rings? Then Kristal had sussed what the score was. Now she was Robbie's missus there was a certain role she was expected to play. Glam and pretty herself up, pop out some kids and keep his home a thing of domestic beauty. Robbie hadn't given a toss about her desires. Missionary most nights, doggy style if he was feeling generous.

Now Dean here…

She glanced at him with a scathing expression that communicated he was shit under her shoes. Dean was wetting himself with lust. Who would've guessed that dopey, half-brain Dean Forest got a rock-hard stiffy with a bit of discipline?

He eagerly led her towards his bedroom. Kristal had other ideas rerouting them to his sitting room instead. The surprised and expectant light showed Dean was well up for a bit of variety.

'What does Mistress Kristal hate above all else?' she demanded roughly.

'Having to wait,' he answered automatically, his voice barely under control.

And that's what Kristal made him do. Wait.

Humming that classic, 'The Stripper', she took her time peeling off her fur coat. As she took it off, she deliberately let her fingertips touch her exposed flesh, especially near her breast. Dean was a tit man through and through. His erratic breathing sounded like a horse galloping towards the finish line at the Grand National. Poor bollocks was going to have a very sticky, messy accident if he wasn't careful.

Dean's breath shattered in the air when he saw what she was decked out in. An Ann Summers push-up bra with peepholes for her nipples, stockings and suspenders, and garter belt. No panties in sight. Talk about all fur coat and no knickers. All the goodies he wanted to play with were there for the taking. He was due a right royal spanking for being such a good boy.

Kristal took out her telescopic soft rubber crop. With a loud smack against her boots, the crop grew to its full length. Calculating smile contorting her lips, Kristal faced Dean and dramatically hit the crop into her palm. Then waved it at him, the signal for him to get his kit off. He couldn't get his clobber off fast enough. His boner was ready for action. She did consider putting the studded collar around his neck … No … That was a treat for another time.

She pointed the tip of the crop at the floor near her feet. Dean immediately scrambled into position on all fours. Kristal leisurely strolled around him as she teasingly ran the crop along his spine. Dean moaned in manic delight.

Kristal sighed heavily. 'Mistress has heard that you've been a very naughty boy. That some girly with a walking stick knocked you on your jacksie during your little visit to Club Class.'

His response fumbled and stumbled from his mouth. 'I didn't realise—'

Impatiently, Kristal unleashed the coiled tension inside of her with a stinging blow to his bum. Dean arched, squealing like a stuck pig.

He glanced up, glassy-eyed with pained pleasure. 'Oh God, Kristal—'

Whack! Whack!

'Who gave you permission to use my name?'

Whack! Whack!

She growled. 'Get on the settee.'

Once Dean was seated, Kristal was on him in two seconds flat, straddling his overeager body and pushing her kitty-kats up north and her vee-jay-jay down south.

Expertly, she rocked her hips. Dean threw his head back with a strangled cry, quickly followed by noisy pants of pleasure. Spurred on, Kristal ground down hard. Rocked from side to side. When she started bouncing, Dean nearly went into hysterics.

They continued to make furious love until Dean could no longer hold his excitement at bay. Kristal's lips spread into a secret, crafty smile. She had this deluded young man eating out of her hand.

Half an hour later, she wasn't so sure. Side by side in his bed, Dean bombarded her with questions, which suggested he might have a brain after all.

'Tell me more about this Mo woman,' he point-blank insisted.

After the attack on the club, Dean thought of himself as a proper gangland villain. A real Face. Lobbing that grenade into the club … Boom! It kept rerunning over and over in his head. That gave him a sense of power that he'd never had before. He was the middle kid in a family of three with a dad who loved a bet down the bookies more than he loved his kids and a mum who worked her fingers to the bone, doing her best to keep her children in decent clothes and enough for their school dinner money. Before she died his mum was a shell of her former self, frazzled and beaten down by life.

Being a middle child, Dean had somehow always got lost in his family. It was as if he wasn't there. When he was twelve, he'd vowed with determination to be a SOMEBODY. He'd spend much of his life thinking how to make it big, not because he really wanted to be a villain, he just wanted the world to notice him.

He'd put his life on the line bombing that club, so the least Granny Big Knockers here could do was answer his fecking questions. Every time he mentioned Mo's name, Kristal went into this airy-fairy 'it don't matter' malarkey. Well, it did matter. And you know why? Because he was da man!

Kristal obviously didn't care for his probing because she stopped teasingly threading her fingers through the hair on his chest and rolled to her back with annoyance.

'I've already told you,' she snapped, 'doing the club was the first step on the road to mega things for you, baby.'

Dean wasn't satisfied with that. 'That girl with the walking stick said I didn't know who Mo was backed up by. What family she came from?'

Kristal gulped. This was all getting too close for comfort. 'That girl,' she dismissed with a hiss, 'I hear is as mad as a fruit fly. You don't want to be listening to the crap coming out of her bonkers' trap. She don't know her behind from her walking stick.'

Dean frowned, considered what she was telling him. Then, 'I know I want to make my mark, but I'm not sure I care for attacking a place that belongs to some woman …'

Kristal twisted to face him, her features wildly contorted. 'She's no woman, that one, believe you me. She's that 666 creature from that Book of Revelation in the Bible who's landed on her hooves in a place she has no business being. My …'

My son, that's what had almost escaped her. Kristal's anxiety levels shot through the roof at what she'd nearly revealed. She scrambled off the bed, desperately grabbing her clothes.

Dean frowned, never taking his gaze off her frantic movements. 'What's the rush?'

Furiously, Kristal swung to face him. And levelled a deadly finger his way. 'I'll tell you what the problem is. I could've chosen any young man, *any* to give a leg up into the bizz. But I chose you. And what do I get for my kind-hearted troubles? A load of flimflam and ol' fanny rolled into one.' Kristal drew a breath. 'You're disrespecting me. Spitting me dead in the eye.'

Dramatically, she sniffed and turned on the waterworks to garner his sympathy. And, more importantly, get his mouth to shut the hell up asking questions that might derail her plan. Kristal was also mindful that she had to do every last thing to make sure that Nico's name stayed out of the mix. There was no way she'd allow this golem of a kid to drop her precious brother into the crapper. Good grief, if Jimmy Southpaw ever got wind that Nico Sinclair from across the river was involved in the plot to harm his granddaughter's affairs, it would mean war between the East End and South London.

That in mind, Kristal changed tack, batting her lashes coyly at Dean. When in doubt, get the sex back out. With theatrical flair she launched her arms around him, flattening her body against his flesh. 'Let's not argue, baby.'

Flutter, flutter, flutter went her lashes.

'I hate arguing when we see each other. Make love to me again.'

But it was more like her making love to him when she climbed aboard Dean again. Her hand might be doing wicked things to him, but Dean's head was buzzing with a single question:

Why wouldn't Kristal tell him who Mo was?

Chapter Nineteen

'A nun walks into a betting shop ...'

That should be the start line of a joke. However, it was no laughing matter when Sister Aggi walked into Jimmy Southpaw's bookies on the Commercial Road. The shocked punters looked like Beelzebub Himself had put in an appearance. In response, Sister Aggi made a sweeping glance of the male gathering, briskly nodding to all concerned. There was one she reserved a squinty-eyed stare for; a family man with a wife and three kids. His poor, embarrassed wife had come begging Sister Aggi for a bit of change from the church's coffers to help pay for her son's school trip to the Science Museum. Fancy that! A God-fearing woman having to beg and borrow for her children when their father had enough to splash the cash in the betting shop.

What a wicked, wicked world!

Still, it wasn't the nun's habit to judge others too harshly. She would pray for the man's soul that he saw the errors of his ways and turned from the sin of gambling to embracing the full duties of a family man again.

Sister Aggi approached the counter where a man called

Sid presided. He resembled a worn teddy bear, huggable despite being a touch moth-eaten around the edges. His tan-coloured skin made it hard to pin down what his ethnic background was. And Sid wasn't telling. As far as he was concerned, those weren't the type of things that mattered about a person.

He lifted a bleary eye from the newspaper he was reading. Sid was a cool customer, not much surprised him in life, including a nun peering down her nose, brow raised on the other side of his counter in the betting shop.

'Now you must be Sid,' Sister Aggi declared. Her small, work-hardened hands flattened on the countertop.

'That I am.' Sid wasn't one to use more words than were necessary. And in this instance, he remained cagey because the only reason a woman of the church would be in here was to cause bother.

'Two things, Sid.' Sister Aggi got into the purpose of her visit. 'First, a Mrs Woodrow, who happens to be seventy-one, was telling me how she thinks she was diddled out of her winnings from this very establishment. She claims Sid wouldn't pay out on a dog that won at the 2:30 at Newmarket.'

Sid pulled a face. 'What's your point?'

'A dog? At Newmarket?' Sister Aggi was obviously not a betting woman, but she knew the difference between a greyhound track and a racecourse. 'How much was it?'

'Forty quid.' Sid had the decency to look sheepish.

The nun held her palm out on the counter. Sighing and muttering, Sid slapped a couple of twenties in her hand. She slipped them into her habit.

'Well, that was easily done,' she said. 'I'm sure Mister Southpaw wouldn't want it to get around that his criminal concerns had sunk as low as ripping off old ladies.'

Sid pretended confusion. 'Jimmy who? Ain't no Jimmy Northclaw here, Sister.'

Sister leant in close. 'You must be taking me for one of those dogs up at Newmarket.'

With that final parting shot, she spun on her heels and started for the door leading to the back stairs with a determined stride. Sid looked like his ticker was about to pack in. He scrambled to get out of his office and reach the stairs before the nun did. They got there at the same time. Sid smartly slipped into her path, barring the foot of the stairs.

Nun or no nun, Sid was apoplectic. And out of breath. Never in all his days of working for Jimmy had he had a battle on his hands to physically stop someone from getting to Jimmy above stairs. People knew better than to behave like that on Southpaw's turf. Way back when, Sid had been in much demand with certain violent types because of a nasty speciality he practiced. Those days were long gone and that's where he wanted them to stay. Sitting behind the counter, an occasional munch on a Havana cigar and a cuddle with his missus at the end of the day was all he needed.

He stretched his spine. So did Sister Aggi. Neither of them willing to give any ground. The standoff lasted until a voice at the top of the landing intervened.

'Let her up.'

Sister Aggi realised that the man standing at the top of the stairs must be Jimmy Southpaw's son. Harry. It was the square, jutting jaw that marked him as being cut from the same cloth as his father. He appeared comically amused at the carry-on between her and Sid.

Sid grudgingly gave way with a mutinous expression, jaw moving from grinding his teeth.

Sister Aggi didn't forget her manners. 'Thank you kindly, Sidney.'

She took each step with a certain amount of swagger. Truth was, she played it confident to hide how nervous she was about this meeting. Harry took his time giving her the eye, along with an undertone of curiosity, obviously trying to figure out what a nun could want with his dad. Then again, Jimmy was well known for supporting a number of local charities, his particular favourite a boxing charity for boys on the brink of falling into crime.

Harry escorted her to his father's opened door. Jimmy sat behind his big wooden desk, reading through a pile of papers.

'Going to confession for your multitude of sins, are ya, Dad?' Harry playfully jeered, ending in a nasty, nasal laugh.

Sister Aggi's hot gaze tore him down a peg or two. 'If it's offloading the badness in your soul you're after, sonny, I'll give you a confession you'll not likely forget.'

Yes, she noted smugly, that wiped the arrogant grin off his haughty face. He wasn't expecting her to give as good as she got. The boy, like so many, thought nuns were a soft touch. A bit of lip from his cheeky gob and she was meant to go scurrying for her life. Not bloody likely.

'Leave her alone,' responded a young woman in a soft, whispered tone, who sat on a chair to the side of Jimmy Southpaw.

Now that would be the daughter. Violet. Lights on, no one ever at home. A bit blank in the brain department. Those and plenty of other unkind remarks Sister had heard said about her. Not in the presence of her father, mind you, or they'd find themselves with a fistful. What she saw was an extremely polite woman who loved her peace and quiet.

'Would you like a cup of tea?' Violet offered.

Sister Aggi hadn't come for tea. 'Bless your heart, but no, thank you.'

She zeroed in on who she'd come here to see. Jimmy Southpaw. Their eyes locked across the room. Even from a distance, this man had presence. Big and raw, muscles clearly defined below his shirt. It was easy to see how he'd carved a place in London's underworld.

'Right, you lot clear off,' he instructed his children, never taking his gaze from his unexpected visitor.

Harry was giggling at the situation. 'You don't want me to stay as your protection?' Seeing his dad's murderous expression, Harry defensively held up his hands. 'Alright, I'm going. I'm going.'

Once the door was closed, there was an uncomfortable silence. Sister Aggi's anxiety deepened as she remained near the door as if thinking twice about getting close to Jimmy.

'Sister, take a pew,' Jimmy told her, waving at the empty chair opposite.

A pew? Funny. Very funny. Neither of them laughed. She took up his offer, perching on the edge of the seat rather than relaxing and getting comfy. Being comfortable wasn't part of her life anymore.

Jimmy pulled out Sister Aggi's greatest sin – a pack of cigarettes. She couldn't take her eyes off them. Milk and honey and manna from Heaven all rolled into one, they were.

Good grief, the greed and love of a puff must have taken possession of her face because Jimmy slowly asked, 'Would you like one, Sister?'

May God and sweet Mother Mary have mercy on my soul. Her mental prayer of forgiveness was because there was no way on this earth she could decline. She needed something worldly to steady her jittery nerves. Sister Aggi took one. Jimmy lit her up. Easing back in the chair, she took her first hit. Momentarily shut her eyes. Pure. Heavenly. Magic.

Jimmy gazed at her quizzically. '"Thou shalt not smoke fags, especially if you're a Bride of Christ". Isn't that one of the Ten Commandments?'

Sister Aggi savoured the smoke on her tongue ... and then let it out. 'I'm a nun, not a saint. I've still got one or two demons I do battle with.'

'Only one or two?' Jimmy Southpaw leant his big self across the table, holding her gaze.

Sister kept her mouth zipped. She wasn't about to give Jimmy Southpaw, of all people, a foothold in her soul.

So, he changed tack. 'You're a long way from the comfort of your convent, Sister.'

'I've come here to ask you a favour.' Suddenly the baccy tasted foul in her mouth. Sister Aggi mashed out her smoke in the ashtray.

'And how would a sinner like me be able to help you, Sister?'

The nun laced her fingers tersely together. Kept her voice steady, which wasn't easy under his intense, unflinching stare. 'This is your manor. You run everything around here. You've got a finger in every pie. People listen to you because you're a man of influence.'

He considered her for a bit, poured a whisky and knocked it back in one. He put the glass down with such a gentle motion it was almost easy to forget he was a powerful man. 'You want me to whisper something in someone's ear? Right?'

Sister Aggi nodded. 'Yes. Into your own ear.'

His body stiffened, coiled with tension. His good-humoured welcome withered and died. 'And what is it I'll need to tell myself?'

The nun glanced directly into his face so that he understood what she was about to tell him she meant with her whole heart. 'Maureen Watson. You have to let her go. She hasn't seen her mum for nearly a year—'

'*I'm* her family,' he ground out, his fury gathering into a storm.

Anyone else would have sensed that was the point when they offered their goodbyes and got out of there as quickly as their trembling legs could carry them. Not Sister Aggi. She understood the strength of fear and never ever again would she allow it to have a foothold in her life.

She refused to flinch beneath his glare. 'She has a mother and …' Her voice wobbled for a second and then was calm. 'Grandfather who worship her. Have looked after and lavished love on her since the day she was born.'

'What are you saying?' His voice was strained. 'That I can't love her? That I can't love anyone—'

'You know that's not what I'm saying.' Sister Aggi jerked across the desk.

The sound of their heavy, noisy breathing was all that could be heard. Sister Aggi could've kicked herself. What a klutz! She'd gone about this all wrong. She should have schmoozed him. Pretty-pleased him and asked him nice as pie to have a word in Mo's ear about at least paying a visit to her mum.

No! She'd not been a 'pretty-please' woman for a very long time.

Slowly, Sister Aggi got to her feet. Looked down at Jimmy. 'I want to thank you for the money you generously give the food bank each year.' At his high-brow-lifting expression of surprise, she added, 'What? You didn't think I knew about that? You're not the only one with eyes and ears in certain places.'

She drew a fortifying breath. 'No doubt about it, you're a generous man. But you're a greedy one too. You see something and you have to have it. There's no problem with that, but in your case, you refuse to share. Mo isn't a possession. She's a human being. She had a life before you decided to acknowledge her.'

He let her say her piece.

'And I thank you for it because that girl has worried about who her father was for too long. Now she's got a whole new family.' Her palms came up as if praying to Him above. 'I heard what happened at the club in town where she has her base. She could've died. You can't keep playing with other people's lives, Jimmy.'

The weight of him getting to his feet so quickly slammed his chair back. 'You. Need. To. Leave.' The clenching of his fists showed he was barely keeping his rage from exploding.

Her chin came up. 'You might boss the East End. But you don't boss me.'

And with that, she strode to the door. As her hand lay on the door handle, she threw over her shoulder, 'I only came here because of Mo.'

She closed the door with care and quiet. Kept walking even when she heard the smashing sound of Jimmy throwing the bottle of whisky against the door.

Chapter Twenty

A deadly silence seized the occupants of the room when Mo entered the Candy Floss Bar in South London. The only sound was the music playing, Missy Elliot's 'Get Ur Freak On'. The place was filled with men who turned their narrowed eyes onto her. *It stinks of the odour of geezers too*, Mo thought with a twitched wrinkle of her nose. The Candy Floss called itself a Gentlemen's Club that featured pole dancing. In other words a stripper joint.

The reason the atmos had suddenly gone tense and very chilling was because the bar was the known HQ of one of South London's most notorious Faces. Nico Sinclair. And Mo's face hadn't been seen here before. She was a stranger.

Knowing Josh and Dell had her back, Mo moved with confident assurance deeper into the bar. Even though it was daytime, the place was painted in the neon-red light of a club that never slept. Cheap fag smoke wafted in the air. On a circular stage was a woman going through her paces next to a steel pole. If it wasn't for the glittering silver-sequin material guarding her pubes, she'd have been as naked as the day she came into this world. Punters gawked at her, licking their lips in 'dirty old man' appreciation. The woman gave it the ol' come-hither routine in spades, but she wore a smile that was as fixed and fake as a Madame Tussaud's waxwork.

The edge of Mo's mouth turned down with disdain and thinly veiled disgust at the spectacle. On the spot, she swore that degrading and using women to make a fast buck was never going to be part of the trade she dabbled in. Her estimation of Nico Sinclair plummeted. She'd only heard bang-up stuff about the geezer. He might be a tough nut and put the fear of God into people who crossed him, but he was fair. Solid, that's what Granddad Jimmy had called him. Mo's lips twisted. Someone should've explained that he liked to live on the sleazy side.

'Back the bitch up.' Josh's warning, growling voice behind alerted her that something was wrong.

Mo spun round. A proper posse of villains stood behind them. Then they menacingly moved, closing in on them. The hairs on Mo's neck stood on end when she clocked another group of men coming at them from the other side. They were trapped. No escape.

Dell acted immediately with her trademark lightning one-two-three move.

Flash! Hands criss-crossed over her shoulder.

Flash! Unzipped her rucksack.

Flash! Two dangerous and super-sharp machetes gleamed in the air, ready to do maximum damage.

Any of these men who decided to take her on would be doing so at their own peril; Dell knew exactly how to use them with deadly efficiency. Josh was about to produce a shooter, but Mo stopped him with a staying hand on his arm.

She reasoned, voice loud and clear, 'No need for any dramarama, lads. We're only here to pay a courtesy call on the man of the house.'

For an instant, silence was the only response to Mo's attempt to cool down the temperature. Then a right scary bastard stepped forward. As big and as wide as Everest, head shaved clean with a wicked scar zigzagging the length of a cheek and hands that could crush a windpipe in one second flat. He did not look like a happy bunny.

His response was cocky. 'Someone's led you down the garden path, love, coz no Nico Sinclair has ever darkened the door here.'

Mo didn't miss a beat shooting back, 'I never said his name was Nico. Or Sinclair.'

What a grade-A plum! The guy obviously hadn't recharged the battery of the single brain cell he used. Dear, oh dear, oh dear! Nico really should take him back to the Jobcentre and trade him in for a newer, brighter model. The man's brows slashed together in confusion. His eyes widened finally twigging the massive slip-up he'd made. He went from unhappy bunny to I'm-gonna-rip-your-head-off bunny.

He surged forward. Dell leapt towards him, machetes at the ready. The insistent ringing of a mobile phone froze the action. It turned out to be mountain-man's phone. He took it out, listened and nodded.

He put it away and addressed Mo. 'You. Come with me. Alone.'

Mo knew she wasn't out of the woods yet. This could very well be a trap. Get her in the back and show her who's boss with a lick down she wasn't likely to forget.

Josh obviously thought the same. 'She ain't going nowhere with you, dickbrain.'

The geezer remained expressionless. Probably been called loads worse over the years.

Mo held up a reassuring hand. 'It's alright. Wait for me here.'

Mo couldn't explain why she was stepping into the unknown with this thug, but she did. She followed him out of the main room and into a corridor, panelled in dark wood, forest-green lino on the floor. Then they climbed a set of narrow stairs and were soon standing in front of a plain white door. He opened it. Mo stepped inside. The door closed behind her.

No one else was there, not that she noticed; Mo was too gobsmacked by the contents of the room. She'd never seen the like in her life. It was like something out of a palace from centuries past. The walls were a stunning, eye-grabbing red, lined with gold trimming that matched the golden furniture. Paintings of men on horses and ladies lounging on chaise longues, some wearing ballgowns and some wearing sod all. A humongous marble fireplace dominated one wall, which faced a French window draped with a startling white curtain. And as for the ceiling … Mo's mouth fell open. It was a beautifully painted scene of the sky complete with stars, pot-bellied cherubs, harps and halos …

'I'm glad you like.'

The man's husky voice startled Mo. She swung smartly around to find a very tall and impressive man with his back against the wall. Mo could've kicked herself. She'd been so caught up in the beauty of the room she hadn't noticed his entrance. How many times had Granddad Jimmy told her to always keep her wits about her? Eyes in the front, sides and back. Nightandbloodyday!

Mo flashed her eyes at him. 'Who said anything about liking it?' Her mouth turned down, knowing full well she was lying. 'Bit OTT if you ask me. Would've popped my shades on if I'd known I'd be a-eye-gazing at all that shiny, trashy gold.'

Instead of getting the nark, he smiled. 'I took inspiration from the Palace of Versailles and Louis the Fourteenth, AKA the Sun King.'

Mo rolled her eyes. 'The Palace of Ver-sigh? What's that then? A bingo hall off the Old Kent Road? And this Louis Sonny character? He run the bingo hall or something?'

He threw his head back and hooted with laughter. Mo didn't have a clue what the Palace of Whatnot was, but she did know it wasn't a bingo joint in South-East London.

He strode towards her, hand held out. 'Nico Sinclair. Welcome to the Candy.'

They shook hands. He had a strong grip, a stark reminder to Mo that she was dealing with one of the most fearsome Faces this side of the river. All that soft chat about palaces and sunshine kings like they were discussing arty-farty stuff in a posho gallery wasn't fooling her. She needed to watch her step with this man.

Mo sat opposite him at a large desk in keeping with the style of the room. The chair was cushy and comfy. She resisted sinking into it. This was business, so she kept her spine ramrod straight. One leg flicked over the other. He offered her a hard drink, which she politely declined.

Nico leant back in his seat. 'So, Jimmy Southpaw plucks you from the gutter,' Mo scoffed at that, 'and plonks you in the prince's chair.' He winked. 'Well now, that would be princess's chair, wouldn't it?'

If he thought he was going to get under her skin, he had another thing coming. 'Princess? Nah! That's for girls who like to dress up for a Saturday night on the razz. What I am is a queen.'

Queen? Nico considered her claim as he took in his fill of Big Mo Watson. She was more like a diamond in the rough. But with a bit of spit and polish, this girl could become a legend. There was an aura about her that commanded attention. Y'know, can't take your eyes off her. She might be a titchy-itchy thing, but she was packing the spirit and bravery of a spitfire. Somehow, he didn't think that his sister's plan to get rid of her rival was going to go like clockwork, even with his help.

Mo caught him off the hop when she pointed at a heart-shaped framed photo on his desk. 'Who's that?'

'My family.' Nico's chest inflated with pride. The snap was an official photo of his wife, son and daughter. He loved them fiercely. If anything ever happened to them, he wouldn't be able to carry on.

Alarm suddenly gripped Nico when he realised that the photo of his family sat next to a smaller one. One of him and Kristal when they were young ones. He was six, and she was fourteen. What a portrait of blissful happiness they were. Now it wouldn't do for Mo to catch sight of it. Not that Kristal resembled the joyful girl in the photo … Still, better safe than sorry.

'I take it your trip across the Thames is because you want a word in my ear about something?' Speaking, Nico casually shifted his body in such a way to block Mo's view of him taking the photo and discreetly putting it away into the top drawer of the desk.

Mo laid her own photo on the table. A still frame from the club's security footage of the baseball-and-sunglass-wearing thug who'd battered her place and put a cherry on top with a lobbed grenade.

Nico plucked up the photo, studying it. 'Who's this then?'

'That's what I'm hoping you can tell me,' Mo shot back. 'Bastard had the brass to come into my place and leave a pineapple on his way out.'

Nico studied the photo closely, his brows slashed together. 'Yeah, I heard someone took against the décor in your club.'

Hahaha-bloody-ha! This guy was a real jester. Borderline jerk too. Mo damped down her frustration, focusing solely on whether this South London gang lord had information that could help her.

'You seen his face before?'

He threw the photo on the desk. Gave her his full attention. 'Can barely see his face, love—'

'I ain't your *love* or anyone else's,' Mo stabbed back.

What a sexist shit. She got to her feet. 'I didn't come over here for you to finger my fanny.'

Mo had had enough of Nico Sinclair and his smart mouth. Annoyed, she headed for the door. As she touched the handle, he informed her, 'The geezer in the photo. If he was from around these parts, I'd have heard something about it by now. Never seen the fella before in my life.'

Mo slowly turned back to face him. Checked out his expression. He appeared genuine enough. Then again, why would he hold anything back from her? The way she heard it, his neck rarely reached in to the business dealings of the East End. He showed surprise when Mo strode purposefully towards him and held out her hand. He shook it. Now it was time for Mo's grip to be strong.

When their hands fell away, he told her, 'If a whisper comes my way about this twat in a baseball cap, you'll be the first to hear.'

Mo bestowed one of her brightest smiles on him. 'If I'm ever down south again, I now know where to come for a cuppa.'

Nico knowingly grinned. 'And if you fancy being fingered in your …'

Mo quietly and firmly closed the door. She couldn't hold back the smile at the nerve of the guy! A right royal cheeky sod! Mo couldn't help admiring that. The smile died on her face. She still wasn't any closer to finding out who the poxy prick was who thought he could take over her turf. She had to sort this quickly before Granddad Jimmy decided she wasn't worthy of his crown.

Chapter Twenty-One

'What was that?' the woman squeaked with alarm.

Her legs were wrapped tightly around the waist of the man in the dark alley behind the Candy Floss bar later that night. Her back muscles hurt; the man screwing her for all he was worth against the rough wall was too lost in his own pleasure to think about any discomfort he was causing her.

She was shit scared. Scared someone would catch her at it. She was one of the club's pole dancers, which meant she fully understood the bar's rule – no opening your legs for the clientele. It was one thing for the Candy's front of house to be known for geezers ogling titties and muff, but open prostitution? A knocking shop? Nah! That was not a good look for Nico's main HQ to be openly associated with.

But this woman was taking her chances. She had four kids to feed, and any opportunity she got to make a few quid on the side she took with both hands. No one had to explain she was playing a dangerous game.

She squeezed her muscles down there to hurry proceedings along.

'I'm coming!' Reaching his completion, the man's eyes rolled like saucers.

The woman couldn't get her legs untangled from his waist quickly enough. Fingers shaking, she dragged her G-string back into place and yanked her miniscule skirt down. Her concerned gaze roamed furtively around. She still had a prickly, uneasy sensation someone lurked in the shadows. She didn't like this. Didn't like it one bit. If one of Mister Sinclair's toughs caught her at it, she was dead meat.

Narrow-eyed, the punter licked his lips, his greedy gaze running over her like she was the dish of the day.

'Second helpings ain't on the menu.' Her hand flashed out. 'But that cash you promised me certainly is.'

The pole dancer practically snatched the notes from his hand. She glanced deep into the darkness one last terrified time. Heart pounding, she yanked the man's hand and tugged him through the back-door entrance and slammed the steel door shut.

She was right to be suspicious. There was someone waiting in the dark. The person stepped out of the shadows. *Thank goodness for that. Thought they were going to bonk for England all night blinkin' long!* The person put the antics of the couple out of their mind. Focused on their primary objective: how to get in to the Candy Floss Bar without being seen.

A laden sigh puffed out of their mouth, frosting in the cold air. The black clothing, including balaclava, was a perfect cover for blending into the darkness. No way could they be discovered here. If they were, there would be major-league ructions.

For a man of Nico's stature and stripe, it was a shocker that he didn't have one of his crew doing sentry duty at the back of the place. Add to that the security cams only covered the entrance to the alley; this was a piss-poor security operation. The person grimly grinned behind the balaclava. This totally inadequate security operation played right into their hands. Beautifully.

The person in black grabbed a drainpipe attached to the building and pulled, testing its solidness. Deciding it would do the trick they shimmied up. Climbed and climbed with the knowhow of a monkey, the damp uncomfortable air wrapping about them. They looked down when they reached the top. And wished they hadn't. The ground swerved beneath like the dark, open mouth of a monster ready to gobble and swallow them whole if they should fall.

The person shook off the fear and faced the window they'd reached. Peered inside the long dark corridor. No one in sight. Perfect! They tried to prise the window up. It didn't budge an inch. The person wasn't fazed. They'd come packing for that eventuality. A screwdriver jimmied the window open. The noise was kept to a minimum.

The bottom of the window eased up with a low snake-like hiss. The burglar moved fast, swinging into the empty corridor. The beat of the music downstairs was faint, but it provided a warning to the intruder; they needed to be in and out in less than five. With soft-footed speed, they moved along the corridor until they came to a door.

Nico Sinclair's office. Tried the handle. The intruder's jaw dropped south in stupefied amazement because the door opened. Then their eyebrows flicked together in a quizzical motion of bemused confusion. What kind of two-bob outfit was this so-called top villain running here? First off, there're no eyes and ears stationed at the back of his HQ, and now boss man's private room where some of his deepest secrets would be kept wasn't under lock and key. Open sesame and you're in?

The burglar stiffened. Maybe this was a trap? Only one way of finding out.

The handle turned. Cautiously, they opened the door. The room was bathed in black. The type of dark that hid someone biding their time, waiting for the right moment to spring. The intruder pressed an ear forward. Listened. And listened. No sound of another heartbeat, or the deep in-and-out breathing of another person. There was a smell, though. Man-scent. Nico Sinclair's natural smell that marked this room out as his territory. Soapy-clean with the hint of designer aftershave.

What are you on? Woolgathering about some bloke's aftershave! Get on with it!

The door shut with a whisper of a click. The person was utterly still for a moment to give their vision time to get its bearings in the dark. Then they moved with long strides, knowing exactly where they were headed. The large desk near the window. The burglar touched the handle of the top drawer. Started to pull…

Abruptly, Nico's Sinclair's office door opened.

Bloody, bloody hell's bells. The person in black instinctively dropped to their knees. Rolled beneath the desk. The many bulbs in the chandelier came on. Light streamed brightly everywhere. Luckily for the intruder the space beneath the desk remained in the dark. Nerves and fear kicked in as the person tried to quiet their breathing. They waited. And waited. For whoever had entered to shout out that the game was up and they should come out.

Waited. Waited.

No one shouted. Whoever had come in walked deeper into the room, bringing their distinctive scent with them. Bollocks. Nico. Of all the effing luck. Nico's footsteps got closer and closer to the desk. Closer … Suddenly stopped on the other side.

Please, please, don't sit down. Don't sit down. If Nico did … Game. Over.

A few minutes later, Nico walked back towards the door. But he didn't leave. The burglar imagined him standing on the threshold looking into the room wearing a puzzled expression. His eyes doing the rounds of his office, suspecting that something was up. Maybe that someone had the brass neck to be inside his private lair?

The light flicked off. Dark covered the room again. The quiet click of the door closing. The person under the desk didn't move an inch. Held their breath steady and silent. Waited a good few minutes to be sure that the South London Boss was really gone. Then they uncurled and emerged from the desk. Opened the desk drawer fully and took something that lay inside. They produced a camera. Snap. They took a picture of the item that lay on the desk. Discreetly, they put the object back.

Wasting no time they re-entered the corridor, slid down the drainpipe, exited the Candy Floss like a phantom disappearing into the night.

Big Mo peeled the balaclava from her face as she settled into the front seat of her Mini Convertible. A self-satisfied smirk sprang on her supremely chuffed face.

'Boss.' It was Josh's none-too-pleased voice in the back seat. His tone bordered on tearing a strip off her. 'You should've let me go in there. I know all about walking through walls without being seen.'

'He's got a point,' Dell flipped in. She didn't hide her annoyance. Mo was also her cousin, her family. You didn't let family waltz into danger on their own. 'Mister Southpaw would have our knackers if he knew what you just did. Our job—'

'I don't need you to remind me what your job description is, especially as I wrote the fecking thing.' Mo twisted to impatiently stare at the very unhappy faces of her two minders. Actually, Dell looked more upset than unhappy.

When she'd revealed her plan to sneak into Nico Sinclair's base on her own, they'd both gone ballistic. Then tried their utmost to talk her out of it. On the one level they had a point. She was a boss lady now, the next in line to Jimmy Southpaw's empire, and therefore shouldn't be placing herself needlessly in danger. However, when it came to Nico, she couldn't seem to help herself. The idea of outsmarting that cocky south-of-the-river sod left her cock-a-hoop ecstatic. As far as she was concerned, the geezer was a legend in his own mind.

She also had to admit she got a real kick out of doing the operation herself. The thrilling opportunity to use the gymnastic skills she'd been so talented at during her time in school because of her small size. That shot of adrenaline as she'd climbed the drainpipe. Even when she was hiding beneath the desk, thinking she'd been caught bang to rights, excitement had rushed through her veins.

Suddenly Dell pulled back so she could scrutinise her cousin's face. Whatever she saw made her features turn fierce and disapproving. 'You and this Nico geezer ain't in a ting?'

'A ting' was a catchall Caribbean phrase for many things, one of which was sex. Dell was asking if Mo was having an affair – a ting – with the madman from the south?

Mo kissed her teeth with a terse roll of her eyes. 'As if! The bloke ain't packing what a gal like me needs. You get me?'

A meaningful girl's glance passed between them. Simultaneously, they clicked their fingers and sniggered in the way only women can at Mo's put-down.

Josh cut through their little happy moment. 'The way I hear it, the King of the South don't play away from home. Devoted to his family is what's whispered.'

Mo's brows rose in surprise. She wouldn't have figured a guy like that would've been able to keep his zip up in a joint like the Candy Floss.

Leaning back, Dell asked, 'So what was tonight's drama all about?'

Mo became dead serious. 'This.'

She passed over the camera and watched Josh and Dell inspect the photo she'd taken.

Josh, clearly baffled, said, 'It's a photo of a young girl and even younger boy.'

Mo's mind zoomed back to her earlier visit with Nico in his office. And how he'd thought she hadn't noticed him pick up the framed photo and squirrel it quietly away into his desk. Mo had played along as if she hadn't seen. Why would Nico hide the photo from her? Did this have anything to do with the attack on her club? Only one way to find out.

She instructed Josh and Dell, 'Be discreet with it, but I want to know who this boy and girl are.' She added, almost as a whisper for her own ears, 'Then I can figure out why Nico Sinclair was so determined to hide it from me.'

Josh spoke. And what he said made Mo's hands curl into fists with her nails digging into her palms.

'While you were doing your *Mission Impossible* routine, I had a call. I've ID'd our slimeball. His name's Dean Forest. He hangs out in a boozer in Essex called the Scarlet Lady.'

Chapter Twenty-Two

This meeting was a bad idea. Blackmail was a bad idea. But these thoughts all came too late for Pockets while he waited on the south side of London Bridge, Big Ben down the river striking midnight. Instead of spilling all that he knew about Robbie Steele's death that fateful night to Jimmy Southpaw's new heir, Big Mo, he'd chosen to withhold what he knew from her and trade it instead for an opportunity to line his pockets on this freezing bridge. Pockets trying to line his pocket! Any other time he'd have laughed himself silly at that. Now, all he felt was his stomach sickeningly lurching.

After speaking to Big Mo, he'd made contact with the one person who wouldn't want it to be known what had really happened to Robbie in the police station. Who wouldn't want Big Mo to know what had really happened to her dad? And the reason why? Pockets suspected this very person who he was meeting was also the culprit behind Robbie Steele's death.

Pockets felt lonely looking out over at the black river flowing around the spans. All that never-ending, bottomless water gave him the willies. He was scared witless. His earlier confidence, boosted by the bottle of high-proof Polish voddy he'd downed this morning before midday, was long gone. Now he was here he didn't think a million quid in used tenners was worth running this kind of risk.

He should've questioned the need for a meeting in the middle of London Bridge at midnight. Should've organised it in a busy caff at the height of the morning. He hadn't been able to see sense because there was only one thing he could think about.

Money! Cash! Wonga!

How much booze he could buy with it? Maybe even go off to stay with his miserable sister outside London until the inevitable moment she screamed at him to sling his hook. His sister properly did his nut in, but he missed her. Missed her potato salad with the fresh chives.

A bus went by, heading south. It could be a matter of moments before Pockets was on one, going home. But there was no going back now, not unless he wanted a phone call in the middle of the night that went along the lines of, 'Hello, bruv, I thought we had a meet sorted? Do you think I'm the kind of person who crosses the bridges of London at midnight because I enjoy the view? I'm so disappointed in you.'

There wouldn't be the need for any open threats. The word 'disappointed' was threat enough on its own.

Pockets took a deep breath and set off northwards.

He didn't spot the person he was meeting until they were nearly on top of him. Tucked under a lamppost in a flat cap and long coat with their back towards the yellow light so that their face remained in the shadows.

'You're late,' the person admonished. Their breath frosted like a ghost in the cold night air.

Pockets hurriedly checked the cheap digital watch he'd thieved off a stall in Whitechapel Market. Time did have a habit of running away with him, especially when the booze was in him.

'Am I? You know how it is with the trains and buses … And all that.'

An impatient sigh was the only answer he received. The hidden face was turned towards the river and the glittering lights that ran beside it. 'London's a beautiful city, isn't it, Pockets?'

Pockets' tongue was too heavy with fear to reply.

'I mean, you could almost forget all the terrible things that go on in this city when you're enjoying a view like this. A bit like checking out a tart in a ballgown.'

Pockets was in a hurry to get away. 'I suppose, yeah, listen …'

But he was cut short. 'And the noises. That kind of hum you get at night-time in our fair city. A bit like crickets when you're in a villa in the tropics.'

Pockets knew it was time to be quiet. Suddenly his bladder felt full.

After a long silence, the shadowy face turned slowly towards him. 'Right then, you say you've got something that might be of interest to me?'

Pockets hesitated. Faltered as he spoke. 'Yeah, but I was hoping, you know, there might be a drink in it for me.' He didn't have to see to know the face in the shadows had become even darker. He hurriedly added, 'I mean, be fair, I've got to live.'

'Have you? Who says? Who says you've got to live? Some people don't have to live at all. Some people are only good for putting in a weighted sack and dumping in the Thames.' The person before him stared menacingly down at the river. 'Their bloated body fished out on a hook by the River Police up Wapping way six months later. Let's face it, bruv, no one has to live.'

Pockets forgot about the money. The booze. Seeing his sister. He was desperate to get away. And if he didn't soon, he'd be pissing himself. 'Whatever you say. The thing is, I'm strolling alone one night minding my own when all of a sudden – bish-bosh – someone grabs me up and drags me off.'

'Who?'

Pockets nervously coughed. 'Never met her before in my life—'

'Fucking who?'

'Mo. Big Mo. Steele family—'

'I bloody well know who she is, you ol' sodden soak. What I want to know is why would she be nabbing the likes of you off the street?'

Pockets took a tentative step forward. 'Talking about her new daddy. Robbie Steele. Except he's gone and all that. Sad business when a child …' The killer expression on the other's face told him to get back on track. 'Asking about the fire that killed Robbie in that police station, she was.'

'And why would she be asking you about the fire that killed him?'

Some of the fear fell away from Pockets as he remembered what he knew. A cocky confidence tilted his chin up. He had the upper hand and was holding all the cards – very close to his chest.

'Coz I was there that night.' If he was high on booze, he would've jumped on his tiptoes doing a jig at the incredulity on the other person's face.

Pockets ran his tongue greedily across his cracked lips. 'I was in the cell next door. Heard it all, didn't I?' He crept closer. 'Now, you wouldn't want me to tell no one what I heard, would ya?' Another step. 'All you've got to do is slip me some notes. Fill my pockets up.'

His greedy request was met with stony silence. Then, 'Have you told anybody else that you were coming here? What you know?'

Pockets crossed his heart. 'Swear on my life, I—'

Hands grabbed him. Hooked him up onto the bridge's parapet while the other gripped the back of his neck and pushed his head downwards. There were only a few dozen yards of cold, thin air between Pockets and the black river.

'So, what exactly did you say to her?'

Horror shook Pockets. The freezing wind smacked his face. 'Nuthin' Nuthin'' he screamed. 'I repeated the story everyone tells … That Robbie Steele died in the fire coz of the old electrics. Come on. There's no need for any of the rough stuff.'

The grip remained tight, the voice a mere whisper. 'You

know what happens to people who tell tales?'

Bone-shaking terror seized Pockets. A river of hot urine slid down his leg. His frozen lips trembled, but no words came out. He shuffled slightly in an attempt to keep his balance like the driver of a van on a cliff edge, but toppled slightly further towards the darkness below. Only then did he realise that he was no longer being held fast. He inched backwards, falling into a shaking heap on the bridge.

Thank God! Thank God!

He shivered so badly he thought his skin was peeling off his bones. When his eyes focused, the other person was looming over him. The darkness shaded their face. 'Why am I relying on you to keep your cakehole closed? I must be going soft.'

Pockets was hauled to his feet. The following seconds fused into one as he was punched into a daze and then fell backwards into thin air. Somersaulting over and over, again and again, like an acrobat into the unforgiving water below.

Chapter Twenty-Three

'You alright, young Mo?' twin voices called out as she walked onto the estate she'd once lived on with her mum and granddad.

The callers were the estate's resident drunks. Milton and Molly, usually to be found on the rusty bench knocking back VP red wine from the bottle. Wandering over to them, Mo felt weird being back here. Freaky! She'd only been gone less than a year, and already this estate felt strange. It was as if she were walking on air. Her gaze darted nervously around, trying to take everything in. For years Mo had dreamed of leaving this place and never looking back. Truth was she'd missed it, including the pair of boozers madly waving at her.

'Ooooh! Get a gander at you,' Molly cooed.

'Ohhh! Done up all hoity-toity,' Milton added.

Mo couldn't help smiling. What a pair! They were twins, in their fifties, who shared a two-bed on the estate. Word was in their young days they'd been part of the dodgy dealings that went on around here. No one knew quite what had driven them both to drown their sorrows in the bottom of a bottle. The cheery, jolly patter they kept up couldn't hide the hurt in their eyes. Whatever had happened to them had damaged them for life.

'Just back for a quick visit,' she told them.

The twins then proceeded to talk as if Mo wasn't there.

'That's right, turns out she's Southpaw's grandkid.'

'Fancy that.'

'Fancy that.'

'Would you Adam and Eve it?'

'Took him long enough to find her.'

'Maybe he spent too much time looking for her down the back of a settee.'

They rocked back with ear-splitting laughter filling the air with wine fumes so potent Mo stepped back, wriggling her nose with distaste.

Mo jumped when Milton's filthy hand clawed around her arm. His stare was scary because his features were suddenly stone-cold sober. 'Don't let him take your soul, Mo. You hang on to it. Lose it and you're doomed.'

Mo snatched her arm back, more ruffled than annoyed. She didn't have time for this mumbo-jumbo. Losing your soul? What a lot of old cobblers. And she really didn't have any time for it due to the fact that she was back to make peace with her mum.

Flipping hell. Just the thought of it made her quake in her Nike trainers. For the last couple of years, they'd had a very rocky relationship. Then the revelation that her dad was Robbie Steele had spun everything out of control. Not seeing her mum was tearing Mo apart.

'Be seeing ya,' Mo cut into the twins' giggles.

As she turned to leave, Molly informed her, 'Your mum ain't in her drum. She's in the washhouse.'

Mo inwardly groaned. As if things couldn't get any worse. The last place she wanted to go was to the launderette. It was a hive of gossip and back-fence talk. Then again, maybe, just maybe, her new status as Jimmy Southpaw's next in line might mean folks in the washhouse shut their gobs and minded their beeswax. Her wish went out of the window when she reached it. The place was chock-a-block, including her mum chatting to Rabina Sweeney. Rabina was the washhouse boss lady who presided over her kingdom with a gravelly voice, a litany of rules to abide by and hands that were made not only to fold clothes but to choke an offending person out.

Mo's heart thumped harder at the first sight of her mother. Precious Watson was and would always be, a beauty. Tall, gleaming brown skin, long thin extensions Alicia Keys style and a figure to die for. Even in everyday jeans and T-shirt she was a pure knockout. Hesitantly, every step filled with nervous trepidation, Mo inched towards the launderette door. When she pushed it back, all convo stopped. Her mum turned.

Precious nearly fell off the metal bench when she saw her daughter. Her first instinct was to leap with joy, run over and hug her to death. She couldn't even put into words how much she'd missed her darling baby. Her tummy tied into knots just seeing her. Then the row they'd had crept back into her memory, every last screaming word of it.

Her lips flattened into a grim line. Robbie Steele's

fecking family had finally come between them. Of course, Precious knew that the day was bound to raise its ugly unwanted head, but she hadn't been prepared for it. Then again, would she have ever been ready?

And Robbie dying like that, in a fire, for Chrissakes! It still left her wanting to sob her guts out. *Robbie, you stupid, stupid bastard!* Standing, Precious mentally made a vow. It didn't matter how many times Mo asked, she was never going to tell her the full story of what went on with her and Robbie. Never!

'Come back, have ya?' Rabina scoffed, clearly a supporter of her mum's. No doubt Precious had given her chapter and verse about what had gone on. 'Hope you've come to apologise to your ol' mum, who grew you up. Put clothes on your back, hot food in your belly, made sure you got to school on time. No one else did that except Precious here and Brother Bertie.'

Mo needed Rabina having a dig like she needed a hole in the frigging head. She sent the interfering so-and-so a sour look. 'You wanna stop sticking that gossip-seeking beak of yours into other folk's business and mind your own. The way I hear it, your Cindy's having to pull in punters on the weekend to top up her wages.'

Rabina shot to her feet, roaring, 'You what?'

Mo gave it to her straight. 'Charity begins at home. You wanna be worrying about your own daughter rather than other people's.'

Precious grabbed *her* daughter by the arm and frogmarched her out. Mo knew how to fight dirty, no doubt about it, but Rabina Sweeney was an animal when riled. The day she'd taken on her ex-husband and his brother, single-handed, and mashed them up until they were a senseless wreck, one piled on top of the other, had gone down in local folklore.

Mo indignantly tugged free of her mum's grip as Precious snapped, 'You ain't back five minutes and already creating.'

That was so unfair. So unfair. She hissed, 'For your info, I'm not back.' She inhaled a heavy shot of air. 'I thought I'd swing by and see you.' The last word was a squeak of heartfelt longing, which her mum couldn't fail to hear.

Precious' mouth popped open in an 'O'. Finally, she said, 'Well, I'm glad you didn't forget me.' She continued; now it was her voice rasping with emotion. 'I thought *that man* would've turned you against me.'

Mo moved in close to her mother and touched her fingers to her arm. 'No one's trying to take me away from you. Certainly not Granddad Jimmy.'

Precious stepped back. Mocked, 'Oh! So that's what it's like now, is it? Granddaddy Jimmy-boy. You bring him his slippers and hot choccie when it's night-time?'

Mo bit her anger back and tried to calm things down. It was clear as the nose on her face that there was bad blood between her mum and grandfather, and she wanted to understand what it was. 'Why is there a beef between you two? Didn't he approve of you and Robbie knocking around together?'

Precious shook her head. 'Jimmy Southpaw doesn't approve of anything he can't control.' She wouldn't tell Mo the rest of it. Couldn't. In some respects, it wasn't her story to tell. But she could quietly say this, 'He won't be happy, sweets, until he controls every part of you. And when he does, the beautiful, gorgeous girl I know will be lost forever.'

A shiver ran through Mo as Milton's earlier words, so like her mum's, came back to her: *'Don't let him take your soul.'*

Tears puffed out the bottom of Precious' eyes. Mo's face crumbled, and she launched herself into her mum's arms. Precious held her tight. There was applause from the many faces pressed against the washhouse window.

And Rabina's big-hearted gob praising, 'That's more like it. That's how it should be. A mother and daughter joined together as one.'

Mo mumbled into the softness of her mum, 'I never meant to leave like that. I was just so cut up about finding out about Robbie. I've wanted to know about my dad for years.'

Precious rubbed her palm soothingly along her beloved daughter's back, just like she'd once done when her Maureen was a babe in arms. 'I know. I just thought it best. Call what I did wrong, but I did what I had to do. And I didn't just do it for me, I did it for you.'

Mo reluctantly eased out of her mum's arms. Both women desperately wiped the backs of their hands across their wet faces.

Then Mo went and spoilt it, innocently putting the kybosh on their reconciliation. 'Mum, I want to take you to meet Granddad Jimmy. He was the one who told me to come over to see you ...'

Precious reared back as if avoiding scalding water. 'Have you gone cray-cray? Me' – she stabbed a finger to her chest – 'meet that man?' Precious was fizzing. 'I'd rather have afternoon tea with Hannibal Lecter.'

Mo got mad all over again. She pointed at her mum. 'So he's not the one with the 'tude, it's you—'

'You need to watch your step—'

Mo's temper went stratospheric, pouring gasoline on what was already an explosive situation. 'I bet Robbie chucked you, didn't he? Got sick to the back teeth of you ordering him around and telling him what to do? Bet he—'

Whack!

Precious slapped her daughter with such force Mo thought her head was about to leave her shoulders. A collective gasp rose from the onlookers in the launderette and Milton and Molly who had left their bench and crept closer to the drama. In fact, much of the estate was openly ogling proceedings from the communal balconies.

Mo's palm flew to her flaming cheek. Stunned, that's what she was. Mo couldn't believe that her mum had walloped her one around the face. In public. How dare she. How bloody dare she.

Mo stretched her neck. Kissed her teeth. The ultimate gesture in dissing her parent. Then Mo demonstrated a new side of herself. A hard side that Precious knew she'd never had before. Precious' heart broke with the knowledge her baby Mo was gone forever.

Mo pointed again, levelling her mother with the coldest stare. 'You want to thank your lucky stars that you're my mother because anyone else who put their hand on me like that would be receiving a very painful midnight call.'

Precious answered with a mash-up of Jamaican and Cockney. 'Little Miss Lady, bring. It. On. If you decide to come around, don't forget to bring that fecking geriatric who hides out in his betting shop with you, coz I'll take his arse down too.'

Precious scathingly ran her hot gaze over Mo, psyching out her daughter, lip curled. 'You think you know everything. You best believe you gwan feel it, gwan feel it, coz when Southpaw's done with you and left you with your bum-bum hanging out of your trackie bottoms, child, you best believe this.'

Her stabbing finger was like the sharpest blade in Mo's heart. 'You go girl! And don't come back!'

Precious turned her back on her daughter and stomped into the launderette into the welcoming and comforting arms of Rabina. The woman who bossed the launderette fired off vicious stares in Mo's direction.

Precious turned her head. Mother and daughter stared at each other, daggers drawn, through the washhouse window.

A line had been crossed. Things had been said that couldn't be unsaid.

Chapter Twenty-Four

'You're not really going in there, are you? I mean, look at it,' Dell stated with disbelief in the driver's seat next to Mo. 'Look at these people. I know we all have to do things we don't like for the sake of business, but this is taking it too far.'

They stared at the crowd gathering in the car park for the Grab-a-Granny shindig in the Scarlet Lady boozer.

Dell shook her head. 'I mean, this Dean character might not even be in there.'

Mo didn't appear any more eager to join in a disco for mature singles than her cousin wanted her to. 'Have you got an alternative?'

'You betcha!' Dell eagerly ploughed on. 'We rush the joint, stick a few shooters in faces, get them to identify this fool, Dean, have him in the boot of the car before treating him to a painful chitchat somewhere. Works for me.'

Mo had come to love her cuz and her route-one approach, but she was wrong. 'I'm not interested in the organ grinder's monkey. I want the guy turning the handle. And I'm more likely to find that out with a lollipop in the gob than a short in the ear.' She peered over her shoulder at the two big guys on the back seat. 'You three, stay here. I'll text you if I need you, although I think that's unlikely.'

Before she got out, Dell pressed her palm against Mo's cheek, leaning in close. 'You alright, cuz? And your cheek?'

Not much got past Dell. Despite the face powder, her cousin had noticed the mark on her face. Mo hadn't told her about the encounter with her mum. And wasn't about to.

Mo whispered, 'It's good to know you're there if I ever need anyone.'

She got out of the car and smoothed down her black leather catsuit, which was unzipped far enough in the front to expose a generous helping of cleavage. She'd Afro comb fluffed up her curls, so they bounced against her shoulder. She ran her finger around the rim of her go-go boots to make sure they were secure and then set off.

It wasn't long before Mo attracted attention from guys hanging around the front of the pub smoking. She walked past one set and an aging admirer cooed, 'Blimey, you look like Emma Peel off *The Avengers*.'

'Who?' Mo was confused.

'You don't know who Emma Peel is? Probably before your time, love kitten.'

Mo walked on, a hint of a smile twitching her lips when one of the guys informed her admirer, 'Emma Peel was white, you dick.'

'Who cares what colour she was when you've got bosoms like that?'

Like Kristal before her, Mo was faced with a choice when

she went into the pub. Upstairs in the function room, aging ravers were getting it on to Donna Summers' 'I Feel Love'. Through glass doors on the ground floor, she saw a mixed crowd nursing their drinks and chatting. She only had a vague idea what her gangland rival, this Dean Forest actually looked liked, but her sixth sense assured Mo she'd know the pretender when she clocked him.

Mo decided to try the upstairs first. The balding bloke selling tickets from behind a table by the stairs studied her in disbelief when she presented herself. 'You know this gig is for the mature kind of single person?'

Mo gave him a sweet smile. 'I'm older than I look, hun. How much is it?'

'It's usually a tenner, although it's half price for ladies and over 60s. Do you want to claim the over-60s rate or are you only half taking the piss?'

'The ladies discount it is.'

She took her money out of her purse, but the guy made no effort to give her a ticket or stamp her wrist to show she'd paid. 'Are you sure about this, sweetheart? With your figure and a get-up like that, you'll be like a fragile bird chucked into a pack of hungry and rather mangy cats.'

Mo shook her hair so it bounced to emphasise her carefree persona. 'I might be a bird, but no one's ever called me fragile. I can take care of myself, thank you very much.'

She handed over her fiver. Mo didn't want to take the chance of alerting Dean by blatantly asking after him. However, seeing the doubtful expression on the doorman's face and the music being loud enough to conceal her enquiry, she decided it was worth a punt. 'Will Dean be upstairs tonight?'

The man's gaze shuttered, his friendliness vanished, replaced by vagueness. 'I don't know no Dean.' But when she turned an artful gaze on him and leant forward to display her cleavage, he confided, 'But if I did know a Dean.' His thumb pointed backwards into the room. 'I reckon a nightmare like this here upstairs is about the last place you'd find him.'

Mo winked at him. 'Cheers.'

He asked, 'Do you want your money back?'

'Nah! Buy yourself a snifter on me.'

Mo pushed open the glass doors into the saloon bar downstairs. From the reaction of the punters to the appearance of this Emma Peel lookalike, it might have been a celebrity making an appearance. Mo posed for a moment, lapping up the appreciative glances before striding, supermodel-style, over to the bar.

'I'll have a Diet Coke, please.'

Mo secretly cased the joint, but there were no obvious candidates for her target sitting at any of the tables.

'Dean in tonight?' she popped the question innocently to the barman. Before he could say anything, she acidly answered her own question. 'Let me guess. You don't know no Dean.'

Mo plonked into on a stool at the bar, ankles crossed, studying the room more closely.

A group of likely lads grabbing quick views of her pins when they thought she wasn't looking. A couple quietly arguing because the woman had caught her boyfriend copping an eyeful of that tart at the bar, otherwise known as Mo. A few commuters eating pub food rather than going home to cook. The inevitable old bloke sitting on his lonesome in the corner.

But there was no sign of Dean Forest.

Disappointment growing, Mo began to wonder if this was a fruitless journey. She picked up her drink and walked to the end of the bar. Around a corner were more punters, but none of them fitted the bill. She was about to turn when the sound of a too-loud voice coming from an alcove, obviously playing court to an audience, made her freeze.

'It's all about having swag. That's swagger to those not in the know. Of course, you need some noodle up top and an eye for style. You'll never see any of the top guys wearing jeans and T-shirts. At the end of the day, if the oppo are coming at you mob-handed, you've gotta standalone against them if you have to.'

Mo put down her drink and headed for the ladies' so she could get a decent view of the alcove. As she walked by, she spotted a handsome young man sitting at the table, an attentive group hung on to his every word. His expensive suit and silk shirt appeared out of place. At the same time, he appeared right at home.

Mo would bet her last bob this was Dean. It had to be.

Mo grabbed a beer mat from an empty table before squealing, 'Oh no! I don't believe it!'

She cantered over to the handsome young man's table like a lovesick puppy, placed one hand on his table and held the other one over her mouth in disbelief. 'I don't believe it! You in here! I thought you'd be Up West with all the other Faces planning your next big blag!'

The embarrassed guy in the suit waved her away. 'Sorry, love, I think you've mistaken me for someone else.'

'No, I ain't.' She cupped her hands to her chest in overkill excitement. 'I know who you are. You're Steaming Dean.'

The poor bloke was well confused. 'Who?'

'Steaming Dean! I know who you are. I read all the true crime books and blogs, watch all the TV shows and that. I've seen your photo on the Net. Here, are you going to sign my beer mat for me? All the top names in the underworld have signed my beer mats. I've got a mega collection.'

She eagerly held the mat out to him. The other lads were divided between those close enough to admire Mo's rear end, which was arched over the table, and those who were enjoying 'Steaming Dean's' embarrassment.

One of them chipped in, 'Go on, Dean, sign the girl's beer mat.'

Mo had no idea how she held back the grin of triumphant elation. Finally confirmation. Here was her gangland rival. The guy who thought he was about to take her down. Who'd fecking well bombed her club.

Looking very uncomfortable, Dean pulled out a gold pen. 'No disrespect, babe, but you've confused me with someone else. My name's Steve, not Dean, and certainly not Steaming Dean.'

Mo's face fell. 'But he just called you Dean?'

Dean glowered at his mate. 'Alright, love, how do you want me to sign?'

'*To Shirelle, loads of love, Steaming Dean.* Loads of kisses, of course.'

Dean made a quick job of signing it and passing it back to her. 'There you go. Now, if you don't mind, I'm busy.'

She pouted. 'Surely you're not too busy to buy a fan a drink and take a selfie? Or do you think you're too important now for the likes of me?'

One of Dean's friends whispered something to him.

Finally, Dean got up. 'Alright, but we need to make it quick. I've got business to attend to.'

Dean and 'Shirelle' were soon tucked away in the corner of the pub. He knocked back his brandy in one, posed for a pixxie and then got up to go.

Mo grabbed his sleeve, tone sultry. 'Come on, Dean, we've only just met. Tell me about yourself and all the ahh-mazing things that are going on.'

Dean was obviously unhappy. 'I've already told you, I'm a car mechanic. Exciting things don't happen in garages.'

'Oh, piss off!' Mo giggled. 'I hear you're going up against that little upstart, Big Mo and her firm. Come on, that's big-time!'

Dean was horrified. 'Where did you hear that bollocks?'

'The true crime blogs have got all the latest news. They say you've teamed up with another crew to take her on.'

Dean shook his head in disbelief. 'This is all over the Net?'

'Yeah! With photos of all the players. Come on, Dean, everything's online these days. There ain't no secrets anymore.'

'You can't believe everything you read on the webz. Most of it is straight-up fake.'

Mo rustled up her best disappointed face. 'So, you're not a big guy then after all?'

Dean seemed as if he was about to carry on fronting his way out of things. But to Mo's relief, his vanity got the better of him.

'I didn't say that. I didn't say that at all.'

'I knew you were big. Just like your muscles here.' Mo squeezed his arm. 'I knew it straight away. So, who are you teamed up with? They're saying on the blogs, it's a gang from Scotland or Liverpool, but I reckon it's got to be a London crew. They know the ground, don't they?'

Dean fessed up. 'Maybe. I have a lips-zipped-tight policy about gassing to strangers about my business. It's not the done thing. For all I know you could be a cop.'

Mo raised her arms, pulling the leather taut over her body. Her voice was soft, husky and very sexy. 'You think I'm wearing a wire? Cop a feel, Dean. You'll soon see there's nuthin' under this catsuit except my … bare flesh.'

Dean laughed, brows shooting to his blond hairline. 'Yeah, I can see that.'

Mo swung their convo back where it needed to be. 'Who are you working with then? Who's the power behind you?'

Dean was still admiring her body. 'I can't talk shop. Unless you want to come back to my place where you might persuade me to engage in a little pillow talk if you play your cards right.'

She had him. 'I reckon I could persuade you to do anything I like.'

But he didn't answer. In fact, he didn't seem to be listening or gazing at her at all. She followed his puzzled stare, which rested on the barman who was gesticulating frantically to him. Suddenly he was close-mouthed as he got to his feet and went to the bar.

Bollocks! His back to her, Mo couldn't see what was happening. Then he was headed back. Mo resumed her adoring fan pose.

He winked and whispered, 'Got to wet my boots. Won't be a mo.'

When he was gone, Mo zeroed in on the barman who was avoiding her eyes. She realised at once what had happened. She'd been rumbled. Someone had recognised her, tipped the wink to the barman who'd tipped it back to Dean.

Mo was out of her chair in a flash. She bombed it through the bar's doorway to the where the gents stood. Barged inside.

An older man, washing his hands, started when he saw her. 'You can't come in here, young lady, this is for the boys.'

Mo pushed past him and went to the back wall where a window was fully opened. Grim-faced, she looked out and saw Dean fleeing into the bushes and trees on the other side of the car park.

Chapter Twenty-Five

'Let me in! Let. Me. In.'

The hammering at the door of the duplex in Wapping woke Kristal up. She'd been curled up with a glass of sparkling wine with a sizeable dollop of brandy, watching some late-night horror flick and fallen into the Land of Nod on the sofa. Rubbing the sleep from her eye, she uncurled her legs.

Kristal prided herself on not doing spooked. But as she looked at the clock in the lounge nearing midnight and felt the relentless hammering on the front door vibrating through her body, she was well worried. She'd relocated at night to the duplex to be at hand if Nico needed anything. The flat was an ideal meeting place.

Who could be on the doorstep at this time? How had this person got past the porter downstairs? One of the reasons she'd chosen to rent a duplex in this block by the river as her fake HQ was because the security was so good.

The hammering started up again.

Cautiously, she moved, although she recognised she needed to pick up the pace before any of the neighbours started making their own noise about what was going on. The neighbours she'd come across were a right lot of triple-barrelled names. Lucinda Smythe-Whatnot. Not her kinda people at all.

She leant close to the door and hissed, 'Naff off or I'll call the plod.'

Chrissakes! The person on the other side obviously couldn't hear her because of the right royal racket they were making.

'Let me in!'

Blimey! Sounded like the Big Bad Wolf! On a side table was a thin glass vase bursting with a gorgeous spray of flowers. Kristal dumped the flowers and water and held the vase as a makeshift weapon.

'Who is it?'

'Open up.'

That's when Kristal could've slapped her forehead because she noticed the security peephole. All she could make out was a distorted, shadowy figure pacing backwards and forwards.

'I'm calling the coppers,' she cried.

'Good! I might be safe then,' came the taunting reply. 'They can lock me up. I might see my next birthday if I'm in the slammer.'

Bloody Dean Forest.

What the heck! Mouth set into a thin line of displeasure, Kristal got lively letting him in. She jumped back in alarm when Dean tumbled straight onto the floor like a dead body. Kristal stood there, her hand over her mouth. Bloody hell!

What if he'd snuffed it? For crying out loud, if he was going to peg it, why did he have to do it here?

He groaned and rolled to his back. Kristal relaxed, teeth gritted, irritated beyond belief. 'I wasn't expecting to see you tonight. You should have rung ahead.'

He stared at her, his face a mix of fear and utter exhaustion. 'Lock the sodding door.'

Kristal didn't care for his tone. All the same, she did as asked, while he struggled to his feet. Instead of heading for the lounge, he stalked and searched both bedrooms and bathroom. Inside the lounge, he peered down at the river. What was he expecting to see? The baddies from a *James Bond* flick come abseiling down the windows?

'You seem a bit flustered, Dean. Is there a problem? Perhaps I can help?' Kristal stated the obvious in a slow tone that suggested whatever was up had zilch to do with her.

Dean's face was pressed against the huge window. He seemed to have forgotten she was there. But when he heard her voice, he twisted on his heels and levelled a furious glare, advancing on her. 'Oh yeah, there's a problem, alright, sweetheart. And that problem is you!'

In an ultra-sexy breathless voice, she declared, 'What have I done?'

Scathingly, Dean looked her up and down. 'Knock off the cougar routine. And don't even go there with the 'mistress riding crop against my bum' set piece neither.'

Who was this tin-plated prick-dick calling a cougar? She folded her arms. 'OK. Whatever's the prob here? Spit it out.'

Dean got in her face. 'You didn't tell me the Mo whose

club I threw a grenade into is called Big Mo. Or that she's the grandkid of Jimmy Southpaw.' The volume of his voice dialled higher and higher. 'You forgot to mention those little details when you were waggling your assets in my face, telling me I was going to be king of gangland.'

Kristal sighed with heavy resignation. So, the kid had finally figured it out. Well, some of it at least. He obviously hadn't sussed who she was yet.

She was not sympathetic. 'Who did you think we were fighting? A crack gang of shoplifters? You want to go to the top, you have to take on the top people. And for reasons no one really understands, that happens to be Mo at the moment.' She couldn't keep the bitterness out of her tone. 'But you don't want to worry about a tiny slip of a girl like her. She don't know her jacksie from her elbow. She'll fold like a pack of cards when the heat's turned on, don't worry about it.'

It suddenly dawned on Kristal what had gone on here. Why he looked like someone who'd been chased through the forest fleeing for his life. Forest! Dean Forest! Haha! Kristal had a little chuckle to herself.

'I suppose the girl's paid you an unexpected visit, has she? And put the wind up you? What kind of villain are you, bruv? She's only a kid.'

Now he was safely locked behind Kristal's door and there was no sign of Mo outside, a red-faced Dean gave full vent to his anger. He was a tinder-dry mixture of embarrassment and fury. 'Yeah, she fucking did. She turned up at my rub-a-dub dressed in a black catsuit, pretending to be a fangirl of mine to win my confidence. In other words, the same stunt you pulled on me.'

Kristal howled with uncontrollable laughter so hard she tumbled onto the sofa.

Dean got properly narked. 'Is my misfortune providing you with more laughs than *Only Fools and Horses*?'

Between gusts of giggles, Kristal told him, 'Mo tarting it up? Hahaha! I wish I'd been a fly on the wall to see that.' Her laughter drained away. 'I can't imagine that po-faced mare pulling that off.'

A sly grin crossed Dean's face. 'Let's see if you're still chuckling when you find out what it was all in aid of.'

Kristal straightened, alert. 'What was she after?'

Dean deliberately milked the waiting silence. Then, 'She wanted to know who was backing up my oppo.'

Dean was proved right. Kristal wasn't laughing anymore. She leapt off the sofa.

'What did you tell her?' If this kid started getting stroppy, she'd bounce him about this room and chuck him in the river. Nothing could happen to her brother. Nothing.

Now Dean was the one laughing. He shrugged. 'You can't blame me for grassing you and your people up. How was I to know who she was? Of course, if you'd warned me we were warring with Big Mo and Jimmy Southpaw, I'd have been on my guard. Since you didn't, I had no idea who the girl in the black catsuit was. So, I might have said a few things.'

They'd swapped roles. Kristal was now nearly as angry as Dean. 'You didn't drop any names? You're stupid, but you're not so stupid that you'd discuss company business in front of a complete stranger. Come on, tell me what's what.'

Dean shrugged like he didn't have a care in the world. 'Can't remember. I might have mentioned your name in the convo. It's slipped my mind.'

He was just quick enough to grab her wrist before she smacked him one. He twisted her arm behind her back so she could feel some pain. 'No, I didn't mention any names. Fortunately for you, someone in the pub recognised her and tipped off the barman who gave me the nod. Know what, though? Wish I had dropped your name in the shit.'

Dean was raging now. 'A bent copper couldn't have fitted me up better than what you've done. Proper kippered I've been, and I ain't happy about it.'

He put a bit more pressure on her arm as he continued. 'You need to get me out of the hole you've dug, otherwise I'll have no choice but to go see Big Mo and confess all. Won't take her long to decide I'm just an innocent victim of circumstance. Taken advantage of by a cougar with sharp claws—'

'You wouldn't dare.' Kristal bared her teeth, visibly shaken.

'Oh, wouldn't I? Give me one good reason why I wouldn't?'

He loosened his grip, and Kristal reeled backwards, rubbing her arm.

She told him. 'It's too late, mate, that's why. You're right, she probably would see you as the fall guy. And since you're falling, she'd think, we might as well put the poor bollocks in the ground. She'd have no choice if she wanted to save face. You know what girls on the telephone helplines say when you ask them why they can't help you out with a simple problem? *I'm sorry, sir, but it's company policy.*'

All the energy worked up in his long evening drained out of Dean, and he withered and sank onto the sofa, head in his hands. 'Fuck me! Jimmy Southpaw!'

Despite her aching wrist, Kristal actually felt a little sorry for the innocent victim in all this. She stood behind him and massaged his shoulders in silence while she tried to work out what her next move should be. As long as Dean wasn't available to grass her up or lay a trail for Mo to find Nico, there was still everything to play for. But it was only a matter of time before Robbie's wrong-side-of-the-blanket offspring tracked Dean down again, so he had to be put somewhere safe rather than wandering around in the wild.

'It was bound to happen sooner or later, babe. And that's OK. So she knows who you are—?'

He twisted out of her soothing hands and examined her over his shoulder. 'Which begs the question, who you are? How's Kristal connected to Big Mo?'

He was getting close. Too close. She was deffo going to need to hide him away. Kristal resumed as if he hadn't asked his pointed question. 'So what if Mo knows who you are? You do what all the top guys do. You find somewhere to operate out of that's got maximum security while you plan your next step.'

His voice croaked. 'There isn't anywhere for me to go.'

'Of course there is. You're sitting in it. Mo's not going to look for you here.'

Dean jerked back into life. 'Are you taking the big p? You think I'm staying here with you after what you've done? I wouldn't put it past you to hand me over to Big Mo and her grandfather for a small remuneration. In fact, I wouldn't be surprised if it was you who put her onto my trail in the first place. I mean, fuck off, treacle.'

He jumped to his feet and headed for the front door. Kristal realised, to her horror, she had no way of stopping him.

She hurried to bar his way. 'Dean, you're perfectly safe here. I'll hire some goons with guns to watch you twentyfourbloodyseven. I admit I should have been a little franker about Mo, but that's all water under the bridge. I'm the only person who can keep you safe now.'

Dean took her by the arm and set her out of his way. 'That's where you're wrong. I know someone who'll shelter me under their protective wing. Someone I can trust. Someone whose promises aren't really day-old shite and who's got my interests at heart.'

Kristal was genuinely stunned. 'Like who? Who do you know who could stop Mo getting her talons into you?'

He opened the door, triumph gleaming in his tired eyes. 'You'd be surprised who I know. You'd be surprised who's got my back.'

The front door slammed. His footsteps echoed away until everything was quiet.

Kristal didn't give chase. It was obvious Dean was very confident that someone out there would look after him. That was clear.

But who was it?

Chapter Twenty-Six

Mo paced backwards, forwards, forwards, back inside her uncle's home in Bow, a top-notch conversion in a block that had once been a matchstick factory. After Dean Forest had bolted, she'd gone on the hunt for that toerag, along with Dell and Josh last night. Mo had resumed the search for him today but had come up empty. Feeling keyed up, as mad as a box of frogs, Mo had needed to let off steam.

She had thought about going to see her other granddad, Brother Bertie, but he'd have probably been tucked up for the night. 'Course, her Granddad Jimmy was a no-no. Letting him know that Dean had not only given her a merry chase but had got away to boot … Nah! It might make him realise that he'd indeed made an almighty misstep putting her in her father's shoes.

So, she'd come to Uncle Harry, who she knew liked burning the midnight oil. And from the looks of the size of his pupils, Mo was realising that he was probably partial to some Californian cornflakes up his nose too. Not that she was judging him. It was his business, but certainly wasn't her style. Especially at this point in her career. In order to prove herself as Jimmy's worthy heir, it was imperative she remain clear-headed.

Harry Steele's apartment was really a massive room held up by industrial-style beams and pillars with a steel staircase to another floor. Mo had expected it to be your typical bachelor's pad, with clothes flung all over the gaff and dishes piled sky-high in the sink. But it was surprisingly clean and tidy, and not for the first time Mo wondered if Harry had a sweetheart he was hiding from the family. Maybe that's why there were two glasses on the table?

Harry looked a bit uptight on the sofa. Usually he'd be lounging about as if nothing mattered. He told her, 'Sit down before you wear a hole in that Serbian oak floor I just got done. It cost me an arm and a leg.'

Mo slung herself into the armchair opposite. Placed her shades hanging off her pocket on the table. She picked up the bottle of whisky and poured herself a generous amount. Then knocked half of it back. And nearly fell off her chair as the fiery liquid seemed to burn through her body. Coughing, eyes wide and watering, Mo sputtered, 'Bloody hellfire, what's in that bottle?'

Harry gave her one of his lopsided grins. 'It's a double oak whisky, with quite a nutty flavour and kick.'

Mo took another swallow, slower, more cautiously this time. Fired up, she banged the glass on the table.

Harry said, 'So what's got your goat?'

Mo let out a laboured sigh, sinking back into the chair. She was still pissed to high heaven that Dean had managed to slip through her fingers. 'This twat who seems to think he's going to take over my empire, I found out where his base is.'

Harry leant over and topped up Mo's glass and then his own. 'What's this jester's name?'

'Dean Forest.' Just uttering his name made Mo want to hit the road again, not stopping until she had him in her clutches. 'I tracked him to some nothing boozer in Essex where, get this, they hold Grab-a-Granny nights.'

Harry stared at her as if she had two heads. 'Grab-a-What?'

'Singles nights for the mature person.' Mo shook her head. 'This Dean prick is a nobody. So where does a nobody get the stones to try to take me on, eh? Where's he getting his mitts on all those shooters and that grenade he threw into Club Class? And, for that matter, where did he get all those men? Coz, let me tell you, when I found him holed up in Essex, he didn't even have any people looking out for him, you get me?' Mo's face was transfixed with brooding realisation. 'The tosser confirmed what I suspected—'

'That someone pretty big is backing him up,' Harry swiftly finished for her.

Mo stood pacing again. 'You haven't heard of anyone fronting someone to play silly beggars with me?'

Harry shook his head. 'Then again, who would be crazy enough to do that? Tangling with you means tangling with Dad. You'd have to have a death wish to go down that path. Or be one step short of East Ham.'

'Barking,' they both said together.

Their eyes caught and then they creased up laughing. It

felt so good to laugh. Since Jimmy Southpaw had taken her under his wing, Mo had been living off her wits. She wasn't even sure if she'd had a decent night's kip in the last year. She'd wanted everything to be oh, so perfect with Jimmy. Didn't want him to think he'd made a mistake acknowledging her as his beloved son, Robbie's daughter.

She observed her uncle from hooded eyes. Mo hadn't really had time to get to know Harry. Not that he stuck around long enough for her to forge a proper relationship with him. He took care of some of Granddad Jimmy's gambling concerns and health club investments. Mo was astonished at how many pies her grandfather had his fingers in. Both legit and under the table.

Never wager all your dosh on one card. That's what he told her. *Diversification across the nation.* When one thing goes belly up, you've still got loads more going on. Obviously, taking care of his father's business kept Harry busy, too busy to have a proper sit-down with his niece.

'What you going to do about this Dean character?' Her uncle's question brought her back to the present.

Mo didn't hesitate in her response. 'I'm going to crush him. One body part at a time.'

Harry raised his glass. 'Here's to that.'

'What was my dad like?'

Mo had been desperate and so nervous for ages, wanting to pop this delicate question to Harry. After all, he'd been Robbie's brother. But Harry was always in and out so quickly, plus it never seemed to be the right time. Mo was soaking up every morsel she learnt about her dad. It still hurt deep inside to think she'd never meet him.

Slowly, Harry placed his glass gently on the table. He leant his elbows on his thighs and cupped his chin in his hands. He stared at her for a long time. 'The truth is, Robbie could be a real shit but was also sugary sweet nice. Bless him.'

Mo smiled at that. She appreciated his honesty and openness. 'Did you get along?'

Harry thought on her question. 'Most of the time. Then again, brothers aren't meant to get along all the time. That goes against the law of nature. It's the way of families, ain't it? We love each other but fall out every now and again.'

Mo leant forward herself. 'Did you like him?'

That Robbie was liked was really important to her. The idea that the man who was her father was some little grunt who people couldn't stand upset her deeply. From what she'd heard, he was on most people's 'top geezer' list. Accolades were all that were heaped on him. Nevertheless, someone his own age who he'd grown up with would know the real man.

Harry nodded. 'I looked up to him. He was a cocky sod, no doubt about it, but that's what I loved about him. He was brave. Fearless.' His face darkened. 'He was caring too. Felt things, y'know, sometimes too much. Took stuff to heart. I remember years back, when we were kids, we went to visit Aunt Beryl.'

Mo's mind went back to the seaside outing Jimmy had taken them all on, including Aunt Beryl. Blimey! What a corker of a character she was.

'She had a pair of rabbits, Brass and Nuts—'

'You are making that up,' Mo interrupted with a shout of laughter.

Harry chuckled back. 'On my life! She swears the first time she brought them home they stood on hind legs and started fighting. Slogging it out until she had to intervene. A bunch of proper bruisers, so she calls them Brass and Nuts.'

His voice grew sombre. 'Anyhow we're around there the day one of the rabbits pegs out from old age. I think it was Brass. Robbie took it bad and wouldn't stop crying. My mum, everyone called her Mini, let him sob for five minutes straight and then told him to pack it in.'

Mini, the grandmother she never knew, sounded like a right character herself. A strong and tough lady. Mo was sorry and so sad that she'd never had the chance to know her. Jimmy said it was Mini who Mo had inherited her height from.

'And did he take her advice and stop crying?'

Harry didn't even know he was self-consciously rubbing his palm down his cheek. He still recalled the stinging burn of his mother's slap against his cheek when he was young on account of him showing up Robbie, the Southpaw heir. Harry had seen it so very differently.

'You alright, Uncle Harry? Is there something wrong with your face?'

He's rubbing his cheek the same way I did when mum walloped me. Did someone hit him? Mo couldn't see Uncle Harry letting someone smack him round the chops.

Realising what he was doing, Harry dropped his hand. 'When my mum asked you to do something, you did as told.

Robbie might've stopped blubbing, but you could tell that bunny's passing had touched him somehow.'

Mo asked, 'So, you're saying he was sensitive?'

Harry shook his head. 'No way! You couldn't be to do what he was doing. But every now and again something would touch his heart.' This ended in a yawn. 'Sorry, girl, but if I don't get any shut-eye, I'm not going to be up for much tomorrow. Got a meeting with a bloke who runs one of our money concerns in Soho.'

Mo stood. 'Maybe one day I can tag along, and you can show me the ropes.'

'Any time, little doll.'

Little Doll. Mo cringed. When Uncle Harry said stuff like that it made her think that he saw her as some young kid. That he didn't take her seriously. Mo bit her lip. The battle to sort out his perception of her would have to wait. The only battle she had armour-plated for was finding Dean and beating it out of him who was his puppet master.

When Mo got back to her motor, she realised she'd forgotten her sunglasses back at Uncle Harry's. That's right, she'd left them on the table. Normally, she'd give him a bell asking him to bring them over the next time he came to Granddad Jimmy's. But the glasses were very special to her. The first bit of money she'd made with Jimmy, she'd used it to buy these shades she'd had her eye on for ages. Vintage, Cat Woman style, with red tinted lenses.

Mo bounced out of the car. Turned the corner … and froze. Uncle Harry stood at the entrance to his building chatting nine to the dozen to someone. The person had their back to Mo, so she couldn't make them out. What she could see was that Harry appeared not best pleased. Money exchanged hands. The person turned around.

WTF!

Dean fucking Forest.

Heart banging, Mo swung around the corner and rested against the bare brick wall. She recalled seeing the second glass on his table, thinking Uncle Harry had a sweetheart when all the time it must've been that Forest fecker hiding on the second floor. This was what people must mean by boiling with rage. The fury inside Mo was an explosion waiting to erupt. Her mind linked up the dots.

Her own uncle was Dean's back-up. He had to be. All this time Harry was telling her homespun stories about her dad, arms wide, welcoming her to the Steele family, when in reality he was plotting her downfall. No wonder he kept treating her like some nipper with no brain.

She could've marched out there and had it out with them. But she didn't. Whichever bright spark had first said revenge is a dish best served cold was bang on.

Now it was Mo's turn to plot and plan.

Chapter Twenty-Seven

Dell and Josh walked into the Caribbean café-style restaurant. Steel Pulse's classic tune, 'Handsworth Revolution', played on a beat-up stereo and a right royal row was going on at the front counter. The place was nothing special to look at with its simple plastic furniture and large posters of Caribbean fruit dotted across the mustard-coloured walls. Then again, folk didn't come from miles around to give the décor a score out of ten. What they came for was the most mouth-watering, finger-licking Caribbean food that would ever touch their taste buds. Most Saturday nights there was a queue around the block. Rumour had it that even some younger royals had been known to pop in for a beef patty or curried goat with rice 'n' peas on a Saturday night.

Josh's eyes widened in shocked surprise at the argument taking place at the old-style counter where a transparent cabinet contained delicious-looking and smelling Jamaican patties heated up all ready to go. Dell showed no such surprise, she'd seen it all before. It wasn't really an argument happening, more like a one-sided severe tongue-bashing being given by the owner to a customer.

The loud, bolshy voice belonged to the owner, Momma Lou.

Momma Lou was one of Brixton's national treasures. Stout, ample-bosomed, muscles on her arms from years of cooking and the same Jerri Curl wig her sister had sent her back from New York in 1983 perched on her head. She'd been dishing up hearty, homemade food to the community since she set up shop back in 77. When her shop got torched to the ground during the Brixton riot or uprising – depending on where you stood on the battle lines – she didn't weep or wail. Crying wasn't for someone who, as a child, remembered her mother on her deathbed. Her last hours on Earth screaming in pain because the family couldn't afford to buy any medicine. Instead, Momma Lou rolled her sleeves up and started all over again. Some went as far as saying that Momma Lou's company rather than the food was the real reason people flocked to the eating hole just off Electric Avenue.

Whoever the customer she was tearing a strip off was couldn't be from around the area because there was one unwritten rule inside this restaurant – Momma Lou Is Always Right.

Momma Lou leant so far across the counter she looked about ready to take off. Her lips stretched in displeasure. 'What you mean? The beef patty was really chicken?'

The customer shook his head. 'It was definitely chicken inside the patty.'

Momma Lou pushed her bottom lip forward in disdain. 'So, where's the patty?'

'I ate it.'

She folded her ample arms. 'Let me get this straight. You come in here to disrespect one of my patties and you don't bring it with you so I can taste it for myself. You think I can't tell the difference between a cock and a moo-moo?'

'Cock?' The customer added with a self-righteous sniff, 'I beg your pardon?'

Momma Lou stared back blankly at first, and then her features slowly changed to fire-breathing outrage when it dawned on her what they thought she'd been implying. 'Cocks meaning cockerels meaning chicken. Moo-moo meaning cows. That's what I'm talking about.'

Suddenly, she brandished a big steel spoon. 'Take your filthy-mouthed self outta my place now before I brain you and then get the broom to sweep you out with the rest of the trash in to the gutter.'

The disgruntled customer didn't need telling twice and fled past Dell and Josh.

Noticing the newcomers, Momma Lou lowered the spoon. 'Delilah-girl, that you?' Swiftly, she placed her makeshift weapon back under the counter. 'What you doing standing there like you're waiting for a firing squad to shoot you down?'

Dell was in her embrace in no time at all. Momma Lou practically squeezed the stuffing out of her, expressing the joy she felt at seeing the younger woman. Momma Lou liked to make a big production of welcoming those she deemed worthy into her shop. As far as she was concerned, there wasn't enough old-style hugging in the world today. Betcha, if more people did it, there would be less trouble and more harmony on this earth. Amen!

Momma Lou set the younger woman aside slightly, her eyes sparkling with pure love at Dell. 'Where you been? Eh? Every night, I put aside one of those saltfish patties you does love to eat, hoping you'll come through the door. I been—'

The words dried in her throat, her brain finally registering that Dell wasn't alone. Momma Lou's gaze took its time sweeping Josh from head to toe. She shifted away from Dell to stand in front of him. 'Well, well, well,' she uttered suggestively. 'Now I know exactly where you've been, Delilah-girl—'

Dell's brows shot up to her hairline in horror. 'What? Nah! Me and him? I'm not—'

The other woman's voice ran roughshod over her explanation, Momma Lou's eyes only for Josh. 'I can see why you've been keeping this one all to yourself.' She was totally captured by Josh's renowned jaw-dropping beauty. 'And what's your name, handsome?'

Josh's whole features lit up with a one-hundred-watt smile. His voice was as smooth as silk sheets sliding on a bed. 'Joshua. But you can call me Josh. And there's no need for you to tell me your name. And you know why?' He leant conspiratorially close. 'The legend of Momma Lou is known from one end of this country to the other.'

He ended his butter-her-up patter by taking her hand and delivering a gallant feather-light kiss to the back of it. Momma Lou squealed with girly giggles, batting her lashes.

Rolling her eyes, Dell muttered, 'For crying out loud ...'

She dialled the volume of her tone to a ten for all to hear. 'Me and him ain't in a ting, you get me? The only business we do together is of the professional variety.'

Momma Lou's gaze shone with a saucy gleam. 'Does that mean you're single, beautiful? Well, so am I. We can be mister and missus by the weekend.'

The riotous gleeful laughter that burst of out of the pair was so loud it probably could be heard all the way to Brixton tube station.

Dell put a spoke in the wheels of the fun and games. 'Momma Lou, we need to pick your brains about something.'

Five minutes later found them at a table, Josh with a plate of Jerk Chicken, plain rice and Mommy Lou's Special Caribbean Coleslaw and Del with a saltfish patty. Momma Lou wouldn't take no for an answer when she insisted they both have some of her fine fare to fill up their tummies. She was part of that older generation who believed in the tradition of providing food for a visitor was basic manners.

'Ummm!' burst out of Josh in appreciation, his expression that of someone who'd just been given a sneak peek into Heaven. 'Now THAT is the BEST jerk I have ever had.'

Momma Lou practically jumped in her chair as she clapped her hands together. Oh, she did love a man who loved her food. It was the most attractive feature on a man.

The mood suddenly changed when Delilah placed a photo of the girl and boy Mo had found in Nico Sinclair's office on the table. The spit in Momma Lou's mouth dried, her tummy twisting into tiny painful tight knots.

Del didn't notice her reaction when she asked, 'Do you know these two kids from back in the day?'

The older woman roughly coughed, keeping her head bowed. 'Do you see me running a daycare centre here? So many of the kids used to come in and out of here—'

An unexpected squeak robbed her of her next words when Josh placed his warm fingers ever so lightly over her hand. Only then did she realise that her hand was shaking like a drunk desperate for a bottle of hard liquor.

Josh's voice was quiet and slow. 'We haven't come here to make trouble. Or to drag up bad memories. We're just trying to track down some info. And Dell says to me that there's only one person who knows all the carry-on that went on down south back in the day.'

So, Josh wasn't just a pretty face, Momma Lou belatedly figured out. Dell glanced at Josh with new eyes. She was amazed at the delicate, caring way he handled the other woman. Sure, she'd witnessed him going on a charm offensive plenty of times before, especially when it involved a woman, but this she was seeing … This was something very different. All that heaving male sex-stuff he usually heaped on in spades was missing. It was like he was speaking to his gran. Dell clenched up. She appreciated what Josh was doing. Momma Lou was very special to her.

Momma Lou raised her eyes. In a jittery motion, she took in Dell and then Josh. Her fretful gaze remained on him. Her tongue wet her bottom lip before she spoke. 'You kids these days … all you dream about is being a movie star, having your face on the telly. Not me. When I was young, all I wanted was my own place to cook.' The memories of her dream made her eyes sparkle with a brightness that belonged on a younger woman.

'There's nothing like seeing people's faces lit up, their eyes half-closed as the seasonings in my food does its magic. But back then it wasn't easy being black and a woman to boot. No one wanted to rent a property to me. Even the council' – she sucked her teeth sharply – 'they didn't want to know.'

Dell started to impatiently butt in, but Josh threw her a fierce look to shut the hell up. Ordinarily, no way would Dell be taking that. Not off him or nobody. However, she reluctantly conceded that he was probably right. Momma Lou might be going about this the long way round, but that didn't matter in the scheme of things. What did, was her ID'ing the two children in the picture. So, Dell snapped her mouth shut.

'You think all those doors slamming in my face was going to stop me? You must be mad.' Her chin defiantly tilted. 'I started operating out of my kitchen. Let me tell you when word went around my back door never stopped opening.'

There was a subtle shift in the tone of the telling of her story. 'Then one day, there's this little girl at the back door. Looking to buy some patties for her, her little brother and her dad who were waiting for her in the car.'

Softly, Josh interrupted. 'The girl in the photo?'

Momma Lou confirmed with a single nod. 'Beautiful child but wore a shield of toughness. Y'know, like she thought the world was going to try to lick her down any minute.' A heavy, weary sigh escaped her. 'Poor kid. They kept coming and going like everyone else, lovin' up my food, but it wasn't until a good while later I realised the man bringing them had changed. Turned out it was their uncle.' Her voice dropped to a whisper. 'Cancer took the father. The mother gone soon after that too. No wonder the girl looked like her heart was breaking.'

Josh asked, deciding now was the time to get straight to the point, 'Was the little boy Nico Sinclair?'

Momma Lou swallowed hard. 'You already know the answer to that question, so you know who he is. And I don't like chatting about his business. *Private family* business.' Her mouth stubbornly tightened.

Dell leant excitedly across the table. 'It's all coming back to me now. The story was a well-known Face about town let you lease one of his properties, this building. I never caught what his name was. But I'm guessing it was Nico's uncle, King Ted?'

Momma Lou's hand slammed over Dell's. 'Keep your voice down. Everything has ears and eyes around here.'

Dell wouldn't let up. 'I'm right, though, ain't I?'

The other woman remained silent and then eased her hand back from Dell's. 'He was the only one prepared to give me a leg up. Let me have the run of this building below stairs while he did what he needed to upstairs.'

'You were running a front for this man?' Josh took over the questioning.

'Front, back, sides, I don't know what it was called. And didn't want to know. I just keep my nose where it belonged

– in my cooking pot.' Her face lit up again. 'Annalisa, that was her name. Me and that beautiful girl became tight. She was Nico's sister.'

Dell tensed up. 'I didn't know he had a sister.'

Josh added, 'You said *was.* Is she dead?'

Without warning, Momma Lou's face crumbled, unshed tears glittering in her eyes. 'I arrived here one morning, early – I like to work early – and there's Annalisa sitting in the doorway round the back. Trembling, she was, so much I thought she was going to break into two. I got some hot broth down her throat and a loving hug around her scared body. Because she terrified. I owned the place by then, so she was safe here. She stayed with me in the small flat upstairs for a few days. Then she was gone.'

A solitary tear escaped, rushing down her round cheek. 'I never heard from her again. Never saw her again. The world out there eats little girls like her up every day of the week. Nico drops by every now and again for some of my dumpling and oxtail stew. He loved his sister to death. I've never told him about Annalisa showing up here that time. She told me never to tell a soul she was ever here.'

Mamma Lou struggled to her feet. And levelled a warning finger at them both in turn. 'Don't be showing that photo around here no more. If Nico finds out you're asking after his sister, he'll hunt you down and put out your lights for good.'

Deflated, Mo's minders headed for the door. Something was niggling away in Josh's head. He couldn't help thinking there was a missing part of the story. Was Momma Lou holding out on them? She was obviously fiercely loyal to Nico and his disappeared sister and Josh could well understand why she might decide to not spill all the beans. He understood and respected loyalty.

Momma Lou's voice stopped them as they started to leave. And what she told them rocked their world.

'Her father had a pet name he would call her because she was like a precious stone to him …'

Mo stood on the street outside the block she'd once lived in with her mother and grandfather and watched her mum through the kitchen window. Mo wouldn't tell a soul, but she came here most nights just to get a glimpse of Precious Watson. Even after her mum had publicly boxed her face. She missed her mum so much it hurt.

Mo's mobile rang. She turned away from the block, taking the call.

It was Dell, who told her, 'We found out who the girl in the photo is.'

Electric excitement coursed through Mo's veins. 'Tell me.'

'Annalisa. Nico Sinclair's big sister. Their father had a nickname for her.'

Mo waited with bated breath.

'He used to call her Crystal.'

Air hissed through Mo's teeth.

Harry. Kristal. Nico providing back-up.

Finally, the pieces were starting to fall perfectly into place.

Dell asked, 'Knowing what you do now, do you still want to do that other job tonight?'

Mo grimly answered. 'Absobloodylootely.'

Chapter Twenty-Eight

'Oh. My. God. Babe! What happened?' Charmaine wailed.

Damien was taking off his polo shirt in Charmaine's room in the Mighty Minge, when she got an eyeful of the fading welts and bruises across his belly and ribs, the result of the beating he'd received at the hands of Carlos Donahue. Most of the pain was gone now. Still, Damien winced at her gentle inspection of his damaged body.

He was too ashamed to confess he'd been demolished by that wank-job. Truth be told, this was the first time Damien had been back to the brothel in a while. He'd hoped that on his next visit he'd have been boasting to Charmaine, playing it large that he'd hammered her attacker down to size. But of course it hadn't worked out like that.

So Damien played fast and loose with the truth. 'Got jumped blind by a bunch of hard-faced doughnuts. Don't worry your sweet head over it.'

With soothing care, Charmaine skimmed her fingertips down a particularly unpleasant bruise. It was her turn to wince. 'This looks nasty.'

He winked at her. 'My body might be a bit knocked

about, but my little friend is hale and hearty and ready to stand at attention.'

'Are you sure?' Charmaine's painted face appeared very doubtful.

Truthfully, Damien wasn't sure. One of the downsides of a sound caning was it certainly put the kybosh on the ol' libido. Still, give it a try, eh?

Gritting his teeth, he unzipped his jeans. 'It's feeling a little tender as it happens. Maybe just a gob job today.'

Charmaine clucked her tongue, shaking her head. 'Tell you what. Why don't we just snuggle down tonight?'

Sometimes that's what Damien loved the best about his visits to Charmaine. Just being held. She was so warm-hearted, caressing his back and finger-combing his hair off his face. His mum didn't so much as hold him as smother him. His mum could never find out about his relationship with the prostitute. If she thought another woman was mothering her son, he didn't fancy Charmaine's chances of seeing the sun rise again.

The door crashed back against the wall. It all happened so fast. Two figures materialised out of nowhere, appearing menacingly at the bottom of the bed. Dark hoodies were zipped to below their eyes, flopped over to obscure the top half of their faces. They had the mark of professionals paid to do someone's dirty work.

A revolver was pressed to Charmaine's temple. She whimpered, staring with wide, crazed eyes at Damien.

Voice muffled, the gunman instructed, 'Don't make a noise, girlfriend. We only want to borrow your punter for a while. We don't want any unnecessaries. You get me?'

Damien couldn't believe what he was seeing. He shot to a sitting position, thoughts only of calming Charmaine. 'Don't worry, baby—'

The gunman swiftly cut him off. 'If that tongue of yours keeps moving, your lady's brains will be redecorating the walls.'

Damien shut up. The other one grabbed his arms, causing him to cry out in pain, and dragged him off the bed to his feet. Damien froze when the gun barrel rested against his head. By this stage Charmaine had scrambled off the bed, hunched over on the floor, tears raking her cheeks.

'You're coming for a walk,' the second geezer told him, 'to get some fresh air. Don't make any trouble. We don't need it and neither do you.'

Although the guy's voice was muffled too, Damien was sure it was no 'he'. There was something about the tone that reminded him of his mum when she was doing her nut.

Frogmarched out of the room, Damien yelled at Charmaine, 'Call …'

Who? Who could he ask her to get on the blower to?

His mum? He'd look a right royal schoolboy.

Big Mo? No chance.

Granddad Southpaw? That would make him appear weak.

His dad? His dad was dead.

That awful burning sensation that ballooned in his belly when he always thought about his dad's death came over him again. Damien always held it back. Never cried. But he wanted to howl at the moon and bawl like a baby that he wouldn't ever see his dad again. He'd adored Robbie. Looked up to him in every way. He would've been able to get word to his old man at a time like this.

There was no sign of Benny or the receptionist front of house. This could only mean one thing. Lucky Lucy, the madam of the brass house, had obviously been given the nod about what was going to go down. Outside, they slung him into the back of a van like a sack of unwanted coal.

'We don't need to wrap him up, do we?' the fella asked the woman.

Spiteful chuckles were the response to that. 'After the pasting he took from Carlos? I don't think he's capable of making any trouble. He's still on the critical-but-stable injuries list.'

Damien hated to admit it, but she was right. And the fact she was a woman only added to his humiliation. These underworld birds were getting out of hand. Grabbing up guys like him was men's work.

One of his abductors drove while the other remained in the back guarding him, the shooter a constant threat. They drove him around for what felt like hours. In reality it was only for about twenty minutes. Damien decided he didn't need to be the *Brain of Britain* to guess who was behind this.

Carlos.

Damien clenched his fists, pondering how to make a move. But there was no energy in his arms and legs. He was as helpless as a trussed-up turkey, but without any truss. He gasped in pain once again as the van ran over some speed humps, circled slowly and came to a juddering halt. Unceremoniously, they jerked him out by his ankles onto a tarmac surface.

It was an industrial estate lined with shady units, pockmarked with stains from dripping gutters and leaking roofs. The van was parked up in front of one. Most of the letters from the sign over the shutters were long gone, leaving the writing a nonsensical: '... ustrial La ndrom t'.

Fear knotted Damien's gut. Once inside that unit there was no telling what they'd do to him. No telling if he'd ever be seen alive again. He was going to have to fight his way out of this.

His attacker with the gun must be clairvoyant because the shooter was back against his head accompanied by a menacing warning. 'Any funny stuff and that mouthy mum of yours will be weeping over your grave for the remainder of her life. Now move it.'

Heart missing a beat, Damien did as told. The hinges of the door screeched open. The interior held the darkness of an endless tunnel. He tried stalling in the doorway. The shooter in his back reminded him to shift it. Damien stepped inside. The metal door shut with a chilling clang behind him.

Their path forward was soon lit by a weak electric light. And that's when Damien saw Carlos. WTF! Carlos was tied to a chair, butt naked apart from a tiny towel across his unmentionables.

Damien turned to his two kidnappers; they'd better have a fuck-off good explanation for this set-up. In the half-light, they pulled down their zips, flipped back their hoods. Josh and Dell. His half-sister's constant shadows. If they were here, that meant …

Big Mo emerged from the darkness.

Fit to be tied, he stormed over to her. 'If this is what I think it's about, you're bang out of order. I don't need you or anyone else to fight my battles. I can take care of it.'

The humiliation of this … this runt of a girl trying to right his wrongs. That she even knew that Carlos had demolished him, good 'n' proper, was bad enough. It left Damien feeling much, much smaller than her.

Mo's steel-grey eyes were a dead ringer for their grandfather's. Glacial. Taking no prisoners. 'If you could take care of it, he wouldn't have knocked you about like a football in the first place, now would he?'

Damien matched her glare for glare. And hissed, 'It's my fight.'

Mo slapped his face. You could've heard a pin drop. Dell, Josh, even Carlos didn't dare breathe. The tension between the half-siblings was electric. Damien's nostrils flared, the imprint of his half-sister's hand blooming red and hot on his cheek. Was he going to belt her back? His jaw clenched so tight his teeth were hurting.

Mo put him straight as Jimmy Southpaw's newly anointed heir. 'No! It's not your fight, not when our family's rep is on the line. I get it loud and clear, you don't like me, *baby brother*.' Mo continued ferociously, 'But, you know what? Build yourself a bridge and GET OVER IT.'

Damien kept schtum while she continued to lay down the Steele family law.

'You should've come to me and told me straight off what occurred across the river. I shouldn't have had to hear it through back channels as I'm going about my daily business.'

She slo-mo turned to Carlos. And spread her lips into a nasty little smile. 'What we're going to do, bruv, is take care of this bag of shite together.'

Damien observed his surroundings more closely. The unit seemed like an oversized launderette with oversized machines and dryers. Then he twigged what the signage over the door had read before its letters had fallen off:

'... ustrial La ndrom t' was once 'Industrial Laundromat'. Why had Mo organised this here?

Carlos ran his bloodshot gaze over her with scornful contempt. 'When Nico Sinclair hears you've been messing with one of his top soldiers, you'll have more than a domestic with your bollockless brother to worry about. But I'll tell you what, if you pack it in and let me go, we can put all this silly misunderstanding behind us. No hard feelings.' His glance drilled into Damien. 'Come down the snooker hall sometime. We'll play a few frames. I've got sweet FA against you, mate, or that scrubber you're humping. Water under the bridge, eh?'

Mo stared him out. Then swaggered over. She took the measure of him, pursing her lips, but said nothing.

Carlos' mouth hitched into a cocksure smile, thinking he smelled weakness. Come on! Mo's just a stupid bint! 'Look, love, call it a day. I won't say boo to Nico about this transgression. Shit happens. It's not your fault you're in over your Tweety Pie head and out of your depth. Do yourself favour, for your own sake.'

Mo suddenly seemed to remember something. She turned to Josh. 'Where is he, anyway?'

'Watching the footie on the box in the office.'

She snapped, 'Time for him to put in an appearance.'

Josh disappeared into the darkness at the far end of the unit and opened a door. A few moments later, a shadowed lone figure emerged. Their silhouette was strapping and tall with broad shoulders. The light slowly crept up their body. The light fully revealed who it was.

South London's Number One Bad Boy.

Nico Sinclair. Decked out in man-about-town perfection as always.

Mo kept it under wraps what she'd learnt about him and Kristal. Mo had asked Nico for a helping hand before she'd found out he was knifing her in the back. His time and that conniving sister-cum-stepmummy was coming soon. Very soon indeed. But for now, she was playing the part of one gangland boss asking another to back her up.

Carlos panicked, eyes widening in shocked astonishment. 'Nico! I don't know what's going on here, but this dopey moo thinks I roughed up her bruv. I hardly touched the cretin. A couple of slaps, that's all—'

Nico held his finger to his lips. Carlos shut it. He knew better than to disobey his boss.

Nico softly warned, 'I'm not interested in a hard-luck story. You were bang out of order. Taking your fist to a woman? Not on my watch, mate. Add to that shouting your tonsils off about Jimmy Southpaw being gaga.' He tutted. 'Go around saying shit like that and there's going to be consequences. Now man up and take your medicine.'

Nico spun on his heels and stalked out of the unit, his role in this done. Mo's heated gaze burned into his disappearing back. Inside, she seethed. She now had the knowledge that he was working with his sister, *Kristal-fucking-Steele*, to take Mo out of the game. Mo mused whether she'd have reached out to Nico if she'd known earlier what he was really up to? Probably. Mo was beginning to understand that in certain circumstances, the only friend a Boss had sometimes was their enemy.

Mo picked up a large box and handed it to Damien. 'Dump that on his head.'

Damien did as he was told. A shower of white soap powder cascaded over a struggling Carlos so that he looked like a very unhappy snowman in a store at Christmas.

Mo leant into his face. 'You are a dirty little toerag. And you know what happens to dirty little toerags? They get a good hot wash to make them clean.'

She gestured to her protection team. Josh and Dell untied Carlos. Predictably, he kicked off. Josh administered a double punch to the side of his face to shut him down. After that, they were able to heave him into one of the large washing machines. A bit of life came back in him then, but it was too late. They slammed the door shut. The washing machine had turned into Carlos' torture chamber.

The screams and yells were muffled behind the thick glass; a squashed Carlos frantically hammered on the door.

Mo looked over at her half-brother to do the honours.

Damien pulled out of his sulk, remembering that this was retribution for Charmaine. With utter pleasure, he pressed the 'start cycle' button. 'If you hold your breath, Carlos, you'll be fine.'

Hot water spraying into the drum, the banging on the other side of the door turned increasingly desperate while his howling became more high-pitched. The drum started spinning, knocking him off his feet. Carlos desperately struggled to keep his head above the revolving water, his terror-stricken, soapy face appearing in the glass like he was looking out of a prison cell window.

Satisfied, Mo beckoned to Damien and took him down the unit into the darkness.

Damien strained his neck in that awkward way, staring at this woman who had taken his place in his grandfather's firm. The child his beloved father had had with another woman. And, worst of all, his dad's firstborn.

Mo closely scrutinised her brother. 'I know we've had our differences and we'll probably have more in the future, but we need to remember one thing. We're family. Families need to stick together or they come undone. A family like ours can't afford to unravel. If we do, we could all end up dead. Do you understand?'

She was right, he couldn't fault her on that score. 'Does Granddad Southpaw—?'

'…Know about what happened between you and drip-dry over there in South London?' she ended for him.

Humiliation stung his cheeks.

'He doesn't,' Mo assured him. 'I made sure it never reached his ears. And he won't hear it from me. Or Nico Sinclair.'

He stared at her strangely. 'Why are you being so matey to me when all I've done is show you my back?'

Mo held his uncertain gaze. 'You're my brother. I'm your sister. The blood of Robbie Steele runs thick in our veins. We're the hope of the next generation of the Steele family.' There was a catch in her voice as she added, 'And I like you. You've got balls to defend the honour of a woman most would spit on. A knight in shining Steele armour is what you are.'

Damien didn't know what to say to that. He could hear the machine's drum spinning in the distance. He'd rather have sorted Carlos out himself, but he couldn't deny Mo had saved him the trouble. Maybe she wasn't all bad after all.

Mo held her hand out. 'Truce?'

Damien hesitated. Then took her hand in his. Neither were under the illusion that they were bosom buddies. Not yet, anyway.

Mo made no mention about his mum's treachery. For all she knew, Damien could be in on it. She doubted it, though. Her brother seemed the type to keep out of messy family situations. On top of that, Damien had shown no signs of knowing that Nico was his uncle. Mo was glad. She didn't want to rock the boat on their potential new relationship.

Tomorrow was going to be a very long day. Time to show those stepping out of line that Mo was the Queen of Crime.

Chapter Twenty-Nine

Twelve-year-old Annalisa and her three friends did some serious moves while they performed a dance routine to Destiny Child's 'Jumpin Jumpin' for the guests at her birthday party. Annalisa sent her dad a spellbinding grin each time she caught a glimpse of him. She had the best daddy in the world and loved him to death.

Nico looked back with a father's pride at his daughter's confidence. What a brave girl. He'd organised a huge bash at one of the properties he owned in Lewisham. The place was a former ballroom that had fallen on hard times until his Uncle Ted had rescued it back in the late 80s. King Ted had done a bang-up job of restoring it to its former beauty. The centrepiece was a massive sparkling five-tier chandelier that made the gold trim on the red wallpaper glitter. It was like something out of a fairy tale, the perfect setting for his darlin' girl to have her birthday party.

Nico also had a son called Victor, named after his dad who had lived too short on this earth. The day his kids were born were the most important days of his life. He didn't understand couples who deliberately decided not to have children. Didn't they know what they were missing out on? The cuddles, the tears, the hugs. A small trusting hand tucked into yours, guiding them on the road to adulthood. There wasn't a feeling like it in the world.

Emotions stirred deep within Nico at the memories of cradling his tiny, wriggling baby girl. It was like The Almighty Himself had gifted Nico something that was more precious than any jewel. And when he'd seen her features, her hair, it had been like seeing his long-lost sister, Annalisa. And that's why he'd named her after his big sister. A frown wrinkled his brow. It still troubled him that Kristal wouldn't tell him why she'd bolted from their uncle's house all those years ago. They had unfinished business between them. After this business with Big Mo was done, he was going to have it out with his sister about what went on all those years ago.

When his daughter's performance finished, Nico was on his feet with everyone else. While people clapped, he wolf-whistled with top appreciation. Annalisa flew immediately into his arms. He hugged her tight. Over her head he saw his wife, Pam, smiling at them accompanied by a teasing roll of her eyes. He spoilt their girl something rotten was her opinion. She knew the story of his sister and over the years had quietly cautioned him that trying to replace one person with another was unhealthy. He needed to let their little girl be her own self. Pam was so right.

Nico had struck gold the day he'd married her. He'd been going off the rails when they met. Beautiful, straight-talking Pamela had sorted him out in no time at all. He adored her, but it was a calm love, none of that wild whirlwind crazy that blew hot for a year, if you were lucky, and then fizzled out for the rest of your married life. Pam was practical, got on with things, none of that drama malarkey.

Nico blew his wife a kiss, let go of his daughter, who scampered over to the other kids who were sitting in a circle waiting for the magician to begin his act.

Nico moved towards the exit. Someone stepped into line behind him. With an impatient sigh, he checked over his shoulder and ordered, 'I don't need an escort to hold my willy while I splash my boots.'

The person behind him was Charlie, the kid from the gang that had put Uncle Ted out of action and come out as the victor when Nico made his crew fight each other gladiator-style. He'd not only liked the lad's shoes, there had also been that certain something about him. Nico had a good nose for sniffing out fresh blood to add to his crew. He'd told the boy to look him up, and there he was, bright and early the next morning, sitting on the steps of the Candy before it had even opened. After that, Nico had let him trail along for various meetings. And, give the kid his due, he was taking his duties very seriously indeed.

Charlie shuffled his feet, his small dreads shuffling too. 'Sorry, Mister Nico. Just making sure you're ticking over nicely.'

'It's a party. Go and get yourself a glass of something. Take the edge off life.'

'Right you are.'

Nico watched him amble off with a faint smile and a good-natured shake of his head and then proceeded to the gents. He pushed the swing door back. Did what he needed to do and then washed his hands at the sink. He looked up into the mirror and saw a face behind him. Shit! His heart went into free fall. He tried to act on instinct to defend himself.

Too late.

A plastic bag was violently thrust over his head. The hold on it tightened. Nico grunted, fought for his very life. Another person captured his hands behind his back and secured them with plastic handcuffs. Hell! He couldn't breathe. The attacker used his hold on the bag as leverage to drag Nico towards a toilet stall. He fought all the way, animal noises emitting from his throat inside the plastic bag. It moulded around his gasping mouth with every frantic breath he took. His face was a grotesque and terrifying picture of suffocating plastic over his skin.

They got him in the stall. Shoved him down onto the toilet seat. That big bastard stood over him while the other kept a tight grip on the plastic bag.

Can't breathe.

Can't breathe.

The air wheezing in his windpipe was audible and horrible in his ears. How could he have been such a berk to relax his protection detail at his daughter's birthday party?

Can't breathe.

Can't breathe.

Nico's vision blurred, his fading mind drifting to images

of his treasured family. The next time they saw him he would be dead, found murdered on a piss-stained floor. His beautiful Annalisa sobbing her eyes out. And Kristal. That's what made him want to scream out the most. He'd found her. She was back. And now he was going to lose her all over again. The outrage of it pushed Nico to fight harder. He swung his legs high until the soles of his shoes touched the wall. With a manic determination, he pushed and pushed against the wall, trying to use the force of it to get out of the merciless grip on his head. No use. The energy sapped away. His legs tumbled to the floor like dead weights.

Suddenly the bag was gone. Nico spluttered and coughed, filling his lungs with air, sagging forward so suddenly he nearly collapsed to his knees on the floor.

The voice that spoke was deep and commanding. 'You're losing your touch, Nico. Thought you was King of the South. By the way, sorry to hear about King Ted being in the ozzie.'

It dawned on him that this was the second time he'd been caught on the hop recently.

Still drawing long, shattering breaths, Nico looked up into the face of Jimmy Southpaw. Behind him stood the East End gangster's longstanding associate, Barker. Nico was pissed. 'This …' Inhale. Inhale. 'This is bang out of order, Southpaw. You know the rules. Bosses stay on their side of the water. Before you swim across, you ask for an invitation.'

Jimmy tilted his head, assessing the younger man. 'I'm glad you recall the particulars, just like I do. Then you might want to explain why you're knee-deep in the foulness that's been causing ructions in my granddaughter's business.'

Nico wore his most innocent, 'Who me?' expression. 'Dunno what you're going on about. It's your grandkid who inserted herself in my life, not the other way round. Paid me a visit, she did, wanting to know about ...' Nico made a big drama of not recalling the specifics of his convo with Mo. 'Some knobhead who'd blown up her club ...'

The plastic bag was back in a flash. This time, Nico was ready. He sucked the plastic deliberately into his mouth and then sank his teeth into it. The material tore, the surprise of it sending Barker slightly off balance. His grip loosened, giving Nico the space he needed to leap up. He might not have his hands, but they weren't the only part of his body that could be used as a weapon. Plastic bag still over his head, he head-butted Barker. The fella went down as Nico twisted to face Jimmy. The older man held a gun on him.

'Sit back down,' was Jimmy's calm request.

Barker was out for the count, and Nico wondered if Southpaw was going to exact retribution for what he'd done. But what happened surprised him. Southpaw pulled the bag off his head. He checked Barker's pulse, which was obviously OK because he straightened again.

He told Nico, 'He's going to be nursing a sore head for a week.' His tone changed. 'I didn't come here for a row, just a chat.'

Nico lifted a sarky brow. 'You always channel your chats through a plastic bag? I must try it myself sometime.'

Jimmy put the shooter away and shocked Nico by taking off the flexicuffs. 'I'm hoping you won't leg it, but stick around to tell me the truth.'

Nico rubbed his wrists, getting the flow of blood back into them. 'The truth being …?'

'This young kid, Dean, who attacked Mo's base and is going around threatening to take down her empire, is a nobody. The kid operates out of a shit-hole boozer in Essex.'

Behind the scenes, Jimmy had made it his business to find out what was happening. But he wanted to see how young Mo dealt with it all. Wanted to see if that brain of hers was smart enough to figure out who was connected to who and the reason it was all going down. Discovering this dimwit Dean had been easy. What was not so easy had been figuring out who was backing him up. And why. Fingering Nico as the source of the muscle behind this no-mark kid's operation had taken Jimmy a while … but Jimmy Southpaw wasn't a man known for giving up.

'What I can't figure out,' Jimmy informed him, 'is why you would provide that numb-nut nipper with back-up? Coz the only way he's been able to go around town blowing out of his behind that he's going to thieve Mo's turf is if he has a big name providing him with the hardware to do it.'

Nico rested against the wall as Barker mumbled on the floor but didn't wake. 'What makes you think it's me? Plenty of other top geezers out there who might decide they want a slice of your East End pie. And maybe they've decided that now's the time to do it since people are questioning whether the Great Southpaw has lost the plot putting an unknown teeny-weeny chick in the seat beside him.'

Jimmy threw back his head and laughed. 'Teeny-weeny?

That girl is one of the toughest people you'll ever meet. She's my Robbie all over again. Whiplash smart. A fighter. Loyal to the core.' His chest expanded in pride. 'Believes in family always coming first.'

Family.

That's what got Nico reconsidering his position. Now Jimmy Southpaw was on the warpath, Nico was frightened for his sister. Sure, she was Southpaw's daughter-in-law, but that wouldn't stop the Big Man from taking his revenge out on her for trying to destroy his crown princess. Maybe he could safeguard her from this powerful man's rage …

'Kristal.' The name burst from Nico's lips. He looked visibly shaken by his decision.

Jimmy's mouth tightened, blood pooling and heating the skin on his face. 'That bobtail bitch,' he ground out. 'She couldn't leave it alone. I've already told her, till I'm sick of the sound of my own voice, that her boy will be sorted out.' His fist thumped the wall. 'To go outside the family—'

Nico leapt up, spitting nails at the way the other man was bad-mouthing his sister. He didn't care who Jimmy Southpaw was. No one, *no one* trash-talked his beloved sister in his presence.

'See, that's where you're wrong,' he fiercely enlightened the other man. 'She never went outside the family.'

Jimmy clenched up, staring hard at him. 'What you chatting about?'

Nico's nostrils flared as it dawned on him what he was about to reveal. Kristal had sworn him to secrecy. Well, at least until her plan to destroy Mo was seen through.

Jimmy wouldn't let it go. 'You better tell me what I need to know.'

Nico wearily sat down again. 'She's my sister.'

Jimmy prided himself on having seen and heard most things in life. Not much surprised him. But this had his jaw hanging open, waiting for flies to take root. 'Your what?'

Suddenly, the stall door banged back into Barker's body. Charlie stood on the other side holding a blade, coiled, ready to spring on Nico's word. His alert gaze quickly took in the scene.

'I didn't see you come back, Mister Nico, so I got to thinking maybe you was in a slight bit of bother.'

Nico smiled. This kid was a bright spark. He'd need to keep him close. He waved his hand at the knife. 'No need for that type of dramatics with old mates.' He nodded over at his unexpected guest. 'This is Jimmy Southpaw.'

Charlie's bugged-out eyes showed he was fully aware of who the East End legend was.

'Come for a friendly chat,' Nico added.

The boy started to apologise.

Nico cut him short. 'Nice one you're looking out for me, kid. Good to know you've got my back. Like I said before, get out there and enjoy the knees-up.'

Once he was gone, Nico picked up the ticking-bomb thread of his incendiary conversation with Southpaw. 'She's my big sister. It's a long story.' He stood. 'Maybe we can take this upstairs and continue over a Scotch?'

Jimmy's mouth was now set into a grim line. 'Sounds good to me.'

Nico just needed to be sure of a few things first. 'I'll withdraw my backing for Dean. As long as you don't touch a hair on my sister's head. And don't mention a word of what I've told you to her.'

Jimmy nodded. 'This is my granddaughter's fight. If she ain't got the balls to defeat her opponents, she ain't got the balls to be the Southpaw heir.'

Chapter Thirty

'Blimey, you sound like you were having kittens on the blower. What's the problem, girl?' Harry greeted his niece as he strolled into her office at Club Class.

His voice was jaunty and upbeat, however, in reality, Harry was peed off. *I mean, who does she think she is summoning me here like her gopher? The girl needs a lesson in manners.* She might be sitting in Robbie's chair, but he was still her uncle. Harry also thought something smelt fishy. Despite their intimate heart-to-heart about her dad last night, Mo had never come looking to him for help before. In fact, she'd made a big production of standing on her own two. Doing stuff the Big Mo way.

His suspicions vanished when he got a proper butcher's at her. Gleefully, he noted that the dopey bint appeared like she really was up Shit Street. Mo sat behind the desk that was so big it nearly swallowed her up, fiddling with her phone, and defensively answered, 'There's no problem. Why would there be a problem? You think I can't cope, is that it? I can manage things. You don't want to worry about that.'

The kid could barely sit still, her gaze darting to the door every two seconds as if she expected the psychos from the *Texas Chainsaw Massacre* to chop it down. Harry could barely believe what he was witnessing. Mo was bending, buckling, cracking up under the strain.

Hallelujah!

Jimmy Southpaw's suit was far too big for this overgrown teenager to wear.

The only mystery was why the ol' man had ever thought she'd be able to get into it.

Although Harry had eventually bought into Kristal's plan, personally he thought it was a waste of time. From his standpoint, it was a waiting game with Mo. Sooner or later, Robbie's girl was bound to fuck it up. It was just a question of biding his time for the day to arrive and for his dad to wise up and face reality.

And then appoint his remaining son to take over.

Harry took the chair opposite his niece, his face a mirror of fake concern. ''Course you can cope. Who's saying you can't? Not me. I never doubted it, babe. Now, what exactly do you need a hand with?'

She sighed, seeming very uncomfortable indeed. 'Granddad Jimmy has got a special job for me. An old couple he knows from back in the day have run into a spot of bother. Some low-rent crew who obviously fancy themselves are putting the frighteners on them. He wants me to take care of business and sort these tosspots out. But also get his friends to a place of safety. I've sorted out a nice, no-questions-asked hotel.'

Harry cocked his head, his confusion showing. 'So why can't you take care of this?'

Mo's answer was almost a whine. 'I haven't got the time, have I? There's too much going on.' She stopped fiddling with her phone and shuffled her chair closer to the desk. Closer to him. 'I'm wondering, Uncle Harry, if you could pick this couple up. Take them somewhere safe where they won't be found until I've got the space to get a grip on things.'

A grip on things? You're already falling, Harry thought with relish.

'I can do that,' he offered, 'but I'm at a loss to understand why you need me to. You're running an empire here. This ain't a big job. Why don't you get one of your runners to do it?'

Mo bowed her head slightly, peering at him through hooded eyes. 'I'm going to level with you, Uncle Harry. I'm not sure who I can trust anymore. There's freaky stuff going on I can't talk about. There's people playing silly beggers behind my back. You get me?'

She raised her head, furtively checking the closed door before settling her anxious gaze back on him. 'This job came from Jimmy himself. He asked me to take care of it. Personally. I can't afford for it to be a botch-up job. Y'know what I mean? I need someone I can trust.'

Harry so wanted to laugh.

'Someone who isn't going to kiss and tell. If Granddad Jimmy gets wind that I fobbed this off onto someone else …'

Mo didn't need to finish. Harry knew all along she wouldn't be able to handle the role of Steele heir, but even he hadn't thought she was this much of a prized plonker.

'This old couple have barricaded themselves in their house,' she continued, 'and they won't answer the door to anyone. Now, if Jimmy's son himself comes a-calling, it's open sesame.'

Poor Mo. She was way out of her depth and in over her head. It was only a matter of time before she was swept away like all the other plastic gangland wannabes who'd come and gone over the years. Harry almost felt sorry for her. Almost. He couldn't forget how the little bitch had nicked his gig as Jimmy Southpaw's heir.

Mo was still gassing away. 'You'll need to take someone with you to carry their luggage and all that. It's got to be someone who's got absolutely no connection to the firm, so nothing gets back to Jimmy. Right? Can you do that for me?'

Harry played along. When the job was over, he'd give his dad chapter and nauseating verse about what really went on, obviously giving himself a starring role as having saved the day.

'You can trust me, Mo,' was Harry's oily reply. 'I won't let you down. Give me the address and consider the job done.'

Mo was relieved. 'When do you think you can get over there? It needs to be soon.'

'Pronto. This evening.'

Mo appeared incredibly grateful. 'Have you got someone in mind to help you out?'

'Yeah, I have actually.'

And he did. It was about time a certain person earned his corn.

To his surprise, not to mention his embarrassment, Mo got out of her chair and hugged him. 'Cheers, Uncle Harry. I'll make it up to you. I'll give you anything you want.'

With his face over shoulder, she couldn't see his twisted smirk. 'Yes, you'll give me exactly what I need.'

'I don't like it. What are we even doing here? And why did I have to come?' Dean groused in the passenger seat.

Sitting behind the wheel of his Merc, Harry ignored him. They were parked outside a run-down detached house in a scruffy suburb of North London. The place must've once been smart but had long since run to seed. The garden was overgrown, the privet hedge needed a trim, and the rusty metal gate hung off its hinges.

The house was dark except for one solitary light behind moth-eaten curtains on the ground floor. That was old people for you, always turning the lights off to save on the leccy bills. Harry guessed that the residents were actually worth a few bob, old friends of his dad's nearly always were. He knew what he was in for, two old skinflints whinging and whining all the way to the hotel.

Harry turned his attention to Dean. 'I'm here to give two old codgers a lift to a hotel. You're here to carry their belongings and, as it happens, I don't give a two-finger salute if you like it or not. Now then, let's get a move on.'

Harry got out of the car, a miffed Dean following a few paces behind. In the darkness it took a couple of seconds to find the front doorbell. In keeping with the run-down vibe, it didn't work.

Harry banged a black metal knocker, bad temper coming through. 'I've had enough of these two already.'

Shadows materialised behind a frosted panel. A thin, weedy and nervous woman's voice demanded, 'Who is it?'

'My name's Harry. I'm Jimmy's son. I've going to take you somewhere safe.'

'Jimmy who?'

Gimme strength! Harry called back, 'Jimmy Southpaw! Y'know, you're ol' mucker Jimmy who's offered to help you out with your situation.'

Silence. Then, 'How do I know it's you and not some gangland assassin?'

Harry tipped his head back, sighing loudly with despair. 'What do you want me to do, love? Put my passport and a set of fingerprints through the letterbox? Now, do you want to get out of here or not?'

Bolts, locks and chains were undone. The door opened slightly and a wizened old dear peered out, her features mostly hidden in the gloom, and only the faint lick of the streetlights showed her nerves. 'You don't look like Jimmy's boy.'

'Turn a light on and you'll soon see the family resemblance.'

'I can't. The bulb's blown. My boy normally comes round to change them, but with all the trouble' – Harry felt her shrug – 'I don't want him popping round. My husband in the sitting room is infirm. He can't do it.' She craned her neck to carefully search her garden path. 'Who's he?'

Harry answered, not bothering to look back at Dean.

'My bag boy. I can't hang around on the doorstep all night. Are you going to let me in or not?'

The door slammed shut in his face.

Dean drew closer. 'First off, I ain't your bag boy. Second, I don't like this. We should have brought some of Kristal's people. It could be a setup.' Although what Dean was keeping to himself was that when he'd called her people, the phone number was 'no longer in service.' Strange that! Stuff was getting more and more whacko.

'A setup?' Harry got sarky. 'Yeah, it could be. I'll tell you what, if the old dear turns nasty, you can take her on while I deal with the infirm husband.'

Properly put out, Dean shot back, 'You won't be laughing on that side of your moosh if I'm proved right.'

The front door slowly opened again. The two men stepped into the blackness. Abruptly, inky black flashed into blinding light. So bright, in fact, that Harry was almost thrown back on his feet. The door slammed behind them. Men appeared as if through the walls. Harry and Dean cowered as they were submerged in a flailing mix of men's fists and boots.

Cringing and groaning, Harry was dragged by the scruff of his neck into the front room. Howling, Dean was hauled in the opposite direction down the hallway towards a door that led to the basement. Harry flicked his head up to check his surroundings. No sign of an infirm husband. The old lady had done a bunk as well. Instead, two massive toughs stood either side of an armchair.

In that armchair sat his niece, legs crossed, looking solemn.

Harry's forehead dropped to the manky carpet.

'Oh fuck!'

Mo spoke quietly. 'You know something, Uncle Harry? I don't really mind you *thinking* I'm dumb. That's worked to my advantage. But I do mind you *treating me* like I'm dumb. That's totally uncalled for.'

Harry was only half listening. His attention was elsewhere. Below the floorboards came the cry of what could be taken for that of an injured animal. It was no animal. It was Dean being worked over by Mo's people in the basement.

His niece followed his gaze. 'That's your mate downstairs. Of course, he'll be singing like the proverbial, but I thought I'd apply a bit of pressure anyway, just in case he's forgotten anything. Strung upside down from a beam, the soles of feet being thrashed with a bamboo stick. Ouch! Bastinado is the fancy name for it. So many of your nerve endings go down to your feet, which explains why it hurts like a bitch.'

As if to underscore her statement, Dean let out an ear-splitting scream. Harry trembled.

Mo blithely carried on. 'There's no need for me to dish out that kind of treatment to you. For one thing, I know everything I need to know. And, for another, despite everything, you're still family. And we all know how important that is.'

Harry felt for Dean, but, hey-ho, at the end of the day, if you played big boy's games, you had to expect big boy's punishment if it all went tits up.

He smiled. 'So, I can go then, can I?'

'Are you having a laugh?' Mo ground out. 'After what you've done? No, Unc, you can't.'

An unearthly squeal from beyond the floorboards made Harry shudder with horror. He warned his niece, 'It's good that you remember I'm family. I'm Jimmy's boy, so don't get too urgent with any retribution.'

Mo stood. 'I've got some business to attend to.' She turned to Harry's guards. 'Will one of you boys get my uncle a cuppa? I bet he'd love a lovely cup of Rosie.'

Chapter Thirty-One

The only sound in the basement was Dean hyperventilating. Short, sharp, painful spurts heaving from his chest as he hung limply, upside down, suspended from a beam.

The basement was dark and dank, not enough room to swing a cat. Enough room, though, to do serious damage to a half-wit who'd been foolish enough to go up against Big Mo Watson.

Urgently, he curled his back and head up, dripping sweat, drooling saliva. Hardly able to catch his breath, he begged, 'Please! No more. I swear I didn't know what I was getting into.'

He was pleading with the man who calmly stood in front of him with a bamboo cane in one hand. Dean didn't even know if he had any feet left. The first lash of the cane, the pain had been indescribable. It was like nothing he'd felt before. Burning, stinging pain had raced through his body like a bolt of lightning.

The exertion of talking was too much, and Dean's head flopped back again, the motion making his body swing. Mentally, he cursed Kristal to kingdom come and back. The day she'd taken him to the caff, and he'd walked away, he should've kept on walking. Ignored her emails and smutty snaps of two women snogging. He'd really landed himself in the doggy-do this time, and it didn't look like there was any way out of it. Dean had never understood when someone said that things were so bad they started crying for their mum. That was coward talk as far as he was concerned. Until now. Now he was on the verge of sobbing and howling for his mum.

Dean froze when he felt one of the men behind him. Not again! An arm locked around his waist to steady him. A hand touched his leg. He tried to wriggle away. *Please! Please! Please, not again!* His foot was caught. Yanked forward.

Dean stiffened. Screwed his eyes tight. Hyperventilating again, the knots of panicked fear tightening in his tummy. *Here it comes! Here it comes!*

The lash that came was Mo's calm voice. 'That's enough, Sid. Thank you.'

Casually, Mo moved off the step, walking into the basement. And looked over at Sid. The same Sid who operated the counter in Granddad Jimmy's betting shop-cum-HQ. In another life, Sid had been in much demand for his skill with whips and canes and the damage he could inflict with them. Foot caning had been a speciality of his.

Sid walked over to Mo, nodding when he reached her. 'I wouldn't do this for anyone else. But I can't stand by and let this wanker take liberties with you.'

Mo patted his arm in gratitude. 'I know this isn't your thing anymore, so big-time thanks.'

Knowing his work for the day was done, Sid took his leave. Mo signalled for the two guys to wait near the door. She now turned her attention to Dean. The place stank of his terror.

She walked over to him, grabbed his hair and pulled his head up. God! What a mess. His mouth and chin were caked in dried spit, eyes bloodshot and bleary.

'Remember me, Dean?'

Mo was expecting him to plead, beg but instead he managed to raise a laugh. 'Yeah! 'Course I recall you. The pocket rocket in the catsuit.'

One of Mo's guys moved menacingly forward, taking exception to what Dean had called his boss. Mo impatiently waved him back. Since she was a kid, Mo had been insulted and taunted about her height. Never had she been called a 'pocket rocket'. She quite liked it. As she'd expected, there was something about this young man.

She let go of his hair and stepped back. 'Cut him down. Bring him upstairs to the kitchen.'

Mo took the stairs while Dean crash-landed to the dirt floor.

Ten minutes later, a very wary Dean eyed Mo across the uneven kitchen table. The first thing he'd done was to inspect the damage to the soles of his feet. He thought they'd be badly injured, covered in cuts, so was shocked to only find the skin on his arches was slightly red. That had been a bonus. Still, he couldn't understand what was going on here. Why was Big Mo providing him with tea and sympathy?

She folded her arms. 'Sid said he didn't hit you too hard,

so the pain should go away in a couple of hours. Maybe soak them in a saltwater bath.'

Dean was incredulous. 'Let me get this straight. One minute you're caning the nuts off me, the next giving me feet therapy treatment tips.'

Mo resisted smiling. She was liking Dean. With the right work and incentive, he could shape up to become someone of responsibility.

'So, which of the clowns approached you, Kristal or Harry?' she asked.

He sipped his tea. After all the crap he'd been through, Dean felt not the slightest bit of loyalty to either one, so he told Mo the truth. 'Kristal. She appeared the same night the Scarlet Lady put on a Grab-a-Granny night …'

Fifteen minutes later, Mo had the lowdown of what had gone on. He finished with, 'They must've seen me coming. They screwed me over, big-time.' He hung his head, defeated.

'What if you were given an opportunity to step up the ladder, so to speak?'

Dean let out a caustic, humourless laugh. 'Yeah! That was Kristal's line too. Do a couple of jobs for her and she'd hand me the keys to the underworld's promised land.'

'The difference between me and her is that I mean it.'

Dean's head came back up, very, very slowly. It took him a while to say anything, and when he did, he was incredibly guarded. 'You pulling my plonker as well as whacking my feet?'

Mo leant forward, her tone dead serious. 'Think about

it, Dean. You want an in, and I'm the lady to open the door. I'm always looking for new blood. Unique talent to take my organisation in different directions.'

What Mo was learning, with speed, was that when you spotted new talent, sometimes it was working behind enemy lines. Sure, he'd bombed her club, but sometimes in life you have to see the bigger picture.

Dean's breath hitched in his throat, his expression half filled with hope. 'You want me' – he stabbed his chest – 'to work for you?' He pointed at her.

Mo allowed herself a full-length smile. 'Sweet as! Simple. If you're willing, we can discuss the specifics another time.' Her brow arched. 'When you've had your foot spa.'

They both smiled broadly at each other. Mo held out her hand. So did Dean.

They shook on it. 'Deal.'

When he would've withdrawn his hand, Mo tightened her grip on it. Looked directly into his eyes. 'In this game, Dean, you've got to learn how to fight dirty.'

Chapter Thirty-Two

Ruddy sniffed back the tears as she cleaned the top of the gravestone. The sun was hot, the sky a pretty blue, and a refreshing breeze blew through the silent graveyard. It was the anniversary of Joy's death all those years ago. Without fail, every year, Ruddy put on her Sunday best and took the trip to the City of London Cemetery to pay her respects.

All those years ago, Ted had made sure that his lady love got a funeral to remember – horse-drawn cart and a procession through the streets of East London she'd grown up in that not many would forget. Bless his solid-gold heart. Joy's send-off was one to remember, not least because that bastard ex-hubby of hers had turned up, tanked out of his head, shouting the odds about what a bang-up wife Joy had been. The nerve! The absolute bloody nerve! The man who used to clump her one on a daily basis. A grief-stricken Ted had jumped the guy, and if it hadn't been for the mourners, he would have ripped Joy's former husband's head clean off.

Ruddy and Brother Bertie had clubbed together to get the headstone. Ruddy looked down and read the inscription:

Joyce 'Joy' Taylor

Mother daughter

Best friend

The love of everyone's life

Ruddy softly announced, 'I've brought Joe along too, just like I always do.'

From her bag, Ruddy took out a small old-fashioned tape recorder. She kept it in her hand and pressed 'play'. Her eyes closed as Joe Cocker's gutsy 'With a Little Help from My Friends' filled the air. Joy had loved the song to bits. Her best friend hadn't been much into shaking a leg, but when Joe Cocker hit the turntable, you couldn't hold Joy back from doing a turn on the dance floor.

'What you pouring on that gravestone?' an abrupt voice behind Ruddy demanded as the song was fading. 'Not a pint of Guinness, I hope!'

Ruddy's heart filled with joy and love, her mouth forming into an 'O' of pleasured surprise. There she stood, Joy's daughter. Casey. It seized Ruddy's heart every time how the girl was the spit of her mother. The same shaped face, the gently rounded chin, the glossy chestnut hair. And as for those eyes ... a complete mirror of her mother's. Staring into them was like gazing into a pool of serene kindness.

Ruddy roughly retorted in a threatening tone, 'You calling me a pisshead, young lady?' Ruddy shook the cloth sternly at her. 'I'll show you what for.'

Both women gently giggled. Ruddy wasn't upset at all but playacting to the hilt. She had established a teasing relationship with Casey since she was a kid. Always pretending to tell her off with a glint in her eye. It had been the poor child who'd found her mum dead with her head inside the oven. Ruddy would never forget seeing the little girl for the first time after the horror. It was etched in her mind as if it had happened yesterday. Casey's small body had shaken and trembled, tears staining her face. Pure terror had transformed Joy's daughter's face into a waxy, marble-white mask, drained of blood, drained of life.

It was hard enough for a child to have to grieve the death of a parent, but Casey had to deal with being the one who had found her mum in such tragic and soul-destroying circumstances. That would've shattered and blighted anyone's world forever. Most kids would've gone off the deep end. Not Casey. She was her mother's daughter, alright. She'd gathered the strength, that formidable steel, to look to the future and make something terrific of her life. A teacher she was now. Teaching the young ones in primary school. And she'd found a good man who treated her like a queen. Two darlin' children they had. Ruddy was so proud of her because her mum would've been beyond proud too.

The women embraced, mindful of the gorgeous spray of daffodils the younger woman held. Then Casey laid the flowers on her mother's grave. They remained in silence for some time paying their respects.

Casey sorrowfully whispered, 'I miss her. So much. Toby passed the next level of learning to play the piano with flying colours last week, and do you know what I said to myself? *I can't wait to tell Mum.*' Ruddy placed an arm of sympathy and love around her shoulders. 'Then I remember, Mum isn't there anymore. That she never got a chance to meet her grandbabies.'

Casey turned so swiftly to face Ruddy, the older woman's comforting arm slipped away. 'Does it ever get better, Aunt Ruddy? Will I wake up one day and not feel like I'm breaking apart?'

Ruddy caught the younger woman's gaze, which was clouded with such pain it made Ruddy feel the ache of falling apart herself. But she didn't allow herself the luxury of doing it. The first day she'd held Casey as a baby, she'd vowed to hold this girl's hand through thick and thin.

She told her, voice light but firm, 'All I recall about my ol' mum was she loved a flutter on the horses. People called her Ladbroke Lil. I'm not saying she didn't love me, but she sure as shit loved a flutter on the horses and dogs.'

Ruddy wasn't one of these people who had mummy issues. She'd long got over the fact she'd come second best in her mum's life. She sure as heck wasn't going to go around moping and ruining her life over it. Get outta here! Or, more pointedly, get a life! Which is exactly what she'd done.

She continued, 'I don't really think about my mum no more. Whereas you, now, you're full of eternal love for your mother. That's why you feel like you're sometimes falling apart because you *feel*.' Ruddy choked up. 'Now all you've got to do is take those emotions and instead of crumbling, use them to raise your chin high.'

Casey's jaw moved, but no words came out. Then she blurted, wrenching out like a sickness deep within, 'I killed her. I killed my mum.'

Ruddy staggered back, her chest tightening. 'What?' There was a roaring in her ears.

Casey's eyes brimmed with swollen tears. 'I might as well have put Mum's head in that oven and turned on the gas—'

'Nah!' Ruddy's voice brooked no nonsense as she waved a forbidding finger in Casey's face. 'You stop it right there. You were a child, a kid, you hear me? There was nothing you could do to deal with the demons riding your mum's back. What those demons were, God above alone knows. I wish I'd have known coz I'd have moved heaven and earth to set your mum free.' She added, 'And your Uncle Ted too.'

The blood left Casey's cheeks, leaving her face as white as a newly washed sheet. Startled, Ruddy added, 'He's in the ozzie, you know. I know you were close to him as a kid—'

Hands balled into fists by her sides, Casey hissed, 'I was never close to … to … That. Man.' Casey had bared her teeth, her mouth a terrifying sight of harrowing pain.

Ruddy's head spun. She didn't like what was going on here. 'But I thought—'

'Well, you thought wrong,' Casey succinctly snapped back.

Ruddy rose to her full height in indignation. 'That's no way to speak to your Aunty Ruddy, girly.'

Casey's face fell in shame and some other emotion Ruddy couldn't figure out. 'I'm sorry, Aunt Ruddy.' Then she made a drama of checking her watch. 'Wow! Is that time? I really need to be off.'

Still in a daze, Ruddy felt the cold press of Casey's lips on her cheek in a goodbye kiss. The touch of Ruddy's fingers against Casey's arm was enough to freeze the younger woman in her tracks. But she refused to face Ruddy.

Ruddy's brows slashed together in confusion. Something was wrong here. Terribly wrong. Why would Casey react so violently when Ruddy told her about Ted? That man had been like a proper dad to the girl, taking her on trips when her mum was busy working or flat out too tired to do anything but rest her weary head. Ruddy could see him now, hoisting a giggling Casey onto his shoulders. That girl had loved her Uncle Ted with all her innocent heart.

Ruddy prided herself on knowing the ways of the world, but she couldn't figure this one out. Casey stiffened as Ruddy proceeded to walk around and face her. 'Have you had a falling out with your Uncle Ted?'

Casey's eyes lethally flashed. 'Don't call him that.'

Whatever was going on here frightened Ruddy. 'What's this about? And stop pussyfooting around. Tell me straight to my face.'

Casey inhaled a deep breath to fortify herself. 'What I said earlier was true. I killed my mum. And I'll tell you how I did it …'

Ruddy listened and listened. What Casey told her next rocked Ruddy's world. By the end, she was shaking her head in denial. Couldn't breathe. Couldn't move a muscle. It was as if she was being buried alive right alongside Joy.

Chapter Thirty-Three

'Open this bloody door,' Kristal demanded between gritted teeth.

She banged both fists frantically against the door of Jimmy's betting shop. The place was dark, locked up for the night. And silent. The only noise was the occasional car that whizzed by on Commercial Road. Kristal was freaking out, big-time. Somewhere inside was Nico. Her Nico. Her darling baby brother. Less than an hour ago she'd received a distressing text from him:

Need you. Now. Southpaw's HQ.

Her heart had nosedived with abject terror. *Need you! Need you!* Kristal couldn't get her brother's desperate plea out of her head. Nico was in trouble. He must be for him to be inside Jimmy's base. Why else would he be here? Despite Kristal and her brother only recently picking up the reins of their relationship, she still knew him well enough to sense when he was in danger. She would move heaven and earth to rescue her baby brother.

But why would Jimmy do this? What beef could he possibly have with Nico? Why would he dare attack another

London boss? Kristal didn't get it. Maintaining order, that's the name of the game for those who bossed the different sections of London's underworld. Not rocking the boat meant that all parties could get on with the business they were all into – the making of money. Her father-in-law would have to have some shit-hot reason to put his hands on another gang lord.

Unless … Unless … Fear for Nico shivered down her spine. What if Jimmy had discovered Nico's part in her plans to take Mo down?

Never, ever, stick your beak in the family affairs of another boss. That was the unwritten rule that the Big Men abided by.

And Kristal had made Nico break it.

Nico could already be dead! Dead! And you're to blame!

Kristal's fist-pounding doubled against the door. She furiously booted it time after time after time. The only response was the violent rattling of the door.

Chest heaving, she nearly bent double, bawling with the enormity of the situation she'd placed her brother in. *Nearly.* Sobbing wasn't going to help her find him. Straightening her shoulders, stiffening her spine, Kristal reminded herself who she was. The teenage girl who'd clawed her way out of a gut-wrenching situation to a prominent place in one of London's most fearsome families. That took courage. Fortitude. Brains. And that's exactly what she was going to use to get Nico out of this situation.

Thinking calmly, Kristal figured the first thing she needed to do was quit trying to bash the door in. The racket might propel Jimmy to finish Nico off, if he hadn't done so already. Plus, she couldn't afford to knacker herself silly banging away at the door when she needed all her strength for what might come.

She stepped back. Looked the building over. There had to be another way of getting in. Kristal strode with purpose around the back and instantly noticed that the light was on in Jimmy's office upstairs. A tiny flame of hope flickered inside her because maybe, just maybe, the two men were talking. The type of chat that got out of hand and that's why Nico had texted her?

Kristal lucked in. A downstairs window was partially open.

Wasting no time, Kristal urgently gripped the bottom of the window frame and shoved it up. Then she scrambled in. One of her six-inch Jimmy Choo's tumbled to the ground outside.

'Heck,' she furiously muttered.

She didn't have the time to go back for it. Instead, Kristal took off her remaining shoe and placed it beneath the window. Now she could creep upstairs on silent feet. The building was dark and cold. It took her a while to get her bearings because it was a rabbit warren of rooms and passageways, including a basement she had only recently realised existed. Finally, she located the foot of the stairs. Gazed up, disgust twisting her lips at the state of the warped banister and dingy carpet. Why Jimmy didn't give the place a splash of paint, a bit of TLC, she couldn't figure out.

Kristal took each step quietly, slowly, hoping the aged

wood wouldn't creak beneath her weight. She reached the landing. Walked on tiptoes to the door ahead. Sod's law there was no glass in the door, which meant she couldn't sneak a look inside the room to see what was happening.

She waited. Caught her breath. Trembling, her hand touched the round door handle.

One. Two. Three. Kristal burst in, almost swinging off the door. And let out an enormous sigh of relief when she found Nico inside. He stood in the middle of the room. Alone.

Kristal would've flown across the room to wrap him in a loving embrace, but she didn't because something was wrong here. Very wrong indeed.

He stalked towards her with relief. 'God! Are you OK?'

She met him halfway, her confusion growing. 'I should be asking you that.'

'I got a text saying you were in trouble in Southpaw's lair.'

'I received the same message about you.'

The hairs on the back of her neck stood to attention when she sensed they were no longer alone. A silhouette appeared in the corridor. Then smoothly stepped inside.

Mo.

In her hand she held up a printed copy of a photo of a young boy and teenage girl.

'Kristal, why did you never mention that Nico is your brother?'

Kristal snapped. With an animalistic roar, she flew and leapt onto her stepdaughter. Mo hadn't been expecting that. The force of the attack sent them both crashing to the floor. Frothing at the mouth like a demon risen from Hell, Kristal delivered a resounding smacker to Mo's mouth. The smaller woman's head snapped to the side.

Nico made no move to intervene. From the looks of things, this reckoning between the women was long overdue. In the world they lived sometimes, the only way to clear the air was with fists.

'I hate you,' Kristal screamed in Mo's face.

She was certainly packing some kinda clout because Mo was dazed and dizzy. The room swam, turning upside down. The hideous 70s wallpaper swayed with the motion of a psychedelic acid trip. Her rival pinned her to the floor. Mo tried to clear her head, but Kristal was back at her. This time with an open-handed wallop to the other side of Mo's head.

Kristal continued to spew her hate. 'You had no right taking my son's place.'

Wallop! Smack! Wallop!

'Robbie could've got the whole world in the pudding club as far as I was concerned. But no wrong-side-of-the-blanket spawn of his is taking Damien's seat at the Steele family table.'

Kristal's hand loomed threateningly in the air, intent on inflicting more damage … Despite the buzzing in her ears, Mo reached up and caught her stepmother's arm. Kristal tried her luck with her other hand. Mo caught that too. They struggled, Mo holding on for dear life, Kristal attempting to shake her off.

Frustrated beyond belief, Kristal leant down, doing her

best to bite the smaller woman's ear clean off.

So, it's like that, is it? Mo thought. *Fighting dirty.*

Bring. It. On.

Mo blinked rapidly until the room came back to rights. Then she kneed Kristal in her belly. Kristal sucked in a torturous breath against the pain. That was the part where her stepmother should've let go. But this was Kristal Steele. She never let go. A new energy ballooned within her and she dug her talons into Mo's hair. Scrambled off Mo. Still clutching her hair with vicious intent, she dragged her stepdaughter across the room.

Nico nimbly stepped out of the way.

'Bitch! Thief! Imposter!' Kristal yelled with feral delight, lips grotesquely and cruelly twisting with every word. 'I'm going to make you rue the day you ever became part of the Steele family!'

The delight was wiped from her face when, in a flash of movement, Mo managed to reverse their positions. Now it was a startled, wide-eyed Kristal who looked up, and a supremely pissed Mo who gazed down. Mo didn't give her father's widow time to attack. She unleashed a swift one-two. A jolting slap to one cheek, a bruising backhand to the other. Kristal stared at Mo, shell-shocked, her eyes round, her open mouth gasping for much-needed air.

'Fuck,' Nico raged beneath his breath, followed by a hard growl deep within his throat. All his instincts rebelled at him standing there doing sweet FA while his sister got the stuffing knocked out of her. Kristal-Annalisa was the one who'd protected him when he was a kid. Read him bedtime stories. Embraced him tight when their mum literally went off the deep end. He restrained himself because she wouldn't thank him for providing back-up in this particular situation.

Mo straddled Kristal, locked her fingers about the other woman's arms, effectively pinning her to the carpet. That didn't stop Kristal from struggling and wriggling like a woman possessed. Teeth clenched, Mo wouldn't let up. Eventually, Kristal's movements turned sluggish, ran out of steam. She stilled.

From her dominant position, Mo read her the riot act. 'You've been wanting to have a pot shot at me, stepmummy dearest, since Granddad Jimmy put me front and centre in the organisation.'

Kristal's features flared with blistering anger. 'He had no right to do that. No right.'

'He had every right,' Mo spat back with equal heat. 'He built this firm up from nothing with sweat, willpower and back-breaking hard work. He decides who'll be next in line—'

'What? You? Some jumped-up street rat who don't know her Chanel from her frigging Versace?' Kristal cut in savagely, scoffing as if she was hawking spit at the back of her throat.

Out of nowhere, a fierce emotion drove up from Mo's belly. 'I'm Robbie's Steele's daughter,' she shouted. It was the first time she was saying it aloud with real pride. Real ownership. 'Your son's sister. Me and Damien have the same blood running raw in our veins.'

Kristal turned her head so she didn't have to witness the

truth on Mo's face. She had to concede what this young woman was saying was the way things were. Were going to be.

Deflated, she faced Mo again. Voice small, she croaked, 'You're not a mother, so you wouldn't understand. I was only trying to make sure that my little boy's future was secure. I was trying to protect my son. Give him the protection I never had when I was a girl—'

'Whoa!' Nico finally made his presence felt, striding closer to them. He couldn't hide his incomprehension. 'What are you talking about? Why would you have needed protection when you were a girl?'

The blood vanished from Kristal's skin. Ashen-faced, eyes darting about, she couldn't hide the panic in her answer. 'Nuthin'. I didn't mean—'

'Bollocks!' His interruption was more brutal than any of Mo's blows to her body. 'Annalisa, tell me what you meant by it.'

Mo's fast-moving gaze snapped between brother and sister. It was as if they were in the room alone. Beneath Mo's pressing legs and fingers, Kristal's flesh had gone cold. Mo didn't know what this was about, but she knew heavy shit when she saw it.

Never taking his gaze off his sister, he told Mo, 'I'd be grateful if you could give us some brother and sister time.'

Mo didn't have a problem with that, especially as it appeared that Kristal had opened a can of stinking worms.

Nevertheless, when she got off Kristal and was back on her feet, she stabbed a stern finger at her stepmother. 'I know your game. But guess what, bitch? We're playing by my rules now.'

Kristal never even heard her because she was locked in another type of hell from the past.

Chapter Thirty-Four

'He would come in the night,' Kristal began.

She didn't get up. She remained on her back lying on the floor of Jimmy Southpaw's office, staring up at the stained patches on the ceiling. The only way she could speak about this was if she didn't have to see her brother's face. Her sweet, sweet innocent boy. She couldn't bear to see his face.

Nico didn't say a word, but she heard his laboured breathing.

Her voice was so soft. So tired. 'I always used to love it when Uncle Ted would visit Mum and Dad. He always had a pocket full of sweets and a mouth full of tall tales.' Her breathing was shallow. 'During those visits not once did he put his hands on me. He behaved how a proper uncle should.'

Nico's strained voice intervened. 'You don't have to say any more—'

'No! I've got to.' His sister charged on. 'See, the thing is, I think this is the only time I can talk about it. I don't think I'll ever have the strength to let this filth dirty my lips ever again.'

Nico was paralysed. He knew what was coming. His head was buzzing so bad it was turning into a full-blown headache. A headache? He was complaining about his fecking head hurting him when his sister … His sister …

Kristal's cool voice washed over his anguished thoughts. 'It didn't start until we came to live with him when I was thirteen and you were five. I didn't sorta get what was happening at first. It began with light touches, big hugs. I didn't think there was nothing wrong with it because that's what you do in families, right? Kiss each other. Put your arms around each other. Smooth your palm down a back, especially if one of youse needs a bit of cheering up. He always liked me to be physically close to him. Y'know, sitting on his lap, cuddling me on the settee while we watched telly. It turned into him visiting my room at night …'

Nico's huge, raging sobs shook the room. He was bent double, head hanging low, clutching the wall for support. He couldn't listen to another word. No wonder Annalisa had bolted for her very life. Kristal scrambled to her feet. Nico looked as if his legs were going to go from under him any second. All it took was one touch of her hand for him to lose it and he slid down the wall. Kristal joined him there.

Tears streaming down his freezing skin, he beseechingly glanced at her. 'Why didn't you tell me?'

Her palm gently cupped his wet cheek. 'And take your innocence away as well? I wasn't prepared to do that.' Her fingertip wiped a single tear away from his skin. 'You were only eight. My beautiful baby brother. I didn't want the rottenness of the world to touch you.'

Nico stared into his sister's large eyes. 'Why didn't you tell someone else?'

Kristal let out a weighty sigh with a helpless shake of her head. 'Who would've believed me that King Ted was doing evil stuff to his niece? Everyone loved King Ted, with his exaggerated stories and exploits of how he got his name. With the money he gave to local charities. Factor in he was a well-known villain, so people were shit scared of him. So even if I'd told one of my teachers, do you really think they would've told the authorities? No chance!'

She breathed in deep and spoke with conviction. 'Looking back, I should've done that. Told someone in authority. Even if the first person did sod all, I should've told the next person and the next until someone believed me. A filthy beast like that should never be allowed to get away with abusing a child.'

Kristal could hear the scary desperation she'd felt all those years ago as plain as day in what she revealed to her brother. 'A couple of days after my sixteenth birthday, he …' She had to take a breath. Momentarily close her eyes. This was so hard to speak of. Horribly painful to dredge up. 'Now I was a woman, he said, he could do other things to me.'

Her hand covered her mouth with the nightmare of what her sixteen-year-old self had been in. 'I had to get out of there. I didn't want to end up like one of those people who call themselves broken. Damaged.' Her voice was suddenly full of strength. 'I. Am. Not. Broken. I. Am. Not. Damaged.' She felt like thumping her fist on the floor to underscore her every word. 'He's the one who's broken. Who's damaged. Who's evil.'

His sister was so brave, Nico thought with emotional pride. She'd been to hell and back and had still come out swinging.

Kristal's mouth thinned. 'That's why I was prepared to fight tooth and nail to get Damien what he's owed. I don't ever want my boy to be in a position where he's powerless like I was.' She shook her head. 'I know what folk say, that I smother him, spoil him something chronic. I'd rather my Damien had every last drop of love I had to give than none at all.' A mutinous expression covered her face. 'I ain't ashamed of what I've become. Never again will I allow *anyone* to make me *less than.* People can call me what they like. I'd rather be a villain than a victim.'

A wrenching silence sat with them for a while, both lost in their own emotions.

'The only thing that nearly broke me was having to leave you behind,' Kristal relayed in a voice so small she could barely hear it. 'You don't know how crippled with pain I was the night I told you your bedtime story. It was going to be our last one together.' She searched his gaze. 'I hope I made it a good one.'

Then, Kristal Steele, who had once been Annalisa Sinclair, did break down. Years and years of holding back all the hideous pain, all the hurt, all the rotten unfairness poured out of her. And she cried. And cried.

Nico held his sister lovingly in his arms. Their roles were reversed now. It was his turn to take care of her.

And that included exacting revenge.

Chapter Thirty-Five

'Been up all night making you more of my potato and leek soup,' Ruddy announced with gusty cheer as she bustled into Ted's hospital room the next day, Brother Bertie closely following behind. Only someone looking closely at her would spot the way the skin strained tight on her face. How pale and shell-shocked she appeared.

The sound of Brother Bertie's stick tap-tap-tapping against the floor with every step he took could be heard, which was strange because he usually moved with a light tread. He moved as if something bad was weighing on his mind.

Ruddy's potato and leek soup was an all-time fave of Ted's. She claimed that the recipe was a carefully guarded secret, passed down from generation to generation in her family. The trouble with Ruddy was you never knew whether she was being straight up or pulling your leg. Then again, in the case of her extraordinary potato and leek soup it didn't matter. It went down like heavenly milk and honey with a splash of molten gold.

Ted, head heavy against a nest of comfy pillows, watched

his friends with relief. He did so enjoy their visits. He tried to muster a welcoming smile, but the muscles around his lips refused to cooperate. Truth be known, he'd had a rough night of it. Tossing and turning, he had only been able to grab snatches of sleep. What puzzled him was it wasn't the usual aches and pains that had kept him wide awake, it was inside his head. Something was troubling him, niggling away at his brain. A sensation of utter dread. He felt off-kilter, a drunk who couldn't walk a straight line. Only one other time he'd found himself in the grip of something this terrifying. The day his niece had done a runner.

Ted tried his hardest to shake off the disorientating sensation. Instead, its claws sharpened, digging deeper. He reached to touch Brother Bertie, his closest friend, for some much-needed support. But his hand was left clasping empty air when the other man sat on the stuffed armchair instead.

He mustn't have seen my hand, Ted tried to convince himself. If that was the case, why did he get the distinct impression that his dear friend wasn't making eye contact with him? Why was Brother Bertie's head bowed instead of looking at him?

Before he could ask if there was a problem, his attention was diverted by Ruddy's emphatic, no-nonsense voice. 'Let's get some soup down ya.'

Bustling away, she was using the bedside cabinet as a makeshift table so she could ladle on a large bowlful of steaming soup. Task completed, she jokingly added, 'Now that will put the hairs back on your chest.'

Ted took his first mouthful. Closed his eyes with

exquisite pleasure. Deeee-lisssh! There was a special spicy edge to today's offering. Just what the doctor ordered. He lapped up every last drop.

'Aww!' His eyes flashed open with satisfaction and glee, his gaze settling with grateful warmth on Ruddy. 'You're a good girl, Ruddy—'

'Like the girls, do ya, Ted?' Ruddy rudely cracked.

Ted was startled, his eyes rounding in shock. The spoon clattered into the empty bowl. Ruddy carried on as if nothing was wrong, took his bowl and filled it up again. It was clear she was wound as tight and taut as an elastic band on the verge of snapping when she placed the steaming bowl back in front of him.

Ruddy gave him a crooked smile. 'Get that down your throat.'

Ted leant forward, inspecting Ruddy's face. 'What did you just say to me?'

Ruddy's congealed smile stayed in place, leaving her looking slightly bonkers. 'I said, get that down—'

He waved his trembling hand. 'You know what you said.' He confronted her, his voice finding its strength. 'You asked me if I like girls? You got something to say, say it!'

Brother Bertie thumped his stick loudly against the floor with such fury it was a wonder it didn't snap in two. Ted recoiled in disbelief when he saw what dwelt within his friend's gaze. Icy rage.

Brother Bertie got to his feet and loomed over him. 'Do you like girls?'

Ted shook his head, scoffing with outrage. 'I'm gonna

pretend I don't know what you're asking me.'

'Time for pretence is over, you scumbag.'

Ted swung to face Ruddy. Her face was a mirror reflection of Brother Bertie's scathing fury. She visibly vibrated with violence. And pain. So much pain it was hard for her to speak. 'When I went to visit Joy's grave, I met Casey. And she says to me …' Ruddy's mouth and the skin around it wobbled, as did the veins in her neck, as she fought to get the words out.

Ted leapt into the space. 'Dunno what that girl's been mouthing off to you about, but she'd have made it up.' His chin thrust out in defiance. He was back to being King Ted, the man feared from one end of London to the next. 'You only ever saw what you wanted, but that girl was trouble from the off. Ran rings around Joy, she did. But she couldn't do that to me. I put that girl right into her place—'

Ruddy pushed her jutting, mottled-red face close to him to shut his trap. 'She says to me that you interfered with her—'

'She means that I told her off. Wouldn't put up with her nonsense—'

Ruddy screamed, 'What she told me in black-and-white detail were things a man should never, *never*, you hear, do to a young girl. It makes me sick to my stomach—'

'You gonna believe a little bitch …' Ted cut in, then sucked whatever he was about to say back with a sharp inhalation of air and a pained whimper.

Brother Bertie had unleashed the sword that was concealed inside his walking stick. Now its vicious tip pressed against the material covering Ted's cock. Both men were breathing heavily. They stared each other down as if they were back being those two young men in a darkened Notting Hill backstreet, circling each other ready to tear the other apart.

A nasty noise emitted from the back of Ted's throat. 'You don't want to play that game with me, Bertram. Put your hands on me—'

'The question is whether you put your hands on an innocent, defenceless child?' Brother Bertie wasn't intimidated. Besides, he knew all the tricks that Ted had up his sleeve to try to put the frighteners on someone. In fact, he'd taught Ted a number of them himself. 'Open your bone-box again before Ruddy has said her piece and I'll skewer you to the bed through your knob just like those kebabs you love to gobble.'

Ted heeded his words. He'd known Brother Bertie for too many years to know he wasn't mucking around.

Ruddy pressed her fingertips against her cheeks as she got her voice back on an even keel. She wet her lips. And started. 'Casey told me that you'd been putting your filthy mitts on her since you were stepping out with Joyce. All those times you'd take her out on her own, it wasn't coz you were trying to help her mum out, it was so you could …' Ruddy wouldn't say it. Oh God! Her heart was bleeding inside. 'She wanted so badly to tell her mum, but she couldn't, she was that scared. Then she picked up her courage and did—'

Ted couldn't keep his evil to himself. 'Stab me all you want, Bertie,' he smugly dared. He waved a menacing finger at Ruddy. 'Joyce comes to see me and spews that kid's pack of lies to my face. The nerve of her! After all I did for her and that fatherless brat.'

Ruddy's voice dialled up and over him. 'Don't you bloody well get it? That's why Joyce offed herself. Stuck her head in the oven because she'd brought a child molester into her home. She couldn't live with what she thought she'd done to her precious little girl. Because she told her mum what you were doing, Casey thinks she's the one who killed her mother.'

Suddenly, Ruddy's voice hitched in a high whine of pain. 'But it was me. I'm the guilty one.' She wildly stabbed her chest. 'Me! I introduced you to Joyce. Me, who brought you into her life. Their lives.'

Brother Bertie let the sword clatter to the floor as he moved to her in a flash to put his arms about her. Ruddy was almost bent double because the pain she was in was so ferocious, eating her from the inside out with guilt and remorse.

Brother Bertie looked over at Ted with disgust. 'You weren't just my friend, you were my brother.'

Ted stared at both of them with lip-curling contempt. He folded his arms. 'You can both fuck off. Believe some lying tart over me? Some mates you turned out to be.'

Ruddy pulled herself free of Brother Bertie to stand on her own two and told Ted, with malicious justice, 'Enjoy the flavour of the soup, did ya? I put in a dash of something very special and spicy in it for you today.'

Ted's face whitened before she'd even finished.

'My piss. Saved it up especially for you from last night. Mixed in some earth from Joy's grave too, you paedo bastard. Animal. Beast.'

He lunged for her, but a deep, authoritative voice from the open doorway sliced through the room. 'Ruddy. Brother Bertie.'

Nico's commanding presence overshadowed the room. He nodded. 'I think that visiting hours are up for you.'

His instruction was backed up by the steel in his tone. Brother Bertie collected and sheathed his sword, took Ruddy by the hand and headed for the door. Neither looked back at the man who had been one of their closest friends. He had betrayed them and those closest to him in one of the vilest ways possible.

Nico smiled high and bright at his uncle making his way across the room to him. He kissed him on his forehead, as he always did. Ted sagged with blessed relief. His nephew obviously hadn't heard what he'd been arguing with those two cretins about. If Nico had … Ted wasn't scared of any soul, except Nico. And it made sense that he should be. After all, it was at his knee that he'd trained his nephew to become the fearsome person he was today.

Nico always had a soft spot for kids, which explained why he doted on his two children. *Spoilt them rotten, more like*, Ted thought. Still, it sent horrifying chills up Ted's spine to think what Nico would do if he ever found out the truth. Ted quietly smirked. He hadn't done anything to be ashamed of. What he'd done went on every day of the week.

Plus, back then things were different.

He caught his nephew's hand before he stepped back. 'You're a good boy. Your dad would be dead proud of you. Business going to plan?'

'Hunky-dory.' Nico frowned. 'Those pillows look a touch uncomfy. Raise your head.' Ted sighed with contentment as Nico fixed and fluffed his pillows, including putting one on the chair. His boy always took care of him.

Nico softly asked, 'What was up with you old timers when I came in? Ruddy and Brother Bertie looked fit to do murder. Was that a sword or something on the floor?'

Ted shook it off with a double wave of his hand and clucked his tongue. 'You know those two, they ain't living if there ain't no drama.'

Ted finished with a raucous laugh. Nico didn't join in. Instead, he drifted to the window. He kept his face turned away from his uncle, speaking while his gaze contemplated the car park below.

'I never forget the first time I sussed out that my Uncle Ted was actually the legendary King Ted. This group of older boys jumped me in the playground, and they're beating seven shades of shit out of me. Outta nowhere, these two other boys fly in and drag the kids off me. I'm lying there, lips dripping claret, watching my rescuers whispering furiously to my tormentors. Know what happens?'

Nico wasn't really looking for an answer so didn't wait for one. 'The next thing I know, the boys who were thumping me up one minute are all now helping me to my feet and dusting me down. Then one of them says to me,

"Please tell King Ted we never meant nuthin' by it." I'm standing there like the joke of the century coz I ain't got a ruddy clue who King Ted is. So, I says, *Who's King Ted*?'

Nico slowly pivoted back to face the room. To face his uncle. 'Since that day, I felt such pride being related to you. The person I raised my chin to look up to.'

Nico walked over to the chair where the pillow lay. 'All these years, I've been cursing my sister from one end of London to the next. Wishing her the baddest, most corrupt evil to drag her into the gutter. Then she comes back—'

Nico had never seen the type of shock he witnessed stun his uncle's face. Ted could barely get the words out of his mouth. 'Annalisa is back?'

Nico ignored him. 'She tells me a story. Similar to the one I hear Ruddy and Brother Bertie testifying to in this very room while I'm listening at that door.' He pointed at it. 'Can't keep your hands off little girls even when they're your niece who's living under your protection. Men like you tell yourself you did nothing wrong. That it doesn't matter coz it happened years ago when it was OK to do those things.' Nico's voice hardened with ice. 'It was never Ok to do things like that to a child.'

Ted desperately shook his head, his fingers flinging off the blanket, trying unsuccessfully to throw his legs over the edge. 'You've got it all wrong—'

Nico wasn't listening. He calmly picked up the pillow on the chair. And then stared at the man he'd respected and loved most in the world dead in the eye. 'It's entirely up to you. You can struggle, which means it will take longer. Or, you can lie back and shut your eyes.'

They were both in no doubt what he was alluding to. What he meant to do.

Nico advanced with the pillow gripped knuckle-white tight between his hands.

Chapter Thirty-Six

What about me?

I'm your son.

I'm still here.

The pleading words of a man in torment bounced against the four corners of Harry's mind until he thought he was going mad. The same words had plagued Harry since the day of Robbie's funeral. He wanted to scream them in his father's face. Wake him up that he still had a son.

Harry held his head in his hands as he sat on the nasty sofa where he'd kipped the night before. A day on, and his nutter of a niece still had him imprisoned in this shit-hole of a sitting room in this crap-end of a house in North London. He knew maybe he should be thanking his lucky stars that Mo hadn't chained him up in the basement, but all he felt was an overwhelming hatred towards her. He despised her for taking his rightful place.

Robbie's git had been creating since Granddaddy Southprick had given her the pole position place in the Steele family. Nearly a year on and Harry was still having trouble taking it all in. Harry was heartbroken. Yeah, heartbroken was the right word. Every time he thought about what his dad had done, his heart cracked in two. He'd always played second fucking fiddle to his bruv when he was alive. Then his dad had twisted the poisoned blade, by now making him play second best to Robbie's hood rat daughter.

Harry was so cut up about it he'd spent most nights blowing his brains out on alcohol and any substance he could sniff up his bugle. When he got his hands on Mo …

Harry swore under his breath. The sweat was running thick and fast down the curve of his back and forehead. If he didn't get a tote on some C soon, he was going to go batshit bonkers. He wouldn't admit that he was addicted to the stuff. He told himself that he only needed a snort every now and again to set his nerves straight, to boost his energy. Y'know, like having one of them energy drinks.

The door to the sitting room opened. The goons got smartly to their feet. Mo waltzed in like she was the mutt's nuts. Harry felt such an overwhelming rage building in him he nearly yelled at her:

Fuck yourself!

You ain't got balls big enough to treat me like this.

Do you know who I am?

But the sweat had turned into a fever that made his very bones shiver and chatter inside his body. The desperate need for a chemical pick-me-up gnawed furiously at his nerve endings.

Bodily needs most pressing, he told her, 'I need to get out of here.' Harry hated the begging he heard in his voice. It would be humiliating if she heard it too.

A wave of relief washed over him when it appeared she hadn't, because he'd assumed if she had, she'd gloat her tits off. Instead, her expression remained guarded. And, let's face it, in her position he'd be gloating for England backed up with some serious strutting around showing her who was boss.

Instead of her answering him, her two personal minders appeared. When Harry clocked the disapproving and ugly looks Dell and Josh chucked his way, he figured he was done for. He'd never seen her in action, but word was that when Mo's cousin, Delilah, got those two wicked machetes out, slashing and chopping left, right and centre, she never missed. Josh was equally deadly with a gun.

Pride went sailing out the window. Harry didn't care anymore. If Mo wanted him on his knees, so be it. 'Look, I never—'

Her finger over her lips shut him up. She told him, 'Let's save the chat for later. I figured you wouldn't mind a bit of time to freshen up. Y'know, slip into something a touch more civilised.'

Harry's eyes narrowed, keenly watching her; he was hardly able to comprehend what she was saying. 'If this is some kind of trick ...?'

Dell charged, threatening, 'What you going to do if it is?'

Josh was swift on her heels. 'Yeah! What you going to do?'

Mo's minders were straining at the leash like two attack dogs ready to sink their gnashers in and maul him.

Some of Harry's stuffing came back. 'Who the feck do

you two likely lads think you're backchatting? I'm still Jimmy Southpaw's son. You best remember that.'

The tension that twisted in the room could be cut with a knife. Dell and Josh and Harry snarled at each other.

Mo stepped in. Raised a palm to her protectors. 'Knock it off.' A subtle nod from her told them to wait in the car.

Neither looked pleased about leaving her alone with her uncle, but they did as she'd instructed.

Harry slowly stood, grabbing the edge of the sofa for support. For a second or two there was silence as they stared, taking the measure of each other.

Harry waited on pins and needles for his niece to speak. Instead, she surprised him by heading for the door. Gobsmacked, he remained rooted to the spot. What Harry had expected was a put-him-down lecture to remind him of her exalted place in the family. That she had the great Jimmy Southpaw's blessing. Demand to know why he'd acted against her. But just turning her back on him and waltzing away … Nah! That he hadn't expected.

He almost jumped when she checked him over her shoulder with a piercing grey-eyed glance, brow arched. 'You coming or what?'

'Whatcha think of the view?' Mo enquired of her Uncle Harry.

They stood on the long, curved balcony of a huge penthouse overlooking the river in St Katharine Docks. Tower Bridge loomed so large it felt as if they were within touching distance. In the light, Harry could make out bruises on Mo's face, making him wonder what she'd been up to since she'd had him locked down in that house. She'd brought him to this swanky apartment to get his opinion – yep, his opinion! – on whether she should buy it or not?

He couldn't get the measure of the girl. One minute she'd got him confined as if he was an animal in her private zoo and the next she's all over him as if he's the answer to her prayers. It confirmed what he'd always suspected – there was something whackadoo about the girl. Talk about coming from the same gene pool, because Robbie had sometimes acted exactly the same. No one else had been able to see it, but Harry had grown up with his bruv so knew him inside out. Now and again Robbie had reeled off useless information. *'Did you know at Pentonville, back in the olden days, prisoners couldn't talk to each other and during rec they had to wear hoods?'* That particular titbit Robbie had told him one day as they'd played snooker. Who gave a toss?

Harry observed his niece beneath hooded eyes. And who gave a toss about where she hung her hat at night? Besides, wasn't that women's business preening over homes, oohing and ahhing about this 'n' that? Harry was livid at her assumption he was remotely interested in houses. Just because … because … Harry viciously shut the thought down.

Instead, he drew his head up and took in the eye-popping view as well. 'One of my first girlfriends used to live down the road.' He pointed along the river. 'In Wapping. Bit of a doss-hole back then. Now, it's a proper Eldorado.'

Mo gazed wistfully at the water gliding by. 'I've always

lived by the river. On The Island. Don't get me wrong, I love living with Granddad Jimmy, but I miss the river. It sorta runs in my blood.'

Harry stared intently at his niece. There was such a longing in her profile he couldn't help feeling her emotion. He suspected she was missing her other family.

'I miss him.' He didn't mean to say it, it just came out.

Mo didn't have to ask who he was talking about. She dared not open her mouth, desperate for any morsel of information she could find about the father she never knew.

'I never told you that the other night. He was so funny. He could have you creasing up for days.' His tone grew sombre. 'The sound of his laughter. That's what I miss the most.'

'Thank you.'

Harry's skin abruptly started crawling again, reminding him that he needed something special in his system. 'I should go—'

'I've laid on a bath, a change of clothes and some additionals to see you straight,' Mo interrupted. 'I've already put things to rights with Kristal. I know that me and you will be doing the same.'

Kristal! His brows shot to his hairline. Really? He thought she'd despise Robbie's daughter for the rest of her days. Whatever was going on here, Harry made a vow. He wiped his hands of ever getting involved in one of Kristal's madcap rackets again.

The bathroom was all black tiles and white floor. The clothes Mo had laid on a chair were bog-standard jeans and

T-shirt. The bath was filled up ready to step inside, which Harry did in less than one minute. Ahhh! So good! He leant back and enjoyed his soak for a time before reaching for the soap. Instead of soap in the dish there was a tempting pile of coke and a red, gold, and green snorting tube.

In shock, Harry froze, eyes shooting to the door. How the hell did Mo twig about his habit? Flipping hell's bells, did he have the face of a cokehead fiend? Harry unconsciously rubbed a palm over his mouth and chin. The girl was obviously more of an egghead than he'd at first thought. She was following in Robbie's footsteps again. His brother had been a watcher too. Always on the lookout to spot a weakness he could exploit. Was this what this was about? Mo trying to have one over on him?

Determined not to give her the satisfaction, Harry refused to look at the coke. But, fuck me, if it didn't start talking to him.

Just one snort, mate.

A pinch to get your balance back.

You've had a bollocks of a time and deserve a pick-me-up.

Harry was on that cocaine faster than a drunk's wages down a boozer on a Friday night. It didn't take him long before half the stuff was whizzing through his bloodstream. Harry suddenly felt like the king of the world.

He was enjoying himself so much, eyes closed, that he never heard Mo enter the room and sit on the chair.

Harry nearly jumped out of the water when he saw her.

'What the ...?' Then his face grew beetroot red. 'Fuck! You're my niece.' His hand swiftly cupped his meat and two veg. 'What are you doing in …?' His words dribbled away when he clocked what she was holding.

A large generator with a long insulated electrical lead that ended in exposed wires. Thick, coated rubber gloves covered her hands. What the fuck was going on here?

Mo calmly explained to him. 'Do you know what kind of damage I could do if I put these' – she rattled the exposed wires – 'into that water?'

Harry could barely breathe he was so horrified. And realised his stupidity. His niece had craftily lured him into her net. There was him thinking she was the idiot of the century when that title rightfully belonged to him.

Flustered, he threatened, 'You better let me out of here—'

'I don't think you're in a position to be flinging out orders.' She stood, which made him swallow convulsively. 'The answer to my question is, it all depends on how long I leave them in the water for. A light touch, like this …'

Mo's rubber-gloved hands nudged the top part of one of the wires into the water. Quickly she let go, stepping back. A shock hit Harry, a tingling of pain and heat that left his heart feeling like it was cramping.

'Stop,' he yelled.

Mo yanked the insulated cable, pulling the wire out of the water. Harry clutched the edge of the bath, heaving and rasping loudly. He couldn't believe what she'd done.

Mo retook her seat, her voice deadly so her uncle understood who was boss. 'I could fry you by dumping the whole fucking thing in. Leave you to burn and bake until every last patch of your skin is burnt to a crisp.'

All Harry's resentment boiled over. 'It ain't fair,' he slammed, teeth clenched. 'After Robbie died, Dad should've chosen me.' His fist bashed down, spraying water into the air. 'Me. My whole life I've always been two steps behind Robbie. Sometimes I wondered if Dad could even see me anymore.'

Mo was on her feet so abruptly the chair fell back. She leant over the bath, wires extended. 'Sounds like you hated my dad. Enough to fucking kill him in that fire so you could take his place?'

Harry stared at her as if she'd lost the plot. 'What? Kill Robbie? Are you off your rocker?'

It wasn't until Harry started mouthing off his resentment about his brother that something terrible occurred to her. What if the person who had killed her dad was someone in the family? Someone who would benefit from his death? In his line of business, Robbie would have collected a string of enemies and it could be one of them. But just say it wasn't. Say it was a member of his own family?

Now she'd crushed the plot against her, maybe it was time to turn her attention back to finding out who'd murdered Robbie Steele? Mo decided it was time to pick up Pockets again for another chat.

She glowered hotly at Harry. 'You're my uncle, but don't let that ever blind you to the fact that if you go against me again, I'll come gunning for you. You don't ever go against your flesh and blood.'

Mo chucked the generator and wires aside, flung off the rubber gloves and stormed out of the penthouse.

Chapter Thirty-Seven

The whizz-bang-wallop of fireworks shooting into the air outside jolted Precious Watson from her snooze on the settee in the sitting room. Her eyes flashed open as she muttered, dazed, not exactly sure what had gone on. Her hand was loosely wrapped around the glass of Taboo she'd been enjoying as part of her downtime. Another firework cracked into the air, the effect of which was to completely wake Precious up.

Her mouth tightened. Those feckin' kids were at it again. When she got her hands on one of them … Vexed beyond belief, she slammed the glass down on the side table and stomped into the kitchen.

She leant out of the kitchen window and yelled with strident indignation down at the group of kids setting off fireworks on the shoreline of the river. 'Oi! Pack it in. Go on. Hop it.'

Bloody little bleeders took not a blind bit of notice. Hardcases, the lot of them. Probably came out of their mother's womb with knuckledusters ready to whack the midwife one. Precious kissed her teeth. How many times had the council told the kids to stay away from the sodding river? There were signs all over the place about the dangers. But those kids wouldn't be told. In fact, the more the council warned, the more the local kids were drawn to it. It wasn't a flipping playground, for Pete's sake. Get caught up in the tide, swept out and that would be it – curtains.

Wasn't that exactly what went on a few years ago? A pack of these teen tearaways decided it would be fun to take a midnight swim. Hijinks soon turned to high drama and eventual tragedy when one of the kids got pulled under … Precious would never forget hearing the screams of the child's mother when she found out her son wouldn't be coming home. The River Thames was such a beautiful thing, but it could turn on you in an instant, its seductive waves twisting into treacherous currents that gripped and sucked you down.

Precious blamed the parents. Some of those kids were below the age of ten, for crying out loud. What business did a ten-year-old have being out this late? And as for the others, well, their parents should know exactly where they were. Have an eye on them. The parents needed shooting, or at least a good kick up the back region was Precious' honest assessment. Call her hardcore, but if you brought a nipper into this world, you'd better be prepared to look after it. Bring it up right. She shook her head with a heavy sadness. The truth was, some people touting themselves as parents around here were on a bender most of the time on junk or booze. What's the world coming to? Eh? Those poor kids didn't stand a chance.

Precious' heart did a series of painful flip-flops recalling her own troubles with her own daughter. She hadn't meant to slap Mo down like that, but the girl had been taking liberties, big-time. God knows she'd tried her best with Mo. Done her utmost to steer her onto the right path. Laid the law down more times than she could remember. Tears sprang, hot and swollen, to her tired eyes. But none of it had been good enough. Her girl had found out about Robbie and was now in the clutches of his despicable father. Jimmy Southpaw, may he rot in everlasting Hell!

Another firework whizzed skywards, dragging Precious back to the present. Its screech shattered the air. She gritted her teeth like a bear who'd been poked one too many times. Right! That was it! It was about time she dished out her own brand of whizz-bang-wallop.

The muffled sound of her faux fur bootie slippers beat against the hallway lino as she marched towards the door. The slam of the cool night-time air in her face had no effect in slowing Precious down. She kept going and going … abruptly, she bumped roughly into someone just outside the entrance to her block.

'Watch where you're going,' Precious snapped. She wasn't in the mood to play nice with someone who'd got in her way.

The hand of the other person suddenly gripped her arm. 'Precious? Is that you?'

Precious' face heated hotter than a summer's day in August when she realised who she'd collided with. Sister Aggi. A simple black coat covered the nun's habit. The poor lady's eyes were redder than raspberries, showing how tired she was. As far as Precious was concerned, God had sent Sister Aggi down as a saint to live among them. Not many folk gave a tuppence about the people of the East End, but this woman served the community with open love, devotion and the occasional clip 'round the ear.

'Sister. I'm that sorry. I didn't realise it was you,' Precious stammered, so embarrassed. She couldn't get the apology out of her mouth quickly enough.

Even though the older woman smiled, the strained tightness of the skin around her mouth showed that she was almost dead on her feet. Precious pursed her lips; the nun worked way too hard. Took on too many burdens. That convent she lived in wanted to have her under curfew after a certain time.

For a moment, Precious forgot all about the children making mayhem by the river. 'You look like you could do with a heart-warming brew. Why don't you come back to mine for a cuppa and put your feet up for five?' Precious added a wink. 'I'm sure even the Lord lets his saints have a bit of TLC.'

Sister Aggi shook her head, stepping back. 'Another time. I really need to be getting back.'

Another time? Beneath her lashes, Precious quizzically observed the nun. This was the first time Precious had invited her in for a cup of tea. And that little step back the nun had taken … A bit odd if you asked Precious. Almost as if her home had demons and devils squatting in it. It was made all the more curious when you factored in how close the nun had been to Mo when she was in school. And the way Precious heard it, those two still had a tight bond.

Precious nodded. 'Well, nice seeing you—'

'How's Mo?'

Precious looked put out. God's truth, it hurt thinking about her girl too much. Then again, Sister Aggi was no stranger. 'I'm sure you've heard of the shenanigans with Southpaw.' She'd never give him the honour of being called 'mister' like everyone else did to him. Spit on that!

Heartbreak broke through her voice. 'She ain't got a cotton-picking clue what she's getting herself involved in. But she won't listen to me.' Precious' hands twisted helplessly by her side.

Sister Aggi placed a comforting palm on her shoulder. 'Sometimes in life the only way some people can find their path is to do it in their own way. Sometimes that includes ending up in the wrong place for a time.'

Precious couldn't hold back the sob. 'I'm frightened for her. Scared witless what will happen to her while she's under his control.' She swiped a hand across her watery eye. 'Looking back, I should've told her about Robbie – her dad – but I didn't want her to have nuthin' to do with his side of the family. Villains, the lot of them.'

Sister Aggi squeezed Precious' shoulder one final time. 'I'll pray for you. And if Jimmy Southpaw crosses my path, I'll give him the telling off of the century.'

A child's high-pitched scream ripped through the air. It came from the direction of the river. Precious' heart dropped to the soles of her feet thinking it was one of the kids in trouble. It gave her no satisfaction to think of her earlier predictions that one of the children was going to end up in a watery grave one of these days might actually happen.

Both women responded immediately, hurrying down the old, worn stone steps, once used by dockers, to the riverbank. Some children stood back from the river, expressions of shock stiffening their features. Another group were gathered together, looking down at something where the river meets the land. Precious clenched up in horror, suspecting her dreaded prediction had come true.

The children parted like the Red Sea when they caught sight of Sister Aggi. Precious followed close behind.

'Oh my God!' Precious whispered in horror at what she saw lying at the edge of the river. Her hand clamped over her mouth.

Not the body of one of the children.

It was the body of a man. Dead. The river had dredged him up and spat him out at its banks on The Isle of Dogs. He was a terrifying sight. A strange colour, and bloated as if he was about to burst. Eyes stared wide and lifeless at the darkened sky. His neck bent at a strange angle.

Sister Aggi made the sign of the cross and then got down on her knees. She let out a quiet gasp. Looked up at Precious. 'I know this man. He comes – came – to the food bank. A harmless soul.'

'Who is he?'

'Willie Robinson. Everyone called him Pockets.'

Chapter Thirty-Eight

'This was another one of Joy's all-time fave songs.' Ruddy's voice thickened and choked.

She sat next to Brother Bertie in their deck chairs on his allotment, Brother Bertie's lethal walking stick resting against his chair. Joy's song was Petula Clark's 'Downtown', which they listened to on his ancient cassette-radio. They each had a glass of 'Lord Have Mercy Rum Punch'. Usually the liquor would be down their throats in no time at all. Not today, though. They were still reeling from the heinous betrayals of King Ted.

Brother Bertie shook his head, his features riddled with guilt and exhaustion. He'd hardly slept. Instead, most nights, he sat on the balcony staring at the river. Some nights he'd simply wept.

'I don't get it. How did we miss it about Ted? He was like a brother to me.' The thickness of tears was back in his voice. 'How did we become sightless every time we were with him?' He was devastated at finding out the truth about his … No! The word 'friend' would never pass his lips again when he spoke of that man. Man? He was an abomination.

Ruddy let out a lengthy sigh, as if living in the world had become too difficult to deal with. 'I'll tell you why. Blokes like him are devious. They go out of their way to make themselves look good, y'know, everyone's mate. But behind closed doors, that's where they're exercising their evil against the most vulnerable.' She spat on the grass. 'I curse him for all eternity.'

A strained noise came from Brother Bertie's throat. 'I don't know if I can do it.'

Ruddy took his hand and held his troubled gaze. 'We're going to go to that bastard's funeral when the time comes, because if we don't, questions will be asked.'

Nico had personally sent word that King Ted was dead. Apparently, he died in his sleep in the hospital. Ruddy and Brother Bertie suspected that the real story of his death was an entirely different one.

Ruddy continued, 'And you know what happens when folks start asking questions? They stick their beaks in even further. And they'll keep digging and digging until they unearth the truth about Joy and Casey. And about God knows who else.'

Her head shook with force. 'Over my dead body, and I'll tell you why. It's going to be those women everyone starts yapping their gobs off about. Everyone will know. Their mates, their family, their kids. Nah! Not happening. Not on my watch. He took their power away. Now we're giving it back to them. *They* should have the power to tell people or not tell folk. It's up to them.'

Her voice trembled as she took in a sharp breath. 'We go

there, pretend like he was the greatest guy in the world, eat a few sarnies and then fuck off out of there.'

The tightening grip of her fingers on Brother Bertie showed how emotionally devastating this was for her.

He said, 'Why is it always family or those closest to you who hurt you the most?'

There was no answer to that.

As the last strains of 'Downtown' played, they both raised their glass in a toast.

'Here's to Joy.'

'To Joy.'

Later that night, Mo leant on the rail of The VIP lounge as she surveyed the clubbers grooving away to 'Do You Really Like It' by DJ Pied Piper and Masters of Ceremonies on the dance floor below. The lilac and electric-blue lights were going crazy-crazy sweeping across the crowd pumping up the feel-good vibe. She was feeling the positive vibes too. For the first time since joining her Granddad Jimmy, Mo truly felt like she was a member of the Steele family. Maybe it was because she'd faced off and seen off the opposition. Proved herself.

She was still getting her head around Kristal and Nico's relationship. That was the thing with the underworld. It was hard to know who was connected to who. News of King Ted's death had reached East London. What had surprised Mo even more was on the grapevine she'd heard that Gramps and Ruddy had been very close friends of the legendary South Londoner. How was it Brother Bertie even knew King Ted? Maybe she'd ask him about it next time she went down to visit him on his allotment. She sure as hell wasn't going to knock at her mum's door. Secretly viewing her mum from afar was going to have to do for now.

'Mo?'

At the call of her name, she turned to find Dell and Josh standing near the spiral stairs. If she was reading their expressions right, something was up. They followed Mo downstairs to her lower ground-floor office for privacy.

'This better not be about Kristal or Uncle Harry,' Mo seethed from behind her desk.

She had a voddy and Coke on the go while Dell drank plain water as usual and Josh a brew from a bottle.

They looked at her from the other side of the desk.

It was her cousin who told her, 'Remember that geezer, Pockets? You asked us to pick him up again.'

Mo had eventually drawn her minders into her confidence about her suspicions about the fire that had killed her father.

Mo put down her glass and leant forward. Remember Pockets? Anything relating to the death of her father she held on to like precious gems. 'What's the story?'

Josh took up the thread. 'Washed up dead in the river.'

Mo was shell-shocked, her gasp audible in the room. 'When? How?' She thumped the table with her fist. 'He was my only lead.'

Her minders' gazes met meaningfully again.

Dell said, 'Word is that he was off his face as usual and fell in.' She averted her eyes from Mo.

Mo looked at her intently. 'What is it you're not telling me?' Her gaze flicked between her two trusted crew members.

Josh said, 'Others are telling a different tale. Some are saying it's all a bit strange because he hated the river. See, he couldn't swim. Add to that he was going around bragging about a wad of cash coming his way soon.'

The implication of what he was saying fell in the room like the grenade Dean had lobbed in the club.

Mo slowly picked up her glass, reclined back and drank. That's what Granddad Jimmy had taught her. A situation like this should never be rushed. Take time to use your noodle and think it through. And then plan, plan, plan.

Mo finished her drink. 'This story of my dad being innocently caught up in a fire is rubbish. I don't know what went on in that police station and I didn't know Robbie, but in here' – she touched her heart – 'I know someone snuffed his life out. I suspect Pockets knew a lot more than he told me that night in the hotel.'

'And someone else found out that he knew too?' Dell tentatively questioned.

'And had to silence him.' Josh picked up her thread. 'Caught up with him and shut him up for good.'

Mo listened to every damning word. Robbie's death was much bigger than she thought. Someone out there didn't want her to find out the truth.

Big Mo Crime Series Book 1

DIRTY TRICKS: A Sneak Peek

#1 Amazon Bestseller

1992

'Knock her friggin' teeth down her throat.'

'Scratch her eyes out.'

'Rip all that curly-wurly hair out of her head.'

The schoolgirls, baying for blood like a pack of dogs frothing at the mouth, savagely screamed and spewed hate and poison at ten-year-old Maureen Watson. Curly-haired with polished light-brown skin, no one called her Maureen. She was known by one and all as Little Mo because she was a tiny, wee thing, still inches off five feet. And that's why the other girls ganged up on her, classic bullies who used their bulk and bluster to intimidate a much smaller girl. Cowards, every last one of them is what Little Mo's grandfather would have told her. Not that he had told her that, because Mo hadn't breathed a word to him about this spot of bother that was being dished out to her at school.

'Titch.'

'Short-arse.'

'Pint-sized dwarfy.'

The other girls tightened their menacing ring around

Little Mo around the corner from the school gates, snarling and abusing her all the way. The other kids, milling out of the school, scented blood in the water. In a flash they encircled Mo and her tormentors, clapping and chanting, 'Fight! Fight! Fight!'

The children loved nothing better than witnessing a proper bashing after being cooped up in school all day.

The boss girl of the bullies was Lulu Lawson, who took pride in her nickname, Loopy Loo. You better believe she was crazy! She was big for her age, broad-shouldered with long arms that ended in hammer-like fists that had been knocking other kids around since the age of four in the nursery. There was nothing she liked better than performing to an audience. It was a reminder to the other children that she was the undisputed Queen Bollocks-Bee of their School. Anyone who thought different ended up with two shiners and a bloody lip.

Loopy's eyes lit up with malicious glee as she went to work with a solid shove that slammed Little Mo into the wall. With all the force she could muster, Mo shoved her attacker right back. The crowd gasped and sucked in their breath with horrified disbelief. Mo Watson must have a death wish.

'You're dead,' the bully barked, a splatter of spit flying from her mouth.

With one of her deadly hands, she yanked a fistful of Mo's blouse, sending a button flying in the process. She lifted Mo to the tips of her toes but before Loopy could deliver a killer blow Mo kneed her in her soft tummy. The other girl staggered slightly back, an audible grunt of stunned air whooshing past her lips. Mo pressed her advantage, swinging and kicking for all she was worth. She was no contest against the much bigger girl who slammed a fist to the side of Little Mo's head. Dazed, Mo wound up face down on the ground. If she'd stayed down, Loopy and her mean-girl crew would've left her alone, no doubt high-fiving each other, congratulating themselves on a job well executed.

But Little Mo didn't stay down. She never did. 'Stay down' wasn't in her vocabulary. Little Mo climbed to her feet, moving her head to shake off the foggy dizziness. Then she tilted her chin with determined defiance, swinging punches left, right and centre. But they missed their mark. The other girls were too big and there were too many of them. The girls steamed in, knocking seven bells out of Mo. So over the pavement she went again.

It was so much easier to stay down. But she got up again. Mo might be small, but she wasn't letting anyone push her around. Never Ever. Sneak over the fence at the back of the school to avoid the bullies was what her friends begged her to do. But Mo's answer was always the same. 'Why should I? I ain't scared of them.'

Mo stood strong and proud despite the wicked pain that pierced through her like the heated blade of a knife. Her school blazer was torn, shoes scuffed, the strap hanging loose from her new bag and her socks marked with the dirt from the kicks she'd taken. Her face was bruised and scraped. She boldly stared Loopy and the other girls in the eye, clenched her fists and gritted her teeth.

As she did so, an angry man's voice in the distance roared, 'Oi!'

The crowd collectively spun round to see who had the brass nuts to interrupt their after-school entertainment. Loopy nastily twisted her lips ready to give the guy a proper, ripe mouthful but when she clocked his face the blood drained from her face leaving her shaken. Her gobsmacked expression was mirrored on the faces of a few of the other kids. The bullies and the other kids scarpered as if a wand had been waved by Mo's fairy godfather.

Surprised, Mo watched them go. When they'd disappeared, she tried to mend the broken strap on her bag. She loved this bag. Her beloved granddad had got it for her down the Leather Market in Petticoat Lane Market or The Lane as everyone locally called the East End institution. And now look at the state of it? It resembled something a dog had mistaken for its dinner.

Mo forgot all about her busted bag when she felt the shade of a dark shadow cast over her. Her head snapped up to find the man who had scattered the crowd standing over her.

'You alright there?' His voice was deep and typically East End. 'What was that row about?'

He was suited and booted, tall, very tall indeed. Muscular and wiry, wearing a baseball cap that shadowed most of his face and shades that hid his eyes. Mo squinted up at him. The guy looked familiar. Then she remembered why. He'd strolled into the chicken-n-chip shop on the High Street, noticed the lengthy line of schoolgirls queuing up, including

Mo, and told the guy behind the counter to let them have their lunch on the house. The bloke on the counter didn't argue. The big guy collected his takeaway on the house too.

Mo's mum had warned her, finger stabbing in her face to emphasise her words, not to speak to any strangers, especially men.

Mo didn't heed her mum's advice as she finally gave him an answer. 'They duffed me up because I'm little. They wait for me, regular like a dose of castor oil, at least once a week at the school gates.'

His lips twitched at the corner like he was holding back a laugh. 'What's a young 'un like you know about castor oil?'

Mo's little nose wrinkled. 'Enough to know I'll bite the fingers clean off the next fool who tries to get a spoonful in my mouth.'

He let out a bark of loud laughter. Then quickly composed himself, his expression turning serious again. 'That's not very nice of those girls to be ganging up on you. Why don't you tell your teachers and get them to do something about it?'

'Tell the teachers? You having a laugh?' Mo snorted in disgust. 'I'm not no grass.'

The man nodded. 'Fair enough. Maybe you could just climb over the back fence instead and avoid them that way?'

Mo snapped back with the same explanation she'd given her mates on that account. 'Why should I? I'm not scared of them. I'm not scared of a living soul.'

'You could get some back-up?'

Mo wasn't having that either. 'I don't need back-up. I fight my own battles.'

The man looming over her smiled. 'Hmm, I can see you're going to go far in life, young lady. What's your name?'

'Little Mo. Coz I'm little and my name is Maureen.'

He folded his arms over his immense chest and sighed. 'Well, Little Mo, why don't you let me help you out? The next time them girls start up on you, tell them I'm a relative of yours. That'll soon put a stop to their little game of soldiers. You'll see.'

Mo folded her arms just like he had. In fact, she shifted her whole body so that she mimicked the way he stood, feet slightly apart. Mo liked the feel of that. It made her feel steadier. Powerful.

'Why should I? Who are you?' Her tone was belligerent.

He seemed to loom even larger over Mo. 'Don't you know who I am then?'

Mo's face screwed up slightly. 'No. Why should I?'

His big hand patted her on the head where her curls were now a tangled mess. 'Don't worry about who I am. Them girls won't be bothering you no more, that's all that matters.'

Grinning, the big guy set off down the street. Little Mo went back to trying to put her bag to rights.

Her new guardian angel was well down the road when he stopped and shouted over his shoulder, 'And another thing, girlie. You'll need to change your name if you want to get on in life. Tell them kids and anyone else who crosses your path that your name isn't Little Mo. It's Big Mo. And if they forget to use your new handle, give them a slap to jog their memory.'

'Change my name?' But Mo was talking to the wind. Her saviour was already gone.

That was the day Little Maureen Watson started thinking big.

Big Mo Crime Series:

Book 1: Dirty Tricks

Book 2: Fight Dirty

Thank you!

Thank you for reading *Fight Dirty.* We hope you enjoyed it!
We LOVED writing it!
Checkout Amazon for all our books
The Mo Crime Series is also available on Kindle Unlimited

Reviews: We write for you!
We adore hearing what you think about our books. Reviews help other readers find books. So do please leave a review.

For news and loads more, head off to our website and sign up.
https://dredamitchell.com

We adore hearing from readers, so please do get in touch with me.
Website: https://dredamitchell.com
Facebook: https://m.facebook.com/dredasaymitchell/
Twitter: Dreda Twitter

All About Dreda

Her Majesty the Queen awarded me an MBE in her New Year's Honours' List, 2020!

After writing five books, I partnered with Tony Mason to continue my writing career. I scooped the CWA's John Creasey Memorial Dagger Award for best first-time crime novel in 2004, the first time a Black British author has received this honour.

We write across the crime fiction genre – psychological suspense, gritty-gangland and fast-paced action books.

Spare Room, our first psychological thriller, was a #1 UK and US Amazon Bestseller. My parents are from the beautiful Caribbean island of Grenada. I grew up on a working-class housing estate in the East End of London and was a chambermaid and waitress before realising my dream of becoming a teacher. I am a passionate campaigner and speaker on social issues and the arts.

I have appeared on television, including *Celebrity Pointless, Celebrity Eggheads, BBC 1 Breakfast, Sunday Morning Live, Newsnight, The Review Show* and *Front Row Late* on BBC 2. I have been a guest on BBC Radio 3 and 4 and presented Radio

4's flagship books programme, *Open Book*, and written in a number of leading newspapers including *The Guardian*. I also reviewed the newspapers every Friday night on BBC Radio 5 Live's *Stephen Nolan Show*. I was named one of Britain's 50 Remarkable Women by Lady Geek in association with Nokia. I am a trustee on the board of The Royal Literary Fund and an Ambassador for The Reading Agency. Some of our books are currently in development as TV and film adaptations.

My name, Dreda, is Irish and pronounced with a long vowel ee sound in the middle!

Printed in Great Britain
by Amazon

57703931R00192